PRAISE FOR SORAYA M. LANE

'With stunning imagery, histor
Girls is a book not to be mis

'Soraya M. Lane brings history to life in ways that take readers into the heart of some of the most frightening, challenging, and inspiring WWII experiences. Unputdownable!'

—Patricia Sands

'*Under a Sky of Memories* is a thrilling novel full of suspense, intrigue, and romance . . . Highly recommended for fans of World War II fiction.'

—Historical Novel Society

'I became so easily immersed in Soraya's poignant, vibrant, visual story, *The Secrets We Left Behind* . . . I loved this novel!'

—Carol Mason

'*The London Girls* is one of those stories that grabs you by the heart and doesn't let go until long after you've turned the last page.'

—Barbara Davis

ALSO BY SORAYA M. LANE:

The
SECRET
LIBRARIAN

The

SECRET
LIBRARIAN

SORAYA M. LANE

LAKE UNION
PUBLISHING

Text copyright © 2025 by Soraya M. Lane
All rights reserved.

Published by Lake Union Publishing, Seattle

www.apub.com

Amazon, the Amazon logo, and Lake Union Publishing are trademarks of Amazon.com, Inc., or its affiliates.

EU product safety contact:
Amazon Media EU S. à r.l.
38, avenue John F. Kennedy, L-1855 Luxembourg
amazonpublishing-gpsr@amazon.com

ISBN-13: 9781662523199
eISBN: 9781662523205

Cover design by The Brewster Project
Cover image: © Richard Jenkins Photography; © Tyler Thomason © Jim Ekstrand © Dhimas Davariza / Shutterstock

Printed in the United States of America

For Victoria Pepe. It's a privilege to be working with you!

Prologue

The woman they called Little Rabbit stood shoulder to shoulder with her husband, their backs pressed against the rough bark of the tree. Her breath was ragged, her chest heaving from running, but she forced herself to stay silent. Their lives depended on neither of them making a sound.

Hugo's hand found hers, his fingers catching against her knuckles, and when she glanced at him, she found his eyes in the almost-dark and held his stare. Someone had betrayed them, and now they were being hunted like animals as they hid in the forest.

Her body began to shake, and she gripped Hugo's fingers with hers as wind whipped through the trees and made the leaves tremble around them.

We're going to die.

As much as she was prepared to sacrifice anything for the cause, she'd never imagined it might happen like this, and as shouts began to echo, the sound of voices coming ever closer, she couldn't stop thinking about the other lives that would now be lost. The family they'd been waiting to evacuate, the documents sewn into her pocket that would now never be used . . . She blinked away angry tears. That family would be shoved into a cattle cart, sent on a train to certain death, when freedom had finally been within their grasp. Children ripped from the arms of their parents, lives shattered in an instant with no one left to save them.

Hugo leaned in close then, his lips whispering against her ear, so close she could feel them touch her skin.

'We have to run.'

She shook her head. 'If we run, they find us,' she whispered. 'They'll know where we are.'

'If we stay hidden here, they find us,' he murmured back. 'We have to go. This might be our only chance to escape.'

She stared at him, his eyes pleading with her as she slowly, *eventually*, nodded, knowing that he was right. But it didn't make the prospect of running any less terrifying.

Hugo silently lifted the edge of his shirt to show her the pistol in his waistband, and she nodded again. It was only one gun against many but it was something, and it might make the difference between them staying alive or not. She also knew that he wouldn't hesitate to use it. They'd both been trained to fire a gun, and she had every confidence in his ability to shoot to kill.

'When I say go, you run. Don't look back and don't wait for me. You have to go.'

'I'm not leaving you,' she whispered.

He shook his head as she gripped his fingers tightly in hers, forcing her to let go when he pulled away.

'*Now!*' he urged.

She sucked in a breath and then pushed off from the tree, moving as fast as she could. She could hear Hugo running just behind her, but she could also hear the ever-louder, urgent shouts of the men looking for them, and nothing could have prepared her for the sound of shots whirring through the forest and knowing that she and Hugo were their target.

4

'They're going to kill us!' Her words were a soft cry as she stumbled over a branch and then righted herself, as more cracks of gunfire echoed around them, the enemy closing in. *They're actually going to kill us!*

It was then she realised that Hugo wasn't beside her.

Hugo was no longer running with her.

Her feet slipped on leaves as she turned, and a scream caught in her throat when she saw her husband's body crumpled on the ground, barely a few paces away.

'Hugo!' she gasped.

She ran back, dropping to her knees and leaning over him, her hand to his cheek. But Hugo was still. His eyes looked past her, and when she held her fingers to his neck to check his pulse, when she lowered herself to feel his breath against her cheek, she knew. There was nothing.

Hugo was gone. Shot dead in the forest, trying his hardest to protect her and get her to safety.

The shouts were more urgent now, the voices clearer, louder still, and she gasped back her tears and reached for his pistol, scrambling to her feet and forcing herself to leave him as another shot echoed out, this time aimed at her and ricocheting off the tree beside her.

He would have told me to go. There's nothing I can do for him now.

She could hear him screaming at her in her head, knew what he'd say if given the chance. *'You need to run!'*

Her eyes blurred with tears as she fired behind her, once and then again, hoping it would buy her some time, before running as fast as she could. Part of her wanted to die in the forest with Hugo, to surrender to the gunfire behind her and end her life with the man she loved so fiercely, but another part of her was already burning. Another part of her was on fire, ready to find whoever had betrayed them and hold Hugo's pistol to their head.

His life had been extinguished as if it meant nothing, but he meant everything to her.

I just have to reach the safe house.

If I survive that long, I'll be able to find out who did this and make them wish they hadn't betrayed us.

The sound of dogs barking spurred her on, her legs covering the uneven ground as fast as they could, even though, inside, her heart was breaking.

I have to run for Hugo.

I have to survive for Hugo.

I have to live for the beautiful family who trusted me, and who will now never live to see another day, because someone we trusted betrayed us.

'He's dead, Benoit!' she cried as she pushed the door shut behind her, her legs giving way while she slid to the ground against it, chest heaving, fighting to catch her breath. 'We were betrayed!'

Benoit ran to her, falling to his haunches and taking her hand. 'What do you mean?'

'I mean that they were waiting for us. Someone told them where we'd be,' she gasped, her lungs on fire as she fought to expel the words. 'They shot him down in the forest and I had to leave him.' She fought against her tears, but it was impossible. 'I had to *leave* him there.'

'They saw you?' Benoit asked, standing up and pacing back and forth, agitatedly running his fingers through his hair. 'You think they know your identity?'

She nodded, wrapping her arms tightly around her knees when she started to tremble again. Every time she squeezed her eyes shut she saw him lying there, on the forest floor. Saw herself running away from his body as if he meant nothing to her, leaving him behind.

'I'm so sorry. You know how much I cared for him, how much I care for both of you, but if you've been compromised . . .'

'I have to go,' she said for him, her voice barely sounding as if it belonged to her. Benoit didn't need to tell her – she knew how dangerous the situation was. She didn't have time to grieve; she needed to keep moving while she still could, make sure that the rest of their cell remained secret, if it hadn't already been compromised.

'You still have the papers?'

She sniffed back tears and wiped her eyes, before reaching into her coat pocket and picking at the lining with her fingernails. It took her a moment to work on the stitches, but eventually she'd opened it enough to pull the papers through. She stared down at the documents, the weight of what she was holding not lost on her, and she felt a now familiar burn of anger deep inside. Those forged visas were supposed to mean freedom for the family she'd been going to meet. They were supposed to signal a new beginning for them; a new life.

'I want to know who betrayed us,' she said, raising her eyes to look at Benoit. 'Someone we trusted double-crossed us and gave our location over to the Nazis, and I won't stop until I find out who that person was.'

Benoit blinked back at her, as if he were trying to decide whether or not to tell her something.

'Benoit?' she asked, wiping beneath her cheeks and holding his gaze.

'We've received information in recent weeks from British intelligence, in the last few days even,' he said. 'But the chance of them double-crossing us seems implausible. What would the British have to gain by betraying those fighting for the same cause? The British are our closest allies.'

'Who was this intelligence from? A spy? A British soldier hiding in France?'

'He was an SOE operative,' Benoit said. 'I know nothing more about him, I wasn't the one to trade information with him, but if they knew where to find you tonight . . .'

'Then they might well know the location of our safe houses now, too, and where I live,' she finished, silent as she listened for noises outside, for any indication that they weren't alone. Their eyes met. 'I know,' she said.

'We need to go,' Benoit said, taking the documents from her and holding a match to them. 'I want to find out who did this as much as you do, but right now, we have a network to protect.'

She watched as flames licked across the paper, before forcing herself into action. He wasn't wrong. Hugo would want them to stay focused on the work they were doing. He would want her and Benoit to do everything in their power to stay alive.

'Where will you go?'

'I'll find somewhere to hide, and then I'll alert the others,' he said, reaching for his coat and shrugging into it, before going to the corner of the room, lifting up a threadbare rug and removing a couple of floorboards. 'I had these identity documents and visas prepared for you when you first joined. I don't know whether they'll hold, but they're better than nothing. You'll see I used your first name, but created a false surname for you.'

She watched as he slipped a document of his own into his pocket after passing her hers.

'Change your hair colour, cut it short, do whatever you have to, to make yourself unrecognisable,' he said. 'You need to make your way somewhere safe and start a new life.'

'But . . .' Her voice trailed away as they both went still, ears pricked, hearing a noise outside that sent a wave of panic like a lightning bolt through her body.

8

Benoit pulled her into his arms and pressed a kiss to her forehead. 'Without you, countless families would still be hiding in France or captured by now. Because of you and Hugo, they have a chance at a new life. Don't forget that.' He paused. 'But the work you've done puts a target on your back, and you know what the Nazis will do to anyone helping Jews to Portugal.'

She blinked at him, knowing what he was trying to tell her, but no matter how many families they'd saved, she knew it would be the one they hadn't been able to help that would forever haunt her, imagining what had become of them. Blaming herself for their downfall. She was also acutely aware of what would happen to her if they caught her.

'Find your way to Lisbon,' Benoit said. 'You're the one on the run now, Little Rabbit. It's time to save yourself.'

'And once I'm there?'

'You can help France in a different way. We'll send more refugees as soon as we can, and you can help them there. Any messages I need to send, I'll send with them,' he said. 'Besides, Lisbon is full of spies. You'll find a way to be helpful to the cause. I know you will.'

He walked quickly across the room then and opened the door, and she waited for him to give her the all-clear signal as he peered out into the darkness. When he lifted his hand and gestured for her to go, she did, hurriedly touching his shoulder on the way past. They'd worked together for more than a year, she trusted Benoit with her life, and yet there was no time to say goodbye, not properly. But in that one touch they both knew what the other meant. Just as she knew how hard he would take Hugo's death, even if he wasn't showing it now. Benoit would never forgive himself for allowing a double agent to infiltrate their network.

'Until we meet again,' she murmured as she left, before hurrying into the darkness and praying that she'd have enough time to change her appearance before she was found. Because one thing was for certain – those men would never stop searching for her now that they'd seen her, and she didn't want to think about what they'd do if they found her.

She would do everything Benoit had suggested – change her hair, her clothes, the way she spoke; *anything* that would help her slip into Portugal without detection. And she would find a way to continue her work – she would never stop fighting for France and the Allies. Just as she would never stop searching for who had betrayed them.

Tears slipped down her cheeks then, leaving her skin wet. She walked quickly across the road, her collar raised and her head bent. Hiccups of emotion caught in her throat and she wrapped her arms around herself as grief rose in her chest, fighting against the sobs inside, too afraid to make a noise.

How will I ever live without you, Hugo?

We were supposed to spend the rest of our lives together. We were supposed to have a family, to open our restaurant once the war was over and be surrounded by children. We were supposed to grow old together.

Now she was fleeing the country she loved, the country she'd fought so hard for, just like the countless refugees they'd dedicated the last two years to saving.

A widow instead of a wife.

Then the sound of a single gunshot rang out in the otherwise-silent night air, and she began to run.

Chapter One

AVERY

Avery smiled at Michael when he reached for her hand. He gave it a little squeeze before letting go and reaching for the serving spoon, and she couldn't help but wonder why he'd paused to touch her when he was clearly more interested in dishing up extra mashed potato. But then she saw her mother watching, her hand held to her chest as if it were possibly the sweetest thing she'd ever seen, and suddenly Avery understood. Michael had always known just what to do to charm her mother, from the very first time they'd met, and he'd clearly noticed her gaze resting on them.

'Our boys will be home by next Christmas, you mark my words,' Avery's father said, reaching for the bottle of wine and pouring himself another glass. 'Germany and the Japs, they don't stand a chance now that we've joined the war. It'll be over before we know it.'

Her mother made noises that indicated she agreed, and Michael nodded along as if her father was an invaluable source of information and couldn't possibly be wrong. It infuriated Avery on a nightly basis that they all just accepted what her father said as gospel. What she wouldn't have given for them all to have a lively debate! The only thing more frustrating was her sister Charlotte's disinterest in politics and world events.

'Speaking of our men, it's such a wonderful thing you've been spared from serving, Michael,' Avery's mother said. 'What a worry it would be for our Avery, for *all of us*, if you had to go and serve.'

'Another reason to be happy we had daughters,' her father said. 'It's bad enough having a nephew serving, but to have a son sent to God only knows where . . .'

'I hear that women in Europe are helping the war effort more and more every day,' Avery said, taking her chance to speak up before the conversation changed. 'I was reading just today, in fact, that women in England are learning to fly fighter planes so they can ferry them about, and that it might be happening soon here in America, too.'

'Nonsense!' Her father laughed, before pressing his napkin to his face. 'You know what I think of women doing men's jobs. It's ridiculous to even talk about it.'

'There are female war correspondents, too,' Avery said, her cheeks burning hot as her father's eyes widened. 'I've been preserving articles from a British paper about them at the library.'

'Here she goes again about the journalists,' he said, exchanging an impossible-to-miss look with her mother. 'Why do young women keep thinking they have to take over the world? In my day, women were happy to be teachers or nurses while they waited to have a family; there was none of this nonsense.'

Avery folded her hands in her lap and lowered her gaze, knowing it wasn't worth the argument. Her father never had any interest in hearing her opinion on anything that didn't align with his old-fashioned views on politics and society.

'We're very proud of our Avery being a librarian though,' her mother said quickly, more likely for Michael's benefit than hers. 'I

12

never thought I'd have a daughter with a degree from Colombia University, so that's something.'

'Well, it won't be much use once she's married,' grumbled her father.

Avery looked up then at her parents, feeling the familiar twist in her stomach that she always felt when they talked about her degree. Her mother was proud of her in her own way, she knew that, but her father had refused to pay her college fees, and so Avery had used her own savings, along with a scholarship, in order to attend, which he'd seemed to take as a personal affront. He'd even asked her to hang her degree certificate in her bedroom rather than the front room, where his was displayed, and she knew that if she'd been a son, he would have had it framed and hung it there himself. Right alongside his, for everyone to see.

'To think both my girls will be married in the summer!' her mother said. 'Now *that's* something we can all agree is exciting, don't you think?'

The knot in Avery's stomach tightened and she felt her cheeks begin to heat. Thankfully her sister came to life and began prattling on about wedding plans and dresses, so Avery was able to sit in silence, pushing the last of her dinner around her plate before eventually escaping when it was time to clear the table. She lost herself in washing the plates, running the water until it was bubbly with soap suds, interrupted only when her mother came in to join her.

'Isn't that Michael of yours just wonderful?'

Avery nodded, blinking away unexpected tears as she scrubbed one of the plates.

'He's going to make an incredible husband, Avery.'

'What if I don't want to get married though?' Avery whispered. 'What if I want to keep my job and—'

'Pre-wedding nerves, that's all,' her mother interrupted. 'Don't go getting all taken with fanciful ideas, because the only thing that will make you happy in this life is a husband and family of your own. Don't you forget how lucky you are, because one day you'll look back and realise I was right.'

'But—'

'You got your degree and you have your job, Avery. What more do you want?' Her mother sounded exasperated. 'There's only so long a man like Michael will wait, and you can't keep playing at this independent-woman nonsense forever.'

Avery held her tongue, knowing there was no use in arguing, not when her mother was set on an idea. The thing was, she was very fond of Michael; she just had the most overwhelming feeling sometimes that she was too young for marriage, and that perhaps he wasn't actually *the one*. That there was supposed to be more to her life than being married with a baby on the way when she was barely twenty-three. Not to mention that she was fond of him in the same way she might have been a brother, or a puppy even, which she was fairly certain wasn't how a woman was supposed to feel about the man she was going to spend the rest of her life with. There was also the fact that she'd rather work than spend her days cooking and folding laundry, which didn't exactly align with marriage.

'You're right,' Avery found herself saying, as much to reassure herself as her mother. 'It's just pre-wedding jitters, nothing more.'

Her mother patted her hand. 'Better to have them now than closer to the wedding,' she said. 'And you just keep reminding yourself what a lucky girl you are, do you hear me?'

Avery rinsed off the final plate and let the water out of the sink, at the same time as her mother tucked something into the pocket of her dress.

'This arrived for you today,' she said. 'I would have given it to you earlier, but everyone was already here when you got home from work and I forgot until now.'

Avery couldn't hide her smile, and she quickly dried her hands so she could hold it. She turned the envelope over, knowing it was from her cousin Jack, and she couldn't wait to read it.

'Don't you go disappearing to read that until Michael's gone, though,' her mother called as she darted out of the kitchen.

But Avery didn't care what she said, and besides, Michael wouldn't miss her in the time it took to read one letter. If they hadn't been subjected to blackout drills, she would have run to the porch and sat beneath one of the outdoor lights, but instead she went to her bedroom and lay on her front on her bed, sliding her nail beneath the seal and hurriedly opening the two small sheets of paper inside. Letters from Jack were as rare as could be, and she always spent days rereading them and imagining the kind of adventure he was on, trying to picture where he might be as he wrote.

Dear Avery,

I know I promised I'd write every week, but sometimes it's all I can do to keep my eyes open to eat something before falling asleep at the end of each day. I can't tell you where I am or what we're doing, it'll only be censored, but let me tell you that I can't believe the places I've seen. For a boy who'd never travelled further than New Jersey, there's a big wide world out here that I couldn't have even imagined.

I showed your photo to some of the boys here, and let me tell you they were hollering and begging to meet you once this war is over. I tried to tell them that you'd be getting married soon, but they wouldn't hear of it. Speaking of marriage, have you told Michael that you want to delay the big day for a bit longer? After the war we can travel together and see the world properly, if that's still what you want to do. We only get one chance at this thing called life, Avery, and we have to make the most of it.

I'm sorry about the mud smudged on the paper, but it's pretty hard to stay clean here. What I wouldn't give for a hot bath right now, or a swim in that lake we always went to in the summer when we were kids. You know, it's scary here and I know it's only going to get worse, but there's something about being away from home that's freeing, you know? Like I'm a different person away from the expectations of my father. You know what I mean, you're the only person who's ever known what I mean, so I won't keep trying to explain it.

Anyway, I have to go, sending love and a big hug. Have a slice of pudding for me and remember to be brave.

Jack.

Avery read his letter for a second time and then held it to her chest, closing her eyes as she rolled on to her back. The letters Jack sent her were everything – they were cousins who'd been best friends since they could talk, and she missed him like crazy every single day that he was gone. But more than anything, she had the most overwhelming feeling that Jack was off living his life and having some grand adventure, while she was left behind, about to try on wedding dresses for a ceremony she wasn't even sure she wanted to be part of. He was also the only person who knew the truth about what she felt for Michael, and why she was so reluctant to get married.

'Avery! Where are you?' her sister called. 'We're going to play a game and we need you!'

Avery took a deep breath before rising and putting the letter on her bedside table to read again later. It wasn't that she didn't love her life, it was just that she had the most overwhelming sensation of wanting more. Of wishing she had more control over her life and the decisions that were being made for her, instead of always having to do what was expected.

'Coming!' she called back, determined to push her thoughts away and enjoy the rest of the evening, playing charades with her family.

Don't you forget how lucky you are. Her mother's words echoed in her mind as she put on a bright smile and went to sit beside Michael, his hand finding hers and squeezing her fingers as Avery's sister leapt to her feet and entertained them with her terrible attempt at acting.

But no matter how hard she tried to stop her mind from wandering, she couldn't help but think about the letter on her nightstand, and how much she wished she was having an adventure overseas alongside her cousin, instead of being stuck in the same place she'd been her entire life.

Chapter Two

Avery

Avery walked down the aisle and held her hand out, her fingers skimming the spines of the books on the shelf. As a child, she'd spent hours in the New York Public Library, dreaming of one day writing her own book and seeing her name emblazoned across the cover, and it was at times like this that she remembered that little girl and wondered whether she might have become a writer if her family had approved. Her other dream had been to write for a newspaper, but her parents had thought that as horrendous as if she'd asked for permission to be a circus performer, which was how she'd settled on becoming a librarian.

She inhaled the familiar smell of old books as she kept walking, slowly and deliberately taking her time. Her meeting wasn't for another few minutes, and she didn't want to appear too eager. Avery had only been working for the library for six months, hired almost immediately after graduating, and she was conscious that many of her peers were much older than her and certainly less enthusiastic about their work – other than her direct superior, Sophie, who was only a few years older and as passionate about preserving history as she was. They were also rather unhappy about Avery's enthusiasm when it came to microfilming, and she'd learnt to bite her tongue rather than constantly spouting the many benefits of her particular line of work. Avery knew it was the way of the future when it came to saving precious texts and newspapers, but they seemed to think she was trying to reinvent the wheel, no matter what she said to convince them otherwise.

'Avery, come this way.'

She looked up when she heard her name called, smiling when she saw Fred, the head librarian, standing beside the open door to his office. He'd always been friendly to her and seemed happy with the work she was doing, although now she was nervous that she was in trouble. She couldn't for the life of her figure out what she might have done wrong to warrant a special meeting, and she'd spent all morning trying not to think about it.

'Please, come in.'

Avery stepped into the office when Fred stood back to let her through, and she was surprised to see a man in a smart suit and tie seated at the table. A sense of sadness passed over her as she realised what was happening. She was about to lose her job, she could just tell. They'd even brought in a senior manager to deliver the news. She fought an overwhelming rush of emotion and tried her very hardest not to cry.

'Avery Johnson, this is Clarke Miller,' Fred said.

The man stood. 'Miss Avery, I'm very pleased to make your acquaintance.'

She nodded and gently shook the hand he offered. 'I just want to say that this has been the most wonderful opportunity, and I know that funding has been difficult to secure, but if you could just . . .' Avery's voice trailed away when she noticed the puzzled looks on the faces of both men.

'Avery, Miller isn't here to fire you, if that's what you think,' Fred said.

She glanced at the man again, receiving a warm smile in reply. Something shifted inside her. 'You're not?'

'Quite to the contrary. I'm here because I've heard great things about your proficiency in microphotography, and I thought it was high time we met and had a discussion about your work.'

She swallowed, looking between him and her boss. But it seemed that Fred wasn't part of whatever conversation she was about to have, because he'd already begun to step backwards.

'I'm going to leave you both to talk,' he said. 'If you need anything I won't be far away, so please just call out.'

Avery was going to make a joke about calling out his name in the library, but decided to keep her mouth shut. And with that, she found herself alone with a man she'd never met before, as the door clicked and she quietly sat down in the chair opposite him. She folded her hands in her lap as he settled back in his chair, elbows on the desk between them, a serious look on his face.

'I understand that you're concerned about the current levels of funding in the Department of Microphotography.'

'Yes sir, I certainly am,' she said. Was that what this was about? Library funding? If so, she wished she'd had time to prepare. 'We can get by on rather little, but the fact is we need sufficient funds to . . .'

She saw the smile creep across his face and stopped talking, feeling as if perhaps he was teasing her. He no longer looked so serious.

'Avery,' he said. 'It is alright if I call you Avery?'

Avery nodded, folding her hands more tightly on her lap as her cheeks heated with humiliation. She didn't know why he'd found whatever she was saying so funny.

'Avery, microfilming is the way of the future as I see it,' he said, leaning back in his chair. 'The ability to preserve texts and books, recording them at a fraction of their original size on film, is quite extraordinary. I'm sure you agree.'

'I certainly do.' It was, quite frankly, a relief to hear someone share her views.

'Well, I'm pleased to confirm that your department will be fully funded from now on, to ensure the preservation of newspaper texts and other works of historical importance.'

Suddenly Avery knew why he'd been smiling. 'I don't know what to say. That's wonderful news!' She grinned, relieved. 'But while we're talking about funding, perhaps a room with a window or two could be found rather than the basement? It would certainly be greatly appreciated.'

He laughed. 'I like you, Avery. You're exactly the kind of girl I'd hoped to meet, if I'm honest.'

She frowned, not sure whether it was a compliment or not. 'And what kind of girl is that?'

'A highly educated girl who's whip-smart and not afraid to say what she thinks,' he said. 'Now, I know all this seems highly unusual, but I'm here to ask you a few routine questions. Unfortunately I can't tell you what for exactly, but I can assure you that your boss wouldn't have permitted me here if it wasn't important.'

Avery's mind began to race, but she simply nodded.

'Avery, why is the art of microfilming so important to you?'

She cleared her throat, watching as he took out a pen, hovering it over his open notebook, and had the distinct feeling that whatever she said next would determine whether he continued to be impressed by her or not.

'Well, most of all I think it's important because it allows us to record documents and books without requiring inordinate amounts of storage space,' she said. 'For instance, if we were to consider how many copies of the *New York Times* are produced each year, and how much space the library would need to dedicate in order to preserve each copy, it's rather daunting. But if we *microfilmed* each newspaper, we would still have access to the information indefinitely, and have it stored safely, without needing space to do so. They're tiny records of information, a photograph of each page, to be viewed in the future if the information is ever needed.'

He glanced up and smiled. 'And you're confident in your ability to photograph and store such documents? You would consider yourself highly proficient?'

'Without wanting to sound as if I'm boasting, sir, I would say that I am. This is what I've been trained to do,' she said. 'My camera of choice is a Leica 35mm, but I have worked using different cameras as well.'

His pen hovered again, and this time when he looked up, he wasn't smiling.

'Avery, I have one last question for you that I'd like you to think very hard about before you answer.'

She hesitated, before eventually nodding. 'Please, go ahead.'

'This is personal in nature, so I do apologise, but I'm wondering if there is anything holding you back from, say, doing something important for your country if you were asked.' He paused. 'I notice you don't have a wedding ring on your finger, which would indicate that you don't have a husband. And once again, I do apologise for such an intrusive question.'

'Something for my country?' she asked. 'You mean, something related to America's involvement in the war?'

Miller stared at her, without blinking. 'I'm afraid I need you to answer the question.'

Avery bristled, but she knew better than to make a fuss. He'd told her at the very beginning that he couldn't disclose what this was all about, and if she didn't give him the answer he needed, she might never find out.

'A colleague of yours was initially the candidate put forward to me for consideration, however it came to my attention that she's expecting her first child, which means she's not suitable for the position I'm recruiting for,' he said, carefully, as if he was being particularly thoughtful in his choice of words. 'So I will ask you again. Is there anything that would prevent you from assisting your government?'

Avery's heart began to beat faster, and she lifted a hand to the base of her throat as she took a deep, slow breath. She glanced at her bare ring finger, knowing that she should be thinking of Michael when she answered, but at the same time feeling the most overwhelming sense of relief that they weren't yet married.

'No sir, there is nothing that would prevent me from assisting my country with the war effort.'

One corner of his mouth lifted in a small smile. 'I never mentioned anything about the war effort.'

'No, you didn't,' she said, folding her arms across her chest. 'But you didn't have to. There's only one reason we'd be meeting in this way, with you asking me questions of a personal nature, and that's because you need my assistance for something important. Something to do with the war.'

He tore a piece of paper from the back of his notebook and scribbled something down, before standing and passing it to her. She stood, too, taking the paper and unfolding it to read an address in black ink.

He held out his hand. 'It was my absolute pleasure to meet you today, Avery. I don't doubt that we'll cross paths again soon.'

Avery placed her palm in his and he shook it, more firmly than he had when they'd first met.

'The address—' she began.

'Be there at twelve noon tomorrow,' he said, already gathering up his notebook and papers. She couldn't help but see her name with the words *Ivy League* underlined. 'Don't be late.'

'But I have to work tomorrow, and that's on the other side of—'

'It's all arranged. You're to be there by midday, and if all goes well, I doubt you'll be returning to work. Now, if you'll excuse me, I have somewhere else to be.'

'Sir, before you go,' she said. 'Are we talking about me possibly working for my country here, or . . .' Avery swallowed. 'Abroad?'

He smiled. 'Just last week I sent a librarian to Stockholm, Sweden. Ivy League graduates such as yourself can be highly useful to our war effort, believe it or not.'

Avery had to force herself not to ask any more questions as Miller nodded and walked quickly past her, his briefcase in hand. He strode through the door and out into the library, leaving her alone in Fred's office. Instead of going straight back to work though, she lowered herself into her chair, taking out the piece of paper again and staring at the address. Never in a million years had she imagined that a librarian like her would have anything meaningful to offer the war effort, and to be posted overseas?

She had no idea what all this was about, but deep down inside she had the strangest feeling that everything about her life as she knew it was about to change.

Avery took a plate of supper to her father and curled up on the sofa beside the wireless radio. Her father had made dinner almost unbearable, having spoken to a pilot he knew to ask whether Avery's information on women flying planes was correct, which had made her wish she'd never brought it up in the first place. It also didn't help that she couldn't stop thinking about what she might be asked to do, and just how she was going to broach that with her father if it eventuated. She couldn't stand the thought that she might do something he'd never forgive.

'Avery, are you alright? You're awfully quiet tonight.'

She looked up to see her mother standing by the door.

'I'm fine,' she said. 'Just pensive I suppose. I've been thinking a lot about Jack and where he might be.'

It wasn't a lie, she thought about Jack often, she just hadn't been thinking of him in that exact moment. If she had, she'd be feeling far more positive, because he would have been the first to encourage her to go.

'He'll be fine, darling,' her mother said, coming to drop a kiss on to the top of her head before sitting beside Avery's father and repeating one of her husband's favourite phrases. 'Those boys will all be home before you know it, just you wait and see.'

Avery reached over and turned the radio up when the announcer's voice rang clear through the speaker, eager to hear what news there was to report on the war. Her parents were both silent too, as they all listened.

'All Jews in France have now been ordered to wear yellow stars pinned to their chests, an order that has also been implemented in occupied Belgium and the Netherlands, a move that intensifies and extends Hitler's mandate for all Jewish people in Germany and occupied countries.'

Avery closed her eyes, not wanting to imagine what those people were going through. She still didn't understand why the Nazis hated the Jews so much. The Nazi Party seemed as intent on erasing Jews as they were books that were written by Jews.

She pushed the thoughts out of her head and turned her attention back to the broadcast.

'Although it will come as no surprise to many Americans, it has been confirmed by the President that our great country has officially declared war on Bulgaria, Hungary and Romania.'

'They won't know what's hit them,' her father muttered. 'The Axis don't stand a chance now that we're in the war.'

She gave her father a small smile, tucking back further into her armchair as she listened to the rest of the broadcast. Avery wanted to be as optimistic as he was, but she wasn't certain that it was going to be as easy, or as straightforward, for the Allies to win the war as her father seemed to think.

Thankfully the news of the day was over, and because it was Tuesday the familiar jingle of *The Pepsodent Show* with Bob Hope began, and Avery found herself laughing so hard at his ridiculous jokes and monologues that her cheeks hurt. Her parents laughed along too, and when the show was over, Avery rose and kissed each of them on the cheek.

'Goodnight,' she said.

'Goodnight, darling,' her mother said, at the same time as her father blew her a kiss, his ruddy cheeks stretching into a smile.

Avery walked slowly down the hall, trailing her fingers along the wallpaper as she imagined not living in the house she'd always called home. They'd moved there when she was a baby, so she knew no other home and also knew how much she'd miss it, just as she'd miss sitting with her family and listening to the wireless at night, but she also knew that she couldn't live the rest of her life wondering what else there was in the world if she was given the opportunity to explore it.

An hour later, Charlotte came tiptoeing into the room. Avery lay there and listened to her get changed.

'How was your night?' Avery whispered.

'Sorry, I was trying to be quiet,' Charlotte said. 'We had fun, you should have come. Michael was there.'

Avery sighed. 'Maybe next time.'

The covers rustled then and she listened to Charlotte getting into bed, fluffing her pillows as she had since they were children before going still. Avery was so used to hearing her sister breathing next to her in the night that she suddenly couldn't imagine sleeping in a room alone.

'Charlotte,' she whispered. 'Are you still awake?'

Her sister didn't answer, and Avery lifted her head and heard the soft sound of her snoring. *Trust her to fall asleep the moment her head hits the pillow.*

'I think I might be asked to travel overseas,' Avery said in a low voice, deciding she was probably better off telling her sister when she wasn't awake. 'And if they do, I think I'll say yes.'

She closed her eyes tight and imagined how it would feel to tell her parents if she was asked, or how she'd break the news to Michael.

'And the best part is, I'll have a reason to call off the wedding.'

Avery turned over on to her stomach and buried her face in the pillow, wishing upon wishing that everything about her life hadn't suddenly become so complicated.

Chapter Three

AVERY

Avery had been awake since well before daybreak, and before that she felt as if she'd tossed and turned all night. But now, after the longest morning in history, she was finally walking up the steps of the Gramercy Park Hotel, double-checking the number on the building before walking through the doors. She was surprised to be meeting at a hotel, but then she guessed that it was a logical place for someone out of town to hold meetings.

'May I help you?' the concierge asked, clearly seeing how confused she looked.

'I'm, ah . . .' Avery cleared her throat and glanced at the now deeply lined piece of paper in her hand. She'd folded and unfolded it so many times since being given it the day before that it was almost falling apart. 'I'm here to meet a Mr Frederick Kilgour.'

'Come this way,' the concierge said.

She followed him to the elevator, where he pressed a button and ushered her inside when the doors opened.

'When you reach your floor, turn right, and room 401 will be on your left.'

Avery nodded, gulping as the doors closed. She was grateful to have the elevator to herself, and she took a few slow, deep breaths until the doors finally opened again when they reached the correct floor.

'Here goes nothing,' she muttered under her breath, before stepping out and walking silently down the hallway, checking the number on each door as she passed, her heels sinking into the thick carpet.

When she finally reached room 401, she stopped, not giving herself time to overthink what she was doing, and swiftly lifted her hand to rap her knuckles against the door.

She stood back, her chest rising and falling with each breath, almost ready to think that there was no one waiting for her on the other side, when it finally opened. A man in a suit, his hair greying at the sides, addressed her with a serious expression.

'Miss Avery Johnson?'

She nodded. 'Yes, that's me.'

'Please come in.'

Avery did as he asked, standing a few steps inside as he shut the door behind her. He held out his hand.

'I'm Frederick Kilgour,' he said. 'Thank you for agreeing to this meeting on such short notice, I'm only in town for two days.'

Avery followed him across the room, surprised to see that it was a large suite and that a desk had been set up in the middle with a chair on either side. She supposed Mr Kilgour was conducting more than one interview for the room to be so well prepared for him.

'Avery, before we get started, I have to ask you to sign these papers,' he said, gesturing to a document on the table, a pen waiting beside it. 'What we're going to discuss today is confidential, and we need assurances that you will be bound by a confidentiality agreement.'

Avery stepped forward and quickly skim-read the papers, before signing. She could see no reason not to.

'Thank you. Please, take a seat.'

She sat down opposite him and nervously fiddled with the strap of her purse, suddenly feeling most out of depth being in a room with an unfamiliar man.

'Avery, your file tells me that you're an Ivy League graduate who speaks three languages, two fluently, and that you've been working for the New York Public Library for a little over six months now.'

'Yes sir, that's correct,' Avery replied.

'You're unmarried,' he said, holding up a manila folder that clearly had a dossier of information on her, 'your family live in New York, and most importantly, you've been working in microphotography since graduation.'

Avery nodded. 'All correct, although I have to say I haven't practised my languages in quite some time.'

Kilgour leaned forward, his elbows on the table. 'Avery, have you heard of the OSS?'

She shook her head. 'No sir, I haven't.'

'It stands for Office of Strategic Services. We've essentially been formed by the government solely for the purpose of obtaining information and sabotaging the military efforts of our enemy nations.'

Avery went very still as he explained what the organisation was, but she forced herself to speak when he finished.

'What I don't understand, is why someone from the OSS would want to meet me,' she said. 'I have no experience in espionage or—'

'You have experience in microfilming and cataloguing publications, Avery, and that's what I'm interested in,' he said, crossing his arms. 'I'm not looking for experienced spies, we have enough of those already, but what I do need are experts in microphotography with top-notch degrees, and the ability to converse in a language other than English for international postings.'

Avery's heart began to race.

'To put it bluntly, we need you, Avery. Specifically, we need you as part of the IDC.'

'The IDC—'

'Sorry, short for the Interdepartmental Committee for the Acquisition of Foreign Publications,' he said, a chuckle breaking his otherwise serious demeanour. 'I'm always rather proud of myself for remembering that mouthful.'

'And what exactly would I be doing, if you were to recruit me for the IDC?' she asked, trying to hide her excitement. 'If I were to be posted overseas.'

'After a short period of training, you'd be sent overseas to a neutral country, specifically to seek out newspapers, books and other texts to help us gather information on the enemy,' he explained. 'You would essentially be operating under the guise of working for the Library of Congress – an innocent librarian collecting all newspapers and other information for the purposes of preservation.'

She smiled. 'Which would essentially only be half a lie.'

'Precisely,' he said. 'Your mission would in fact be to photograph and send back copies of enemy publications, on microfilm of course; however no one other than you would know that. To put it bluntly, our agency strongly believes that accessing enemy publications could provide vital information that might help us win the war. It's important we read Axis newspapers and recently published books as quickly as we can, and we need those publications here, for our intelligence bureau to access in Washington.'

Avery took a deep breath. 'Would I be in danger, if I agreed to such a role?'

'Yes,' he replied bluntly. 'There's little doubt that you would be in some danger as a foreign national, but I'm confident that if you go about your business, focusing only on doing the job assigned to you, then you would be unlikely to draw attention.'

Avery blew out a breath this time, hardly able to believe what he was telling her.

'If I agreed to this opportunity,' she began, thinking through her choice of words carefully before continuing, 'would I be able to tell my family where I was going? How exactly would I explain this to my parents? Would it be a secret?' She half laughed. 'What I'm trying to say is, I'll need a way to explain this to my father.'

'Well, the answer is yes and no. They will know your cover story, which means they're aware of your location, but they won't know the full extent of your work. All you'll tell them is precisely what you'd tell anyone who asked wherever you're posted – you're there to obtain all newspapers and texts from all countries, as a record of history, for your work as a librarian. They don't need to know that we're in fact searching enemy publications for clues, but they can be told how badly your government needs you.'

'For the Library of Congress,' she said.

'Precisely.'

Avery suddenly felt hot all over, and she dabbed at her upper lip with the back of her finger. She also moved her arms from her sides slightly, hoping she didn't have sweat marks on her blouse.

'Do you have any further questions for me?' Kilgour asked.

She interlinked her fingers, frantically trying to think of intelligent questions she could ask and failing to come up with any.

Kilgour cleared his throat and glanced at his watch, as if he had somewhere else to be or perhaps someone else to meet.

'The crux of the matter is that we need men and women with special skills to join the IDC. Being overseas isn't for the faint of heart, but my understanding is that you've fought your way to succeed in a man's world already, Avery.'

She met his steady gaze, understanding that he was probably a man few people ever said no to.

'So can we count on you, Avery?' he asked.

She felt her hands begin to tremble and she balled them into fists, taking a deep breath and meeting Kilgour's steady gaze.

'I'm flattered that you think I'd be suitable for the role, truly I am, and I'm immensely interested in helping my country,' Avery said, feeling an unfamiliar flutter inside of her as she forced her words out. 'But I need to think about it.'

His lips formed a tight line as he stared back at her, before finally speaking again.

'I'm only in town for one more day,' he said. 'I'll give you my card, but I have to tell you that you won't be offered this kind of opportunity again if you turn this one down.'

Avery rose, smoothing down her skirt before reaching for the card he extended. 'Thank you,' she said. 'And I understand the time constraints, I just need time to consider your proposal.'

He blinked wordlessly at her, then rose and walked a few steps behind her to the door, quietly, as if waiting for her to fill the silence with words. She couldn't tell if he was disappointed or whether he'd expected her not to give him an answer on the spot anyway.

Her heels sank into the carpet as she walked, and her heart sank at the same time, feeling as if she'd already made a mistake in not giving him a straight answer.

I need to be braver. I came here hoping to be offered an opportunity. I walked through this door hoping to be given the chance of a lifetime. This is everything I've ever wanted. What's stopping me from giving the man an answer here and now?

Avery reached for the door handle, but then just as quickly dropped her hand and slowly turned around. She knew if she didn't make a decision now, if she wasn't brave enough to just say yes, she would regret it for the rest of her life.

'I'll do it,' she said, sounding breathless even though she wasn't.

A smile spread across Kilgour's face. 'You had me worried there for a moment, Avery.'

'Thank you for the opportunity,' she said, as he shook her hand a little too vigorously. 'I promise I won't let you down.'

'I'm counting on it,' he said. 'I'll have a car collect you from your home on Monday. Training will be in Washington, DC, and once you've received your posting you'll have the chance to return home before flying out to wherever you're posted. I look forward to seeing you again next week.'

She gulped. '*Flying* out?' Avery hadn't ever even imagined getting on a plane before.

'It'll be the experience of a lifetime, trust me.' He chuckled. 'Pan American will look after you, I promise. Do you have a passport?'

'No sir, I don't.'

'I'll have one issued for you, then, leave it with me.'

Avery nodded politely even as her stomach churned, and this time when she lifted her hand to the door, she opened it and stepped through into the hallway.

'Good luck with your father, Avery.'

She glanced over her shoulder, suppressing a groan at the thought. 'Trust me, I'll need all the luck I can get where he's concerned.'

But maybe it was her mother she should have been concerned about – her mother who was so fixated on there being two summer weddings that perhaps not even the government recruiting her daughter would be enough to deter her.

'Absolutely not!' her mother cried, slapping her hand so hard on the table that Avery feared the meatloaf and peas might fly into the air and land in someone's lap.

'Avery, I'm aware you're a grown woman, but you have no right to speak to your mother that way at the table,' her father cautioned. 'Look at how upset you've made her.'

Avery shut her eyes for a moment, before taking a breath and levelling her gaze first at her father, who looked as if she'd just said something beyond reproach rather than tell them about the job offer she'd received, and then at her mother, who was now dabbing her eyes.

'I know this is a shock, but all of us, men and women, are being asked to help with the war effort, and I'm honoured to be one of them. Aren't you at least proud that I've been asked?' She turned to her father. 'I thought you'd be proud, at the very least, that your daughter has been asked to fulfil an important role for our country.'

'I should never have let you get that degree,' her father muttered, and Avery felt her face fall. 'Look what it's done, having her head filled with such nonsense. That was the start of all of this, and now she thinks she can help us win the war!'

She wasn't entirely certain she knew who he was talking to, because her mother was now clutching the little gold cross she wore around her neck as if a terrible sin had just been committed that Avery needed forgiveness for, and her sister was looking the other way.

'What about your wedding?' her mother asked, her eyes wide and filled with tears. 'What about Michael? Does he know about any of this?'

Avery swallowed. 'I wanted to tell you first, but my intention is to call off our engagement. I'm going to see Michael tomorrow.'

'You could get married quickly, put an end to all this,' her father said, taking a large sip of wine. 'They wouldn't ask a married woman to go, so that's what we'll do. We'll bring the wedding forward.'

Her mother's eyes widened, full of hope, and Avery knew she had to let her down gently right now, before they both got carried away.

'Yes, that's exactly what we'll do! Michael doesn't ever have to know about all this!'

'I mean to call off the engagement, not to delay it.'

Avery looked sideways when Charlotte squeezed her fingers, surprised by her sister's sudden show of affection. Avery had had plenty of arguments around the dinner table with her parents over the years, but her sister had never once showed any interest in supporting her; she'd always sat there quietly and kept her eyes on her plate. Until now, it seemed.

'We should be proud of our Avery,' Charlotte said. 'Shame on you both for acting as if she's done something terrible. I can't believe how brave she's being to even consider this.'

The table fell silent then, and Avery mouthed 'thank you' to her sister as she squeezed her hand back, wondering how she'd ever repay Charlotte for standing up for her when she most needed it.

'We only have a few more days with Avery here, and I'd personally like to make the most of it,' Charlotte continued.

'You're certain this is what you want?' her mother asked. 'You understand what you're throwing away?'

'Yes, this is what I want, and I'd much rather do it with your support than without.'

Her father grumbled to himself and her mother dabbed her eyes again, but they both quietly picked up their cutlery and slowly went back to eating dinner as if Avery hadn't just told them she was leaving.

And it wasn't until later, when they were both in their beds, that she finally had the chance to thank her sister properly for her show of solidarity.

'Thank you, for what you said tonight.'

They were lying in the dark, whispering so their parents couldn't hear on the other side of the paper-thin walls, just as they had since they were girls.

'I wish I was as brave as you, Avery. I could never consider leaving home and flying halfway around the world.'

Avery felt tears prick her eyes. 'I'm going to miss you.'

She heard Charlotte stifle a cry. 'Not half as much as I'm going to miss you.'

Chapter Four

LISBON, 1942

CAMILLE

Camille turned the little sign at the front of the shop to 'Open', pausing to look out at the morning sun and the people going about their lives outside. She smiled at two young girls skipping side by side – their long hair bouncing around their shoulders – as if they didn't have a care in the world. Camille watched them until they disappeared around a corner before turning away, hoping it wouldn't take long for her bookshop to fill with customers. It was when she was alone that it was hard to keep her memories at bay, which had made her busy little shop the place she loved most. She always had an eclectic range of people coming through the door, from Jewish refugees to locals, and walking along the shelves and tracing her fingers across the spines of books with her customers kept her mind occupied, for which she was grateful.

Camille had barely returned to the counter when the bell above the door jingled, and she looked up to see an older gentleman walking in.

'Good morning,' she called out, noticing the way he leaned heavily on a cane.

He nodded and started to browse the books she'd arranged at the front of the store that morning, and Camille went back to checking her inventory. She was careful to mark off which books she'd sold on her list each day, but sometimes she found herself too busy to double-check her own notes, and so she wandered around the store to check some of her most popular titles. Orders were sporadic at times, but she did her best to keep the shop full of new stock.

'Is there anything I can help you with?' she asked.

'I'm told you know what books people like me might want to read,' he said gruffly, but loudly enough for her to detect his French accent.

Camille smiled, immediately sympathetic towards him. 'Well, many of my customers have thoroughly enjoyed *For Whom the Bell Tolls* by Ernest Hemingway, although it's not the lightest of reads,' she said, looking over the row of books as she gave him a little nod to tell him that she understood what he was referring to. 'I doubt I'll be able to get any more of his books, so it's somewhat of a collector's item now.' His eyes met hers, the words unspoken between them. This man was a Jew, and the Nazi book burning and banning wasn't something that needed to be explained to him. He was testing her to see if she was who he was looking for, and she was doing the same to him.

'I want to read books that no one wants us to read anymore,' he muttered.

Camille looked over her shoulder, as if expecting someone to be watching her. But the bell had only jingled once, and no one could enter without it making at least a small noise. It didn't stop her heart from beating just a little bit faster though.

'I have to be very careful about what books I stock these days, even though I don't approve of censoring what my customers can purchase.'

The way he looked at her, his eyes glistening, told her that there was no chance he was with the PVDE, Portugal's secret police. This was a man who'd experienced loss – she could sense the depth of his pain – and she beckoned for him to come with her. Portugal might not be at war, but their policies and policing were anything but neutral. Camille often wondered if the rest of the world truly understood that, far from being a shining beacon of neutrality, Portugal was in fact brutally sympathetic to fascism.

'I do have a book I think you might like,' she said. 'It's by a British author by the name of Graham Greene, and it's quite something.'

The man hobbled along behind her, and within minutes she was wrapping a copy of *The Power and the Glory* in brown paper for him, having taken it from its hiding place in her office out the back. In exchange, he passed her a scrap of paper with information written on it, and she quickly ran her eyes over the words, her hand hovering over her cash register. To anyone else, it would have looked as if she were counting money, but this exchange was far more important. The paper contained the names and personal information of a woman and two children – this man had come to her shop under the guise of shopping for books, when in fact he wanted her to create false visa documentation for him.

'Not one for you?' she asked, glancing up from the paper.

'I don't care about myself, only them,' he said.

She shook her head. 'No. I will do it for all of you.' Camille lowered her voice. 'Quickly, write your details down, too.'

He grunted and begrudgingly gave them to her, and she slipped the paper into the register quickly in case anyone should walk in. With the book tucked under his arm, he told her where she'd be able to find him, said his thanks and left, and Camille found herself busy for the next hour with a trickle of customers looking for all manner of things. Some wanted volumes of poetry, others were looking for a newspaper, and even more were simply browsing as a way to fill time or to stave off the breeze outside. But it was the regular customers who brought the most joy to Camille; she forgot all about the memories that haunted her at night as she welcomed an elderly lady who visited every day with her tiny dog tucked under one arm, and the young teenager who always smiled shyly when Camille offered her a cup of coffee to sip as she browsed, guessing that she perhaps had nowhere else to go.

Camille spoke to all who came, letting them know she was always ready to help anyone find the right book. She paid for the day's newspapers when they arrived, and opened the shipment that had come from overseas, which was always a treat. Camille tucked those ones behind the counter, knowing there would be a handful of foreigners looking for them before the day's end. Foreign newspapers always seemed to be in high demand these days – almost as much as the secret visas she forged late into the night by candlelight, using her expensive black ink so that it closely matched that used by Portuguese officials. She was only thankful that she didn't need photographs for the visas, which would have made them so much harder to create.

This time when the bell jingled, though, Camille was sitting behind the counter, her head bent as she glanced over a crumpled clandestine French newspaper that she most definitely shouldn't have been reading so openly. She glanced up, expecting it to be another local, but instead she saw a very tall and very handsome man striding towards her.

She quietly tucked the paper away, not wanting to draw attention to what she was reading, before standing and running her hand down her skirt to smooth out any creases. Camille fixed a smile and stepped forward, holding out her hands in greeting. If he asked her, she'd tell him she was filling the hours by keeping up to date with the news in *Avante!*

'Kiefer!' she said, trying to sound bright. 'What a lovely surprise. You should have told me you'd be calling in.'

He took her hands, leaning in and kissing her cheek. 'If I'd told you, it wouldn't be a surprise now, would it?' His German accent was thick, so there was no mistaking where he was from despite the lack of uniform. He was tall and blond, his skin kissed by sunshine and his eyes blue – a shining example of Nazi perfection if ever there was one.

She kept hold of one of his hands, and led him to the back of the store. 'Let me make you a coffee,' she said. 'Or I can put up a sign for the door and we can go out for a late lunch?'

He shook his head. 'I don't have long, I just wanted to call in and see if you'd received any newspapers today?'

Camille swallowed, feeling very much as if she might be walking unknowingly into a trap. Her overseas delivery today had been uneventful, her *Combat,* a paper produced by the French Resistance that she'd almost been caught reading, coming in via a newly arrived Jewish refugee rather than the scheduled delivery. She cleared her throat as nerves wound their way through her body.

'Was there something in particular you were after?' she asked, keeping her voice even. 'I did have a box with British postmarks arrive, but I've been so busy I haven't had a chance to look through it.' Camille quickly realised the error of her words, the inconsistency that a man such as Kiefer would be sure to notice. 'Other than the short break I took just now to read my book, of course. I figured I deserved fifteen minutes of sitting after being on my feet all day.'

She held her smile even as her stomach lurched. But she was well used to showing restraint when it came to her true feelings, and it seemed her performance had been satisfactory.

'Good. I was hoping for *The Times* or the *Daily Telegraph* if you have them.'

'Let me see,' she said, squeezing his hand one more time and receiving another smile. 'There's every chance *The Times* will be in this package.'

Camille walked away, hoping that he was too fixated on watching her figure to notice how many papers she had tucked behind the counter, or to see the paper she'd been reading. She also hoped he hadn't noticed the unusually high pitch of her voice.

Kiefer stood with his legs apart, hands folded in front of him, and she tried not to grimace as she remembered the other men she'd seen like him – the Nazis who'd patrolled the streets of Paris and stood menacingly on street corners. Sometimes just the sight of him made her body start to tremble.

'Ahh, here we are,' she said, trying to sound as bright as could be as she opened the box and sorted through the packet of papers. 'Would a copy of the *Daily Express* be helpful?' She did indeed have the *Times* newspaper he was seeking, but she tucked it away at the bottom so he couldn't see it, intending to keep that for another customer. *A customer who isn't a Nazi.*

Kiefer put down the book he was holding and came back towards her. 'Excellent, thank you.'

Camille didn't ask why it would be that a German living in Portugal might be in need of a British paper – it was as good as implied that every foreign man in Lisbon was spying for his country, there to trade in secrets and collect information – but she just couldn't imagine what truly useful information he'd find in a newspaper. She wondered if perhaps there were secret messages contained within, as far-fetched as that might seem.

'Could I tempt you with a book as well?' she asked. 'Perhaps a volume of poetry? What caught your eye there?'

'You could tempt me with a kiss,' he said, boldly, even as the bell rang behind him.

Camille didn't want to make a fuss, but she certainly didn't want anyone to see her being passionate with him in the shop either, and so she planted her hands on his shoulders and stood on tiptoe, gently pressing a kiss to his cheek.

'How about I see you tonight,' she whispered in his ear, hoping that would be enough to please him.

From the look in his eyes, all she'd done was tempt him more, but she'd rather have to deal with him after-hours than while she was at work.

'You'll meet me for a drink?'

Camille nodded and smiled sweetly. 'I'm looking forward to it.'

And she held her carefully curated smile until Kiefer had turned and walked out of the store, standing there until she could no longer see him, before letting it slide from her face. She pressed a hand to her stomach, feeling physically unwell and hating herself for her duplicity.

'Excuse me,' asked the new customer, a young woman with a boy on her hip who Camille recognised from earlier in the week when they'd been in looking for children's books.

Camille's smile was genuine this time. 'I'll just be a moment,' she said, as she hurried past the counter, snatching the Resistance paper and taking it to her office, where she quickly hid it beneath the floorboards.

Don't be so careless again. If he catches you, he won't give you the chance to explain yourself. You'll be floating in the harbour or hanging from a lamp post by daybreak.

And with her own words berating her, she went back out into the shop to do her job. Her only regret was that she'd agreed to meet with him, which meant she wouldn't be able to get started after closing on the forged documents for the man who'd visited earlier in the day.

An hour later, Camille turned her key in the lock and checked the door to the bookstore before starting the short walk to her apartment. Whenever she was on her own, she had a sense of safety that she doubted most women walking without company felt in other parts of Europe. During the day, the outdoor tables in Lisbon were full of people drinking coffee and reading the paper, eager to discover the news of the day or simply to sit in the sunshine. But Lisbon felt like a contradiction of sorts, with natural enemies passing each other on the street; a city with fascist leanings that quietly allowed Jews to populate the square, knowing that to persecute them was to risk an uprising among the people of Portugal.

In certain parts of Lisbon, large numbers of Jews congregated, most relying on the kindness of locals as they waited for weeks or even months to sail for America. Thousands had reportedly left for New York the year before, but Camille often wondered whether there were any more ships coming for those who were waiting. It wasn't lost on her that she'd once risked everything to get some of these families to Portugal, and some of them were still stuck in limbo in Lisbon. *At least they're alive. They might be stuck, but they're alive.* And with her help, those who'd arrived illegally, who were many, now had documentation that was almost as good as the real thing, or at least she liked to think so.

Soon she reached her apartment, walking quickly up the stairs and unlocking her door, careful to secure it behind her as she dropped her bag on the single armchair in the living room, kicking off her shoes and wriggling her toes. She longed for the soft carpet in the house she'd grown up in, remembering the way her feet had always sunk into it, but she tried not to think about that and instead concentrate on being light-footed as she trod across her threadbare rug.

Kiefer would be waiting for her, which meant she needed to get ready as quickly as possible. She sliced a piece of bread from the loaf, spreading it thinly with butter, and then went back for another when her stomach continued to growl, before hurrying into her room and taking off her work clothes.

Camille slipped into a dress she knew Kiefer would love – a midnight-blue, silk design that clung to her curves, the very same dress she'd worn when they'd first met. She'd heard that the locals thought women who dressed like her were prostitutes, hating the fact that foreigners showed bare legs and didn't wear hats, but Camille wouldn't be alone in dressing for a man tonight, not where she was going. She reached for her red lipstick and then looked at her reflection in the mirror, staring into her eyes – eyes that somehow no longer seemed to belong to her, a gaze that no longer felt like her own.

You can do this, she told herself. *He'll be there waiting for you, and you can do this.*

But she didn't go so far as to tell herself that it was what Hugo would have wanted, because if he were here, he'd have told her to hold a knife to Kiefer's throat and not hesitate to use it.

Barely an hour after closing the bookstore, Camille stood under the twinkling street lights outside the Hotel Aviz, squaring her shoulders before walking up to the door, her heels clicking with every step.

'Good evening,' said the doorman.

'Good evening,' Camille replied, before walking into the loud bar and peering through smoke strong enough to sting her eyes. She paused as she surveyed the room.

And then she saw him. Sitting with two other men, his head tipped back in laughter, a drink in one hand and a cigarette hanging from his lips. But when she caught his gaze, Kiefer immediately stood, dropping his cigarette into a tray and holding out one hand, ever the gentleman. Sometimes she wondered how a human being could be so unfailingly chivalrous, while at the same time part of a regime of such cruelty.

'Camille,' he said, catching her fingers in his and drawing her in to kiss her cheek when she stepped towards him. 'I was afraid you weren't coming.'

She noticed the champagne bottle on the table, not his usual whisky, and the two men with him considering her with appraising glances. Camille reminded herself to stand tall – there was no way they would touch her if she was with Kiefer, which meant she had no reason to wilt under their scrutiny. They could admire her all they liked so long as they didn't think they could try anything on with her.

'It was never a question, I just had to stay until closing, that's all,' she assured him, running her hand up his arm. 'I see you started without me. Are we toasting a special occasion?'

'Can't a man just order champagne?' he replied with a wink.

Camille smiled and held out her hand in greeting to his friends as he introduced them. *Gunther. Carl.* Names she committed to memory in case she ever had need to recall them, but at the same time hoping she wouldn't.

'You're certain you don't mind me joining your group?' she asked, sliding on to the seat beside Kiefer. 'I'd hate to interrupt.'

'There's always space for a beautiful lady, am I right?' Kiefer asked, raising his brows and receiving laughter and raised glasses from the two men seated with him.

Camille realised all three men had already had a lot to drink, but she smiled along anyway, not at all surprised when Kiefer ordered another bottle of champagne at the same time as asking for a glass for her. *French champagne.* It seemed he had a penchant for her country's champagne. And her country's women.

'I'm so happy you could join us, Camille,' Kiefer said, his hand falling over her leg, fingers splaying across the thin fabric of her dress.

She leaned in to him, tipping her head forward so that her hair obscured her face. Anything to stop him from kissing her in public.

Thankfully one of the men at their table said something that made him laugh, and she took the chance to glance around the hotel bar, taking in the eclectic mix of people filling the space. Some were drinking champagne like Kiefer, others were staring into short glasses full of amber-coloured liquid, and one man seated at the bar was drinking what appeared to be an American soda in a bottle. It was fascinating, the sheer number of men from different countries all in the hotel bar at the same time – American, British, German, Japanese and most likely more, mixed with only a handful of affluent locals. And as fabulous as the nightlife was in Lisbon, with hotels, supper clubs and a casino nearby, she doubted they were all here for pleasure.

Camille absorbed it all, taking the smallest sip of the champagne Kiefer poured her and tuning her ear to the conversation at her table, keeping her face impassive as Carl said something vulgar about her in their native tongue. They'd presumed she couldn't speak their language – a pretty girl on their friend's arm and nothing more. But perhaps it would all be worth it, because two

47

hours later, after drinking enough champagne to have them all staggering, Kiefer whispered in her ear.

'Come back to my room with me?'

Fear knotted her stomach. She'd played a cat-and-mouse game with him, always putting him off, coming up with an excuse, but tonight Camille knew she was all out of excuses. If she didn't go to his hotel with him tonight, she feared that he would lose interest, and she would lose her chance to extract information from him.

Camille placed her palm in Kiefer's outstretched hand and let him pull her towards him, tucking close into his side. He swayed slightly from drinking so much, but she pretended not to notice, slipping her hand into the crook of his arm instead and hoping that he was so drunk he'd fall asleep while she was in the bathroom of his hotel.

'I would love to,' she whispered, as he bent down to kiss her.

Forgive me, she thought, blinking away tears as they walked arm in arm to the door, stopping only to retrieve her coat, before stepping out into the cool night air.

She only hoped it would be worth it.

Chapter Five

AVERY

Dear Jack,

You won't believe it, but I'm onboard a plane right now and I'm flying to Lisbon, Portugal! I know war isn't an overseas adventure, even though sometimes you make it sound like you're just away travelling with a bunch of new friends, but this feels enormous to me. My parents barely spoke to me when I went home for the week before flying out; I think they thought that if they gave me the silent treatment they might guilt me into staying. But honestly, Jack? Nothing was going to make me stay. I thought the IDC had the wrong person in the beginning, but I can see now that everything has led to this point. All my studies, my job, it was all worth it.

The worst part was calling things off with Michael, and even though I knew we weren't right for each other, it still broke my heart seeing how upset he was. It was like he couldn't begin to imagine how or why I didn't want to get married. Then my mother had the worst idea to invite him over for dinner just before I left, which was incredibly uncomfortable for everyone, but at least I was able to give him back the engagement ring. Anyway, it's over now, and I hope he meets some lovely girl who adores him and can't wait to be his wife. Because this is going to be the adventure of a lifetime for me, and nothing is going to stop me from making the most of every second. Even if I'm so nervous I actually think I could be sick on my shoes right now!

With all my love. I wish I could see you. Avery.

PS Don't forget to write me back!

Avery folded the letter and placed it in an envelope, tucking it into her bag and then settling back into her seat. She tried not to grip the armrests too tightly, smiling at the woman next to her when she felt her gaze.

'I can't even imagine how this thing is going to land on water,' Avery muttered as she turned to peer out the small window and looked at the long wingspan of the plane, wondering if the propellers ever stopped turning.

'Relax, Pan Am does this flight every other week,' the woman said, gently patting her hand and making her laugh. 'I'm sure they have an excellent safety record.'

Avery glanced at her. 'You're *sure*? That doesn't sound very convincing!'

The woman shrugged. 'Nothing we can do about it now other than sit back and enjoy ourselves.'

Avery sighed. She supposed that was her only option at this stage, although she did wonder how everyone else onboard seemed so relaxed, as if they travelled by air regularly.

'Come on, it looks like we're being served dinner, and then the beds will be turned down for us.'

Avery unbuckled her seat belt and followed the woman's lead, walking past a group of men smoking, the haze lingering around them and making her cough a little, before they made their way through to the lounge where dinner was being served. It was like nothing she could have imagined before, although she'd probably never considered what it would be like to fly in the first place. There were luxurious seats, a dressing room and restrooms, as well as the lounge, dining room and sleeping areas. It was far more luxurious than her house in New York, and she knew that it was an experience she'd never, ever forget, not to mention one she'd never have been able to afford if the IDC hadn't been paying for the fare.

'How long until we arrive in Horta in the Azores?' Avery asked the stewardess as she took her seat at the table.

'Long enough to eat a six-course meal and have a lovely long sleep. We'll be landing before you know it.'

Avery did sit back as she was served her first plate, marvelling at the fine china being used and the petite bread roll placed to one side. Suddenly she didn't care how long it would take to complete the first leg of the flight to Portugal; all she could think about was the delicious smell of warm ham wafting up from her plate.

I'd better not get used to this.

'Would you like a drink?' the stewardess asked.

Avery was almost tempted to order a whisky, imagining that the strong liquor might help her to sleep.

'Coke, please,' she said firmly.

'Honey, it's not every day you're onboard a Boeing 314 Clipper. You sure I can't tempt you with champagne?'

Given how uncertain she was about the big plane staying in the air, she had a feeling she might need to keep her wits about her in case she needed to don a life jacket and leap into the ice-cold water below. Just the thought alone sent a shiver through her. But the idea of champagne was tempting – she'd only been offered it once before, at a cousin's wedding.

Avery sighed. She doubted anything would save her if the plane came down, anyway. 'Just a half glass,' she said. 'I wouldn't want to get tipsy in the air.'

By the end of the second leg of her flight to Lisbon, Avery was ready to stretch her legs and get off the plane, regardless of how luxurious the trip had been. She'd eaten so much food she thought she might pop, been tucked into bed by a stewardess with as much care as a mother would her own child, and eaten a breakfast fit for royalty, not to mention slept like the dead, thanks to the second glass of champagne she'd consumed with dinner. And now the plane was beginning to lower, the sound of the engine changing as they descended towards the water for landing, and she tightened her seat belt and held on to the armrest.

She'd already experienced it once when they landed in Horta, where a handful of passengers had disembarked, but this time felt bumpier and Avery wished she hadn't eaten quite so much for breakfast as her stomach began to lurch. But soon they were hitting the water, not quite the seamless glide of the first time but still bearable, and taxiing towards the floating pontoon. Avery had her nose almost pressed to the window, trying to glimpse as much of Lisbon as possible, and felt so relieved they'd made it without incident.

She'd been shown photos and given maps during her time in Washington DC, but they'd all been taken pre-war and she imagined that the city would have changed somewhat since then. It was almost impossible to see anything other than the water and some buildings in the distance though, try as she might.

'It's time to go,' a pretty stewardess said, gesturing for her to follow. 'I'll help you off and your bags will be taken from the cargo hold and waiting for you on the pontoon.'

Avery stood and followed, thanking the stewardess and about to say something else when she arrived at the plane's door. Her jaw dropped. The first thing that struck her was how strikingly blue the water was, and the second was how different the air smelt in Portugal compared to home. It was somehow fresh and salty at the same time, and she might have stood and stared all day if the stewardess hadn't touched the small of her back and urged her forward.

'It's quite something to see for the first time, isn't it?' she murmured.

Avery nodded in agreement. It was quite something, alright, and somehow not at all as she'd imagined.

She collected her bags, pleased she'd followed the advice given to her during training not to pack more than she could carry herself, although it was certainly still a lot to lug on her own. *Now all I need to do is find my way to the apartment.*

An hour later, Avery's hair was sticking to her face and the perspiration on her body was making her feel as if she was very much out of her depth, not to mention reminding her that she was in a foreign country with a completely unfamiliar climate. She stood outside the address she'd been given, scrawled on a piece of paper that she'd been told to dispose of once she'd found her way, staring up at the two-storey building and hoping it was the right place. It was nondescript, with a number etched into the concrete outside, and she double-checked the address on the wall yet again.

She hadn't been given a key, only the address, and her greatest fear was that she'd end up stranded, waiting for the inhabitants to get home. Hoping very much that wasn't the case, Avery knocked, and then waited. Tears began to well in her eyes when no one answered, and she stepped forward and knocked again, refusing to crumble now.

They picked you for a reason, Avery Johnson. Don't give anyone a reason to think you're not fit for the job by whimpering at the first hurdle. You're made of stronger stuff and you know it.

It was almost as if she could hear her cousin Jack in her mind, spurring her on, telling her that she was made for this. He'd never been happy about her marrying Michael, not because he didn't like him but because he knew how much she wanted to travel and see the world before even thinking about becoming a wife. *Well, this is my chance. If I have to sit out here in the damn sunshine for the rest of the day waiting, then so be it. This one moment doesn't define my entire adventure.*

'Hello?'

The door swinging open and the man's face appearing took her by surprise just as she was about to turn her back and plonk herself down on the concrete step. She quickly ran her hands down her skirt, hoping she didn't look too dishevelled after so long travelling.

'Ahh, I'm Avery. I was told you'd be expecting me.'

He ran his fingers through his hair, which made it stick up even more. He was American, perhaps a little older than her, and she noticed how bloodshot his eyes were, and wondered if he might be unwell or had just gotten out of bed, despite the advanced hour.

'*You're* the new microfilm man?' He looked thoroughly confused. 'From the IDC?'

'That's me, aside from the *man* part, of course. I was told the apartment at this address was where I was supposed to stay. I take it I have the right place?' She grimaced. 'Although I'm feeling more and more as if perhaps you weren't expecting me.'

He cleared his throat and immediately opened the door wide, coming out far enough to take Avery's largest suitcase from her. 'Sorry, you've taken me a bit by surprise. I was told you'd be here this week, but I actually didn't think you'd be here before I left. Not to mention the whole gender misunderstanding, which I apologise profusely for. I'd intended to leave the key under the flower pot.'

'Left?' She hoisted up her other bag and shut the door behind her, following him up the stairs. 'You're leaving here?'

'I've been posted elsewhere; I leave the day after tomorrow. Didn't anyone tell you?'

When they stepped into the apartment, it was very clear that whoever this man was, he'd been living alone and most definitely hadn't been expecting company. There were things strewn everywhere, including bowls and cutlery, and an open bag on the small dining table was stuffed full with belongings, not to mention stacks of newspapers piled high on the floor.

'Excuse the mess. If I'd known you were arriving . . .'

Avery kept hold of her bag, deciding not to put it down on the floor, which looked equally in need of a good clean. 'If you could just point me in the direction of my bedroom . . .'

'Sorry, where are my manners,' he said. 'Tom.'

'Avery,' she said, reluctantly letting her bag go and sticking out her hand. 'You're a librarian too?' she asked.

'No, I was a research assistant at Harvard before they recruited me for this job. It's a pretty good posting, if I'm honest. Lisbon is an easy place to enjoy yourself.'

Avery nodded, not sure whether she was pleased he was leaving or sad. She'd certainly never lived alone before, but then she'd never shared accommodation with a man other than her father either.

'The bedroom?' she reminded him.

'Ahh, yes, sorry, I have a few things in there. I'll clean them out straight away.' He dashed down the hall ahead of her. 'I've been here a month on my own now. There were two of us but he was posted elsewhere – Stockholm, I think?'

Avery stood and waited, pushing her damp hair off her face and wishing she could draw herself a bath and soak in the hot water until it went cold. She felt as if she'd been travelling for days.

'Sorry, one more question. Where would I freshen up?' she asked, when he came past with his second armful of things and announced the room was ready.

'Down the hallway and to the left. We share with one other apartment, but he's barely ever there.'

Avery nodded and took her bags into the room, pulling the drapes wide and letting some light in. It was small but comfortable enough, with a narrow wardrobe and a desk and chair in the corner. She had a few possessions from home to liven it up, and she was certain there would be things to buy locally to make it feel more like a home. Either way, it was her own space, and for that she was grateful.

'Avery?'

She looked up expectantly. Tom stood at the door, his face hovering between a smile and uncertainty. She realised that, despite his mess, she'd immediately warmed to him, and was starting to wish that he was staying simply because she was nervous about being alone.

'I'll let you get settled in tonight, but tomorrow night me and some of the guys are heading to the Hotel Avenida, a going-away drinks of sorts in my honour. You're welcome to join us if you'd like?'

'I'd love to, thanks for asking.'

He gave her a long look, as if there might have been something else he was going to say, but she spoke before he did.

'Tom, I was told that someone would walk me through the process here – how to get the microfilm back to Washington and such. Is that person you?'

He laughed. 'They didn't walk you through all that during training?'

'You could say that my training was rather expedited, and although I know we use a diplomatic pouch, they told me there'd be someone on the ground to help with logistics when I arrived.'

'You only had a few weeks of training?' he asked.

She grimaced. 'More like one, then I was sent home on leave until my passport was ready and my flight organised.'

'They must have been in quite a rush to get you here. Tomorrow afternoon suit?'

'Perfect. It'll give me time to explore and try to find my first publication.'

'I'll make a list of the best places to go each day. Remind me tomorrow.'

Tom gave her a wink then and left, and she sat on her bed and listened to what she imagined was him frantically tidying the living room. Avery smiled, despite how tired she was, and lay back on the bed for a moment, the fatigue of travelling very much catching up with her. She would rest a bit before freshening up, and give him some time before reappearing in the living room.

I'm actually here. In Portugal. In my own apartment.

It was almost impossible to believe it, but she'd done it, and she wasn't going to let anyone wonder if they'd sent the wrong girl. This was exactly where she was supposed to be.

Avery opened her eyes, taking a moment to remember where she was. It all came back in a flood of memories – the plane, the apartment, lying down – and she realised that instead of exploring her new home, she'd fallen asleep. It didn't take her long to change her clothes, and when she walked out into the living area she was surprised to see it looking as tidy as could be, with a note for her on the table along with a key.

> *There's some leftover food in the kitchen, help yourself, and if you wake up in time, the market is the place to go. Head down the street and turn right when you see the vendors set up on the roadside. See you tomorrow (don't wait up tonight!). Tom.*

She put the note down, grateful that Tom had been so considerate to think of her, and glanced at her wristwatch to see the time. It was very late in the afternoon now, so she doubted that anything would still be open, but she was determined to at least have a look around. Within minutes she'd fixed her hair and applied a sweep of red lipstick, and then she was locking the door and stepping out on to the street, her eyes wide as she watched two women with straight backs and big smiles balancing fish baskets on their heads, a man sitting on his doorstep smoking a cigarette, and a group of children laughing and running in the opposite direction. The city immediately felt alive to her, and it was like nothing she'd ever seen before. Until that day, she'd barely gone a few miles out of New York, other than her recent trip to Washington, and it felt as if she'd travelled to another world, it was so different. It was colourful and bright, warm and quaint, all at the same time. It was exactly as she'd hoped it would be, and more. And perhaps most surprising of all, there were no signs of a world at war.

Avery began to walk, taking in all the different people around her, her low heels clicking on the cobbled pavement. She had the distinct feeling that she could walk for hours, taking in the sights and breathing in the scenery, and she only wished she had someone with her to share the experience with, and that it wasn't quite so late in the day.

She rounded a corner then and saw a few small stores, wishing she'd brought her map with her so that she could figure out where everything was. There were two bookstores that she was supposed to frequent as often as possible, as well as a newspaper vendor another street over, and she was certain that one of the bookshops was in the area closest to her apartment.

Avery headed towards the shops, eager to look in the windows even if they were shut, and sure enough she soon came to a bookstore with a little sign in the door turned to 'Closed'. But she could see that it was jammed full of books, with shelves lining the far wall and tables set up through the middle, and she couldn't wait to go in and explore the next day to see what she could find.

She kept walking, eventually circling back and finding the market Tom had written about, watching as the stallholders tidied up and left for the day, carrying baskets and talking in rapid-fire Portuguese that she hadn't a hope of understanding. Brushing up on her language skills was going to be her first task, other than sourcing the publications she'd been sent to discover.

But then the most magical thing happened. The street lights began to click on, one after the other, just as the sun began to lower in the sky. Avery burst out laughing, her hand over her mouth, as she twirled on the spot and looked up and down the street. It wasn't even dark yet, but she could already imagine what it must be like at night, with the lights twinkling in the dark and illuminating the city.

After months of blackouts at home – and all around the world from what she'd read – Portugal was like a little beacon of light amid the darkness, and she couldn't wait to write home and tell her parents about it.

'Are you lost or just enchanted?'

She turned at the man's voice, obviously directed at her because he'd spoken in English and with a very British accent.

Avery shook her head, realising how silly she must have looked twirling around to see everything – so much for blending in. She was the most obvious tourist in all of Lisbon.

'Not lost, but thank you for asking.'

The man was tall and lanky, with dark hair that fell slightly on to his face. His skin was golden, as if he spent a good deal of time enjoying the sunshine, and his smile was easy.

'Your first time in Lisbon?'

Avery laughed. 'Is it so obvious?'

He just gave her a lopsided smile and went on his way, a newspaper tucked under one arm, and Avery decided to retrace her steps and head for home. She couldn't wait to explore Lisbon more in the morning, but for now she needed to find something to stop her stomach from growling, and set up her bedroom.

Thankfully her mother had packed enough baked goods to last her for days, so she wouldn't have to raid Tom's supplies in the kitchen, but as she walked back to her apartment, it wasn't food she was thinking of. It was the devilishly handsome man who'd spoken to her on the street and then disappeared.

Her footsteps quickened as she wondered if perhaps he lived in the area, because she certainly wouldn't mind seeing him again. But then she remembered what they'd called Lisbon when she'd been in Washington – the 'city of spies' – and she wondered if perhaps he was someone she shouldn't hope to run into again, no matter how handsome he might have been.

The last thing she wanted was a complication. She was in Lisbon to work, and that was exactly what she intended on doing. Avery most certainly didn't have time for distractions.

Chapter Six

CAMILLE

Camille woke early. She'd drawn the curtains when Kiefer had fallen asleep the night before, and she was grateful for her foresight now as she carefully extracted herself from beneath his arm. She held her breath as she wriggled silently away from him, waiting to check his breathing hadn't changed before quietly sliding out of the bed. As it was the first night she'd gone to bed with him, she had no idea how deeply he slept, and how easily she could slip away without him noticing. All she wanted was to bathe and wash the scent of him from her skin, to scrub the memories of what she'd done from her body, but if she did that now, it would have all been for nothing.

Her pulse raced as she tiptoed across the room to where he'd discarded his clothes the night before, his jacket and trousers flung over the single chair in the hotel room. Camille glanced back, knowing that she was taking a big risk as she reached for the pile of clothing, her breath silent yet ragged. This was the only reason she'd accepted his invitation, and she had to take her chance.

But before she could check the pockets of his jacket, her fingers inches away from the fabric, she heard him stir. It was just the slightest rustle of sheets, but it was enough to unnerve her.

Camille took a quick step sideways and opened the curtains to let a small amount of light filter into the room, her heart thudding away in her chest. If he caught her . . .

'Good morning,' she murmured, turning around and heading back to the bed, stretching her arms above her head as she pretend-yawned. 'Did you just wake up?'

Kiefer sat up, his hair messy and his eyes half-lidded. But she didn't miss the question in his stare, telling her that he didn't trust her. 'What were you doing?'

'I was just peeking through the curtains to see whether the sun was shining yet or not,' she said. 'I don't have a wristwatch to check the time.'

He grunted, and she hoped that he'd bought her story. To distract him, she slid back into bed and leaned down to kiss him. He grabbed hold of her wrist as she did so, kissing her back and then examining her arm immediately after, as if to check whether or not she was telling the truth about the watch. Camille forced herself to hold her smile, as if there was nothing unusual about him doubting her.

Seemingly satisfied, he pushed up until he was propped with pillows behind him. He was incredibly handsome with his thick, dark-blond hair and bright blue eyes, his shoulders broad as he sat before her, but no matter how good-looking he might be, nothing could distract her from who he was. Every time she looked at him, he was a reminder of what she'd lost and what had happened to France under Nazi occupation.

'Come here,' he said. 'Spend the morning with me in bed.'

'I wish I could,' she murmured, leaning in to kiss him one last time, but quick to evade his hold on her. She smiled down at him, her long hair falling over her shoulder.

'What's the rush?'

'I have a bookshop to open,' she said. 'And I need to bathe and change my clothes first. I can't exactly turn up smelling of my lover and dressed like this, can I?'

'You're certain you can't take the day off?' he said, looking most put out.

'I'm certain,' she said. 'Maybe another day.'

'What if I came and helped you? I could stack books or something.'

'Help me? What a waste of your day off that would be,' Camille said, immediately suspicious of why he'd want to spend a day in her shop with her. Only the smallest part of her believed it was because he wanted to be with her, even though there was a chance that he was simply being kind and liked her company. More likely he wanted to spy on her or her customers.

She smiled and turned, going around to his side of the bed so he could zip up the back of her dress for her. His kindness towards her was at odds with the man she expected him to be, and she always found that she was reminding herself of who and what he was.

'Can I offer you my jacket to walk home in?' he asked.

Camille faltered, not expecting such thoughtfulness from him. 'Thank you.'

She turned, still barefoot, and reached for the jacket he'd left on the chair, but Kiefer was too fast. He was out of bed and crossing the room with a speed that surprised her, taking the jacket and emptying the pockets. She saw two folded pieces of paper and a card, along with a carton of cigarettes and matches, and she wished she'd been able to go through his things before he'd woken. It was even worse knowing there had possibly been something in there to discover.

He leaned in and pressed a kiss to her bare shoulder, skimming a hand down her side and over her hip, before holding the jacket for her to shrug into. Camille spun around and looped her arms around his neck, kissing him slowly on the mouth, knowing that the key to his heart was to make him feel wanted. She'd already gone so far, which meant she needed to keep up the pretence.

'Perhaps you could come past the bookshop this afternoon?' she asked. 'I'll have your jacket waiting for you.'

Kiefer made a sound in his throat that she took as a yes, given the hungry way he was looking at her.

'I have a newspaper coming in that you might be interested in, too.'

His eyebrows raised. '*The Times*?'

She tapped her nose. 'It's a secret. But visit me and I'll have it for you.'

'In exchange for borrowing my jacket?'

Camille grinned. 'Well, there was something else I hoped you might be able to procure for me, in exchange for the very best British papers,' she said, knowing she was taking a risk by asking anything of him, but doing it anyway. After spending the night with him, she was hoping he'd be more pliable. 'Although I do appreciate the jacket, regardless.'

He turned and reached for his cigarettes, taking one out and lighting it. Camille nodded when he offered it to her, taking a long inhale and slowly blowing the smoke out before passing it back to him. His eyes were narrowed, but she could see the beginnings of a smile playing across his lips.

'A diamond? A fancy wristwatch?' he asked. 'What bauble are you coveting?'

'A wireless radio, actually,' Camille said. 'I so miss listening to the radio, especially on the nights when I'm alone. It would mean the world to me if you could get me one.' The truth was that other than the snippets of information she received from the newly arrived refugees from France, who were few and far between these days, she wasn't hearing any current news. The papers in Portugal were mostly empty of any news on the war, as if their neutrality translated to a blanket ban on even mentioning world events.

He narrowed his gaze again and she watched as he blew an almost-perfect smoke ring into the air, clearly something he'd spent many hours practising. It was somehow impossible to look away from, as much as she didn't want to be impressed by him.

'A radio?' he asked.

She nodded. 'Yes, a radio.'

'Very well. I'll see what I can do. But you have that paper for me today, yes? And anything else you have coming in this week?'

Camille smiled and took a step backwards, and then another, not wanting him to try to lure her back to bed. 'I will. I've also added your subscription to the German papers to my orders, so you will be receiving them regularly from now on.'

He grunted. 'Good.'

'I'll see you this afternoon,' she said, pausing only to push her feet into her heels, closing his jacket around her body and then slipping from the room.

She shut the door behind her and kept walking, even as her legs trembled, not wanting to stop until she was well away from the building. Her hair was loose about her shoulders when usually it was pinned carefully into place, her dress was too tight for daytime, and it was obvious she was wearing a man's coat – but worst of all, she felt as if she'd betrayed her husband. All this time she'd led Kiefer on but never had to go to his bed to get what she wanted, and now the smell of him on her skin, the scent of his cigarettes and aftershave on his jacket, it was all too much. It made her want to be sick.

When she rounded the corner, Camille pressed herself against the wall, her breath coming in fast hiccups as she fought for air, as if there wasn't enough space in her lungs. She'd told herself it would be easy to seduce a Nazi, and by and large it had been, only she hadn't thought about what it would feel like for her to be with another man, to feel as if she were betraying her husband even though he'd been gone for so long now. To let another man touch her, a *German* man do things to her that she didn't want anyone who wasn't her husband to ever do to her again.

'Once all this is over, we're going to live the life we've always dreamed of.'

Camille tucked closer to her husband, her leg thrown casually over his as she trailed her fingertips across his chest. 'Sometimes I wonder if this will ever be over though. Freedom feels like a distant dream these days.'

'Of course it will be over, and then we can find that house we've always talked about. Your father can come with us, and—'

'You're certain you want him to come?'

Hugo laughed. 'I think we'll be grateful to have someone to mind all those children we're going to have, don't you? We won't want to leave them with a stranger.'

They both laughed, heads tipped together. And when Camille kissed him, she touched her lips slowly to his, taking her time, not wanting to ever leave their bed. She'd loved Hugo from their very first date, talking so late into the night that it had become morning, their fingers intertwined as he'd walked her home at daybreak, promising to see one another the very next day. Already imagining a life together after hours of being in his company.

'I wish we could stay hidden here until it's all over,' she whispered against his skin. 'Our little love nest.'

'So do I,' he murmured back, his hand around the back of her head, gently drawing her closer. 'But they need us. France needs us.'

She nodded. Despite her desire to stay tucked up in bed with her husband, he was right, and there was nothing she wouldn't do for her country. She wanted her freedom back like everyone else, and that meant staying to fight, no matter what. Because she wanted freedom for everyone, not just for them personally.

Camille sighed and kissed him once more, knowing that they didn't have long before they had to leave, and wanting to make the most of every moment, wishing they could have longer, just the two of them.

'For France,' she said with a sigh. 'And then *for us.'*

Hugo grinned and pulled her down on top of him, and Camille didn't resist, loving the feel of her husband's body against hers, the weight of him, the strength of him. She'd been drawn to him from the moment they'd met, a friend her brother had brought home for dinner; their eyes had immediately locked across the table as if they were the only two people in the room.

'I love you,' he said, his mouth against her neck.

'I love you, too.'

'Just keep remembering our dream. The house with the big garden, the restaurant we're going to open, surrounded by all our children.'

Camille straightened, pushing off from the wall and hurrying down the street as memories threatened to consume her; memories that usually only plagued her during the night when she tried to sleep, but were now chasing her while she was awake. Sleep was no longer something she could count on, the terror coming for her night after night, no matter how hard she tried to forget. Right now, though, she had to forget, because if she didn't, her memories would make it impossible to fulfil her mission.

They'd called her the Little Rabbit for a reason in France, because she was so good at sneaking around undetected, and she intended on living up to her codename. It was all she had now that Hugo was gone, and it had to mean *something*.

She kept her head bent, obscuring her face with her hand as she dashed down one cobbled street after another, not slowing until she was at her apartment. It was time to wash and get ready for work, because the bookshop wouldn't open itself, and rather than being a chore, it was the one thing in her life these days that made her smile. And smiling was no longer something she ever took for granted.

Her bookshop was also a lifeline for those Jewish refugees who needed her, and nothing, not memories nor nightmares, could stop her from doing everything she could to help them.

The rest of Camille's morning was uneventful, serving a handful of people every hour who were trying to find books to keep their minds off things, and talking with her regulars, until the bell jingled and a young woman in her early twenties stepped into the store. Camille glanced up from the letter she was writing, following the woman with her eyes and noting how nervous she seemed, which was unusual. Most people relaxed the moment they stepped inside, as if the very sense of being surrounded by books was enough to calm them, but it appeared that the opposite had happened in this case. Camille immediately wanted to find out more, and knew she'd never seen her before. The woman was too pretty to be forgotten, and looked different from her usual clientele. She also seemed to be of a similar age to Camille, maybe a year or two younger.

Camille assessed her for a little longer, before finally calling out.

'Good morning,' she said in Portuguese, even though she was certain the woman wouldn't know the language. Her dress was fashionable, and she was wearing heels, her dark-blonde hair half up with soft curls falling from the pins. She looked . . . Camille narrowed her gaze. She looked distinctly out of place, and it immediately made Camille suspicious. If she wasn't local, and she wasn't a refugee, then who was she?

The woman nodded, her eyes meeting Camille's.

'You're French?' Camille asked, in her native tongue, just to see whether the woman could understand her or not.

'American,' the woman replied, flashing Camille a small smile. 'But my grandmother was French and my grandfather Portuguese, so I speak a little of both languages.'

'And what brings an American girl all the way to Lisbon?' Camille asked, frowning.

She'd seen all sorts come looking in her shop, usually British, German or even Japanese men, as well as an increasing number of Americans lately, and they were all looking for foreign newspapers or magazines, all eager to obtain the same material it seemed. The last American had offered to trade her chewing gum and candy if Camille made sure to keep certain papers behind the counter for him alone, on top of whatever price she charged. It didn't take much guesswork to know they were spies, and with Portugal being one of the few places they could move around without sanctions, in a country almost entirely unaffected by the war, it was like a melting pot of nationalities. The fact they seemed to have an unlimited amount of money to spend was another giveaway.

'Actually, would you believe that I'm a librarian?' the American said. 'I've been sent here to find and preserve history for our Library of Congress. They're determined to document the war as carefully as possible, for historical purposes, so I'm going to be very busy . . .' The woman laughed. 'Sorry, I talk too much when I'm nervous!'

Camille didn't buy the story for a second. The woman's eyes were wide and she looked more nervous than a girl on her first date, which told Camille that there was more to the story than she was letting on. Camille certainly wasn't convinced the woman was a librarian, and the last thing she needed was trouble around her shop, or another reason for the police to come looking.

'Well, that's all rather interesting,' Camille replied. 'I dare say you're the first American librarian I've met before, although perhaps there are more here and they simply haven't introduced themselves?'

The woman smiled. 'Perhaps,' she said. 'All the others would have been men though, so they might not stick out like a sore thumb in the same way I do.'

'Ahh, I see,' Camille said, considering the woman before her and trying to ascertain whether she was genuinely nervous or playing a very convincing part. Perhaps the talking-too-much nerves were part of her cover story. 'And this endeavour, it is helpful to your country?'

The American frowned. 'Yes, it's very helpful. They've sent me a long way to complete the task.'

Camille forced a smile, considering that she'd been too direct with her question. It wasn't her intention to be rude to customers, especially not American ones with deep pockets when she very much needed the money. 'And how are you finding Lisbon so far?'

'It's beautiful here. Nothing at all what I expected. We keep hearing stories of fallen cities and ruined buildings back home in America, but to think war hasn't touched Portugal is almost impossible to believe until you see it with your own eyes. It's certainly something else.' She paused for breath. 'I've heard that Jews and Nazis might even pass on a street corner here. Is it true?'

'Yes, it's true,' Camille said. 'But don't for a moment think that those Jews aren't terrified, just because they're in Lisbon, because they are. They've seen things, experienced things, that you couldn't even imagine if you tried. So the fact that they might be standing on a street corner side by side does not for a second mean they're not still scared, that war hasn't touched here, because it has.'

The woman's eyes widened and her cheeks turned a deep shade of pink. 'I'm sorry, I didn't realise. That was incredibly naive of me.'

But Camille found she couldn't stop now that she'd started speaking, anger bubbling up inside of her. 'Those French Jews who've made it here? They are only a handful, a lucky few who managed to flee and find safety here. If you'd seen Nazi soldiers marching the streets in Paris as if they owned the place, hungry children starving and begging for food, the mothers lined on street corners . . .' Camille blinked away a tear, knowing she should stop but not able to; she was so angry. It was all too much – this naive American, the night she'd spent with Kiefer, the memories she was trying so hard to bury. 'War has touched here,' she said, softly this time, restraining herself. 'Just because the Jews don't have yellow stars pinned to their jackets and the buildings are still standing, doesn't mean it hasn't touched the people here.'

The American's eyes were filled with tears now, and Camille regretted how harsh she'd been with her words. But after everything she'd been witness to, she couldn't stand that anyone could be so naive.

'Please accept my apology,' she said, taking a deep breath and holding out her hand. 'The war has taken a lot from me, but I should have held my tongue. I'm Camille.'

'Avery,' the woman said, her palm soft against Camille's. 'But there's no need to apologise. You were right in speaking frankly, and it's me who should be sorry. It was a silly question I asked.'

They both stared at each other for a long moment, before Camille finally spoke again. 'May I help you find something while you're here? A book perhaps? It's the least I can do.'

'Well,' Avery said hesitantly, as if she wasn't sure what to say, or perhaps she was trying to be careful with her words so she didn't receive another sharply worded lecture. 'I'm interested in books, but I'm really looking for newspapers.'

'Foreign editions?' Camille asked. 'You mean British? German? Or our local Portuguese paper that's delivered every day?'

Avery's smile seemed more relaxed now, and Camille found herself curious all over again about who this woman actually was. Given how Avery had reacted to the tongue-lashing she'd given her, Camille was starting to wonder if she *was* perhaps just an innocent librarian and not a highly trained spy.

'Well, anything you have would be a great start,' Avery said. 'I'd also, well, the book burning in Berlin . . .'

Camille waited, not filling the silence and letting Avery continue talking instead.

'The types of books that were destroyed, well, it would be a great shame to not preserve them for history's sake, if you know what I mean. If you ever had a copy, I would most certainly be interested.'

Camille didn't imagine for a moment that an American woman had been sent all the way to Portugal for history's sake, but she went along with it anyway.

'The books you speak of, if I were to have anything like that and the wrong person discovered such a thing . . . Well.' Camille paused and lowered her voice, realising just how ill-informed Avery truly was. It was as if she didn't even understand how careful she had to be, that a person couldn't just speak their mind in such a way. 'Avery, you can't go around asking openly for those types of books. Lisbon, all of Portugal in fact, leans very heavily towards fascism.'

Avery visibly paled. 'I thought, I meant I didn't—'

'I'd be thrown in a cell by the PVDE if I were to sell you such a book and they found out. They take censorship very seriously, and I cannot have anything like that in my shop. They raided me only last month, and another bookshop that was openly pro-Allies was closed down only weeks ago.' *Before I took up with Kiefer. When they were more inclined to wonder if I was a Jewish sympathiser.*

72

'I-I thought Lisbon was neutral, but I'm guessing that's just something else I'm wrong about?' Avery asked.

Camille nodded, glancing around her shop at the wooden shelves heaving with books, considering her words before speaking again. 'The authorities tolerate the Jews being here because they have to, because most of the locals are sympathetic, but we have to be careful about what we do, what we say, and certainly what we read. The authorities might let the Jews inhabit the streets, but they certainly don't want their publications, or I dare say anything else that might paint Germany in a bad light. It's a very fine line to walk, and one you'll have to learn to tread carefully if you're going to live here.'

Avery nodded and turned, walking slowly down the closest row of books, her fingers trailing over their spines. Camille watched as she glanced around the store, as if to check they were alone before she spoke again.

'Are there many other French women living here?'

'In Lisbon?' Camille shook her head. 'No, unless you count the French Jewish refugees waiting for boats. There are few French women living here.'

The American woman looked crestfallen, and Camille felt at least partly responsible. It was impossible not to be cynical and suspicious after what Camille had been through, but she could have been a little softer in her approach. She could see that now.

'How about I take a look for the types of newspapers you're searching for. I'm sure there will be something in yesterday's delivery that will be of interest to you, and I'll be sure to include a copy of our local paper as well. That's published daily and I have them delivered every morning.' Avery's face lit up and Camille went out the back into her office and took out the foreign papers she had sorted there, glancing through them and selecting a German one, as well as the British *Daily Mirror* and the local newspaper.

When she walked back out, Avery was glancing at a book, and Camille moved closer to see what she was looking at.

'You have good taste.' Avery was flicking through the first few pages of Virginia Woolf's *Mrs Dalloway.*

'The best part about working at a library is discovering authors. But I spent most of my time microfilming old books and newspapers that would otherwise have been disposed of.'

Camille's eyebrows lifted in question. 'Disposed of?'

'There simply isn't room to store everything forever, but—' Avery stopped talking, as if she'd suddenly realised she'd said too much. 'Anyway, it's nice to spend time looking at all your lovely books; you have an impressive inventory. Tomorrow I might come back and find something to read for myself, if I have the chance.'

'This microfilming you speak of—'

'Oh, it's nothing. Something for another day,' Avery said quickly. 'What do you have there?'

'It's a German book on military tactics I thought might be of interest.'

Avery's eyes widened as she reached for it, flicking through the first few pages and then smiling. 'Thank you, this is definitely what I'm looking for.'

Camille was about to ask Avery another question, curious about what microfilming was, when the little bell above the door announced a new visitor. And her American customer must have noticed how still she had gone, because she immediately held out the book.

'I'll take it,' Avery said.

Camille quickly folded the newspapers against it, wrapping them in brown paper and passing the package back to Avery. The American had been in her store for long enough – she didn't need anyone who might be watching to think she was collaborating with an Allied spy.

'I'm certain you'll love the book,' Camille said as she rang the sale up on the cash register and took the money Avery passed to her, trying not to look nervous as Kiefer stepped up to the counter.

Avery turned when Kiefer cleared his throat behind her. Or perhaps she was more perceptive than Camille had given her credit for and could sense the change in her, and wanted to see who was the cause of it.

'Oh goodness, I wasn't expecting such a handsome man to be standing so close,' Avery said, clutching her book to her chest and moving quickly past Kiefer.

If Camille had doubted the woman's ability to pass as a spy in the beginning, she didn't now.

'Oh dear, look at me being all clumsy,' Avery said, knocking into a table and turning to give Camille a quick smile as Kiefer bent to collect the fallen books. 'You've got me all flustered here.'

'Be sure to come back when you're ready for another good book,' Camille called out.

'A romance next time!' Avery said. 'Put something aside for me when you get a chance.'

With Kiefer's attention diverted as he watched Avery leave the shop, Camille took a deep, shaky breath, grateful for the reprieve before readying herself with a practised smile.

'Kiefer,' she purred when he turned to her, the bell signalling that Avery had left. 'What a wonderful surprise.'

'Who was that woman?' he asked, striding towards her and running a hand through his hair.

Camille shrugged. 'A woman looking for a book to read, that's all.'

'An American?' he asked.

She swallowed, knowing there was no point in lying to him. If he wanted to find out who Avery was, he'd follow her himself, so she may as well tell the truth.

'An American librarian, actually,' Camille said, reaching for the jacket she had folded behind the counter for him. She'd even dabbed a little drop of her perfume inside the collar. 'This is for you.'

He took it from her, and before he could ask, she took out a small bundle of newspapers for him. 'This is a copy of *The Times* from last week and today's Portuguese newspaper.' She smiled. 'I also have a very recent copy of an American *Time* magazine that I was able to procure. I thought it might be of interest.'

His smile told her that he'd already forgotten all about the American girl, and she realised that it had most definitely been worth giving him the single copy of *Time* that she'd had delivered. If anything, it would help him to trust her.

'Well, aren't you full of surprises today.' He took the papers and tucked them under his arm.

'Will I be seeing you tonight?' she asked.

Kiefer shrugged. 'Perhaps. But I have work to do today and it might spill over into tonight.'

'Well, perhaps tomorrow night then,' she said, relieved that she'd have time to work on her forgeries rather than having to see him, and just then the bell rang again and one of her regular customers entered – a mother with her young child on her hip.

The woman looked nervous, as many did when they saw a man like Kiefer. With his blond hair and height, it was obvious he wasn't local, not to mention his thick accent giving away that he was German. If it had been a Jewish customer, she didn't doubt that they would have run straight back out the door and disappeared on to the street, perhaps never to enter her bookshop again.

'I should have what you asked me for later this week,' he said. 'You just keep these papers coming to me, yes? And I'll see you another night.'

Camille nodded and waved goodbye to him, exhaling the breath she hadn't even known she was holding and taking a moment before going to help the mother and son with their book selection. But even as she talked to them and found books the young boy might like, it was Avery she kept thinking about.

She might just be the librarian she was claiming to be, and if that was the case then Camille wanted to find out everything there was to know about her pretty new American customer. And she especially wanted to find out what this microfilming was that she had spoken of, because she had the strangest feeling that if the woman's sympathies were strong enough, she might be one of the few people in the city who could be useful when it came to Camille's late-night forgeries. Most especially if she had a camera at her disposal and experience at developing film.

It was after dark when Camille reached the square. She'd worked late, and the forged visas she'd penned were now drying, but when she'd left her shop, a little boy had been waiting in the shadows. It was the boy she was still following now, but she was careful to walk a long way behind him just in case she was being watched, not wanting to put him in danger.

It wasn't a crime to liaise with the large numbers of Jewish families now populating the square, but she was reluctant to give the Portuguese police any further reason to be suspicious of her.

The little boy dashed into one of the many makeshift tents – the square had become almost like a city of refugees – and Camille waited for a moment, looking behind her before following him again.

'She's here,' the boy whispered in French, and a woman's head emerged barely a second later.

'Thank you for coming,' the woman said. 'You are the lady from the bookshop? The French lady?'

Camille nodded.

'We were told we could trust you.'

'I can't be here for long. Do you need visas?'

'Yes, and I also need identification papers for my daughter,' the woman said. 'She's only a toddler, but we won't be able to leave without papers. I'm afraid of what the authorities will do if they catch us.'

'Do any of you have visas to be here?' Camille asked.

The woman shook her head, tears filling her eyes, visible in the glow of the street light. 'No.'

'Without the right documentation for all of you, they could send you all back,' Camille told her. 'The PVDE raid the camps here often, looking for those who are here illegally. You're not safe without entrance visas.'

'I have no money to offer you, I can't—'

Camille reached for the woman's hands and held them tightly, the conversation reminding her of the last time she and Hugo had said the same words she was about to whisper now. 'I don't want payment from you. Your safety is payment enough, and you'll need everything you have for your passage out of Portugal.'

The woman's hands were cold in Camille's and she kept hold of them, wanting to warm them as much as she could before she let go.

'Do you need blankets? Is there anything I can do to help you be more comfortable?'

Tears slipped down the woman's cheeks then, and Camille felt emotion building up in her throat as their eyes met. They had both known pain, and they had an immediate bond over what they'd suffered.

'I knew who you were. When they were talking about you here in the camp, I knew.'

Camille studied her face, but she was certain she'd never seen this woman before.

'You helped my brother and his family, a long time ago. You and your husband.'

Camille's breath caught at the mention of Hugo. 'I helped many families, but your brother . . .' She closed her eyes, wondering if it was him, seeing the man and his family in her mind, remembering the hope shining from their gazes when she and Hugo had promised them that they'd take them to safety, before everything had turned upside down. She wanted to ask, but the question stuck on her tongue.

'I'm told my brother made it to New York. It's why I'm hoping to follow him.' The breath the woman let out shuddered from her lips. 'It's why I risked everything.'

Camille's shoulders sagged with relief. 'Then we need you to be ready. I'll make the visas for you first, and then your daughter's identification.' She frowned. 'I don't have a camera for passports, but I'll find one. You can trust me, I promise I'll find a way.'

She had the woman write down details for her, and Camille carefully placed the paper into a hidden pocket in her coat, before disappearing into the dark again. Women like the one she'd just met, mothers fighting to keep their children alive, gave Camille a purpose in Lisbon, and the moment the sun came up she would be back in her bookshop working on their visas. Because if they were caught without the correct paperwork because she hadn't completed it fast enough, they'd surely be sent back to where they'd come from, and that wasn't something she wanted on her conscience.

Chapter Seven

AVERY

Avery walked down the street with her pulse racing and a spring in her step. She'd done it, she'd actually acquired her first two foreign newspapers! But something about the man who'd entered the bookshop had made her nervous. And the way the bookshop lady had bundled the book and newspapers up so quickly made her wonder who he was; perhaps the PVDE she'd spoken of? Or, Avery gulped, a Nazi. The very thought sent a shiver down her spine. In hindsight, he *had* looked Aryan, which meant she may have just rubbed shoulders with the enemy. It was so hard to tell when his English had been so heavily accented.

She hurried back to the apartment, her mind full of everything the bookshop owner had told her, stopping only on the street corner to see what the vendor was selling, but quickly realising it was the same local paper that Camille had already given her. Everything else had either sold out or not arrived yet, and she needed to return rather than search for more publications. Tom's departure had been delayed by a day, as had the drinks he'd invited her to at the hotel, but he'd still promised to walk Avery through everything she needed to know that afternoon, so she didn't want to be late. He'd been sleeping when she left, but it was almost noon now and she doubted he'd still be snoring. If he was anything like her cousin Jack, it would be his stomach that eventually woke him.

When she finally reached the apartment, she found Tom nursing his head at the table, a piece of bread spread thickly with jam in front of him.

'Late night?' she asked, going to pour him a glass of water and setting it in front of him.

'Thank you.' He groaned but sat back and mustered a smile. 'Far too late.' He glanced at her brown paper package. 'What do you have there?'

'Well, I'm not entirely certain as the bookshop lady wrapped it up so quickly, but—'

'The French lady?' he asked. 'What's her name? Camille, is it?'

Avery nodded slowly, as if she wasn't sure whether to confirm or deny the fact. 'Should I not have? Her bookshop was on the list I was given and—'

Tom waved his hand. 'No, it's fine. She seems to stock all types of interesting books and newspapers there, but . . .' He made a noise in his throat. 'Someone said she's linked to a Nazi, although it could be nothing more than a rumour. They seem to spread faster than the truth here.'

'*Romantically* linked?' Avery asked, aware that her voice had become very high-pitched.

'Look, I'm sure it's not because she's a Nazi sympathiser. Women have to do certain things to survive in wartime, if you know what I mean, and I've heard she was widowed.'

'Well,' Avery said, digesting what she'd just been told and hoping she hadn't sounded too prudish in her initial reaction. 'That's interesting, but would she help me find the foreign newspapers I wanted if she were a Nazi sympathiser? She was rather scathing, and that's putting it lightly, about people she perceives as being naive about the war when it comes to the Jews in particular.'

Tom shrugged and massaged his temples. 'Take whatever anyone tells you here with a grain of salt, if you know what I mean, and just be careful to show as much interest in Allied publications as enemy ones, just like you were taught. Our budget allows us to do that, so that if we were ever questioned, we can honestly say that we were simply preserving all works. No one needs to know that we have intelligence agents back home scouring the newspapers for clues or hidden messages, although I'm sure they covered all this in your training.'

They sat for a moment, and Avery watched as he gingerly ate his toast. She hoped he wasn't going to throw up right there at the table, and she inched her chair back a little just in case, at the same time telling herself not to get carried away and drink alcohol at the hotel tonight. She did not want to be nursing a sore head come the morning.

'So, tell me about how to get the microfilm back to Washington,' Avery said. 'How often do I send the film back? And what do I do with all the papers and books once I'm finished with them?' She was starting to realise that buying a cross-section of all papers, including unwanted Allied ones, was going to result in a lot of material that needed to be stored. 'Actually, no one has even told me if acquiring all these texts is even legal here. Could I get in trouble if I was found to be in possession of too many foreign papers?'

'Don't overthink things, you're not a real spy, Avery. If anyone does find what you've acquired, they'll just think you're some weird bookish lady,' he said with a laugh. 'Now, the time-sensitive or most important film goes in the diplomatic pouch, and the rest—'

Tom opened his mouth as if he were about to continue speaking, then leapt up and ran for the bathroom door.

Avery sighed and reached over for his toast, not about to let all that jam go to waste. It was going to be a very long day by the looks of it, although it wasn't as if she didn't have a lot to think about. Her conversation with Camille had certainly opened her eyes, and she found herself determined to find out more so that no one could accuse her of being so woefully naive ever again.

The next night, Avery had never felt so out of her depth. Not being plucked from obscurity by the IDC, not flying to the other side of the world – *nothing* had made her feel so unsure of herself as walking into the Hotel Avenida that night. The building itself was impressive, with a concrete facade and glass doors, and as she'd walked up the low steps to enter, a doorman had welcomed her and told her how stunning she looked. That had set her cheeks on fire and had her all a-fluster before she'd even walked into the hotel bar, which appeared to be full of people. Or not so much *people*, as men.

She might have been engaged to be married once, but she certainly didn't have experience in being around so many members of the opposite sex. *You're alright, Avery. Just look for Tom and everything will be fine.* She sighed. Her internal pep talk wasn't working.

The trouble was that she couldn't see Tom anywhere through the haze of smoke, which lingered in the air as if men had been in the bar smoking all day and the place had never been aired out. She shifted on the spot, keeping her chin high in an effort to at least appear confident as she glanced around the tables and then at the few men seated at the bar. He was nowhere, and if he was keeping an eye out for her like he'd promised to, he was doing a very bad job. Either that or he was already drunk and had forgotten all about her.

Avery decided that her best option was to order herself a drink, to at least give her something to do while she surveyed the room. The bartender made his way down to her almost immediately when she lifted her hand, and she ordered a soda, not sure what else she was supposed to drink in a place like this, having decided to wait for Tom until she tried anything alcoholic. But the damp line of sweat across her top lip didn't abate when she sipped her drink and turned to look around again, torn between wishing she'd never agreed to meet him here, and feeling thrilled at the prospect of being somewhere so thoroughly exciting.

Someone moved in beside her at the bar, to her right, and Avery glanced to see who it was. She quickly looked away though, immediately recognising the handsome man from her first day in Lisbon, the one she'd bumped into on the street, and she was still embarrassed that he'd seen her twirling around like a girl.

Avery took a quick sip of her drink, even more flustered than before, and then immediately felt as if he were watching her. She angled her body slightly so that she could see him from the corner of her eye, and she realised he was most definitely looking at her, seemingly without a care for being discreet.

'Gin and tonic,' he said, leaning casually against the bar as he held up his hand with two fingers raised. She wondered who else he was ordering for.

'Relax,' he murmured, sliding one of the drinks down the bar to her when his order arrived. 'You're being too obvious, you need to loosen up a little.'

'I'm sorry?' Avery wished her cheeks wouldn't set to fire so easily.

'Look around,' he said, gesturing with his hand. 'How many locals do you see?'

Avery tried to feign innocence, wishing she'd received training in Washington about what to do in situations such as these instead of being told that she wasn't a spy so she was simply to be herself.

She racked her brain, but came up with nothing, other than hearing Kilgour in her mind saying: *'Always tell the truth as much as possible.'* If this man asked her questions about why she was there, she had little to hide. That was what she was supposed to remember.

Avery stood a little taller, although it wasn't much good given her height difference with the British man beside her. He was tall and lean, dressed in a dark suit like the rest of the men at the hotel, but somehow standing out all the same.

'I'm afraid I don't know what you're talking about,' she said, keeping her voice as level as possible as she attempted to slide the glass he'd ordered for her back down the bar. 'And I'm quite capable of buying my own drinks, thank you.'

'No one comes to the Hotel Avenida and drinks soda,' he said, nudging it back in her direction. 'But I promise not to buy you another, if that helps. It would be a shame for this one to go to waste.'

Avery relented and picked up the drink, taking a sip. As much as she didn't want to accept it, she also needed something to do to give her time to right herself, not to mention settle her nerves. She had no idea what she'd done wrong, what she'd said to give herself away, but somehow she was being too obvious, and all she'd done was walk into a hotel bar. Had this man followed her? It suddenly seemed too much of a coincidence that they'd bumped into one another again.

'Can I give you a tip?' he asked.

She glanced up at him, wondering if he'd had too much to drink or whether he was always in the business of talking too much to women he met at the bar.

'I'm not sure what advice you think I need when you don't even know my name, but certainly, go ahead. You seem rather taken with speaking your mind.'

'It always pays to ask the doorman on the way in who's ordered champagne,' he said, his voice low as he leaned in closer to her. 'You see, whoever orders a celebratory drink was the winner of today's battle.'

85

Avery's heart started to beat a little faster as she interpreted what he was telling her. Why was he not even being discreet about it! 'You're a spy?' she asked. *He's a British spy?*

'No, my dear, I'm a *journalist*,' he said with a wink. 'And you are . . . ?'

'A librarian,' she said, hearing the shake in her own voice.

'Am I the first person you've told your cover story to?' She bristled at his laughter. 'Because you're not terribly convincing, even though part of me thinks you could be telling the truth.'

'I am a librarian! I'm in Lisbon to collect publications of importance for the Library of Congress, to ensure we preserve history.'

He shrugged. 'You say you're a librarian, you're a librarian. Just like I'm a journalist. We all have to be something in this town.'

Avery took a gulp of her drink and regretted it almost immediately. It made her feel giddy the moment she swallowed it.

'I haven't the faintest idea what you're trying to insinuate, or why you'd think I have a cover story,' she said, anger tainting her voice. 'But I'm the most librarian of librarians. I have a degree from an Ivy League university, I'll have you know, and I'm very proud of it.'

She cringed. *The most librarian of librarians? Why couldn't I have come up with something more compelling than that!*

'Better,' he said, downing his drink and ordering another. 'You sound far more convincing when you're cross, by the way.'

Avery's fingers tightened around her bag and she went to turn, but the British man straightened and reached out, his hand covering her elbow for just long enough to stop her.

'I'm sorry, I didn't mean to offend you. It's been a long day and I couldn't help myself,' he said, holding out his hand to her. 'James Anderson.'

She stared at his hand for a moment, tempted to turn on her heel and leave him standing there, but she was in a strange city with no friends, and she was inclined to at least introduce herself. Not to mention Tom still hadn't found her, despite the fact she was one of very few women in the bar.

'Avery Johnson,' she said, pressing her palm into his and appreciating how gently he shook it. She couldn't stand a man with a rough grasp. '*Librarian*,' she said, receiving a chuckle in response.

'You're not even lying, are you?' He laughed.

That made Avery laugh, too. 'I'm truly not! When I said I was the most librarian of librarians, I was being deadly serious!'

'Well then, Miss Avery the Librarian, who might be the only person telling the truth in this entire hotel, what do you say we have another drink and start over? I fear that I've spent so long away from home that I'm starting to lose my manners and expect that everyone is telling lies.'

She sighed and took another little sip of her drink.

'So, what brings you to the Hotel Avenida? Have you been before?' he asked.

'I'm supposed to be meeting a—' She stopped herself before she said *colleague*. 'A friend. But I haven't located him yet.'

'Ah, well, perhaps I can keep you company until you find said friend,' he said.

'You're British?'

'Guilty as charged. American?'

Avery nodded.

'This bar is full of Brits, Yanks, Germans and Japs,' he said. 'Heck, there's probably a few Russians as well. It's the only place in Europe that you'll find enemies smiling politely under the same roof, which is why I'm used to finding almost every word that comes out of most people's mouths here to be a complete and utter fabrication.'

Avery digested what he was saying, looking around and immediately trying to pick out the Nazis. She'd known before she came that Portugal was home to the enemy as much as it was to the Allies, but actually being in a room with them was most unsettling.

It was as she was glancing around that Avery saw an elegant blonde woman holding on to the arm of an equally good-looking blond man. She recognised her as the bookstore owner, and him as the rather intimidating man who'd walked in while she was there. Avery turned, about to ask her new friend if he was acquainted with Camille, when a hand clapped over her shoulder.

'Avery! You made it!'

Tom was standing there, a drink in hand and a big smile on his face, looking like the happiest man in the world now that he'd set eyes on her.

'I thought I was never going to find you,' she said. 'I can't believe how busy it is here.'

'Well, I heard there was a very attractive American at the bar, so I knew where to look,' Tom said, before turning to James, who was facing the bar now, his focus very much on his drink as he stared into it. 'This a friend of yours?'

Avery gestured to James. 'Just a gentleman who's been keeping me company while I was alone,' she said. 'James, this is Tom. Tom, meet James.'

The two men shook hands, and she stood rather awkwardly as they made small talk.

'I expect I'll see you around,' Avery said. 'Thanks for the drink.'

'Watch out for those Nazis,' James murmured, and she shook her head and laughed, not sure whether he was teasing or being serious.

Avery took Tom's arm when he offered it, happy to keep hold as they navigated their way to the far corner where his friends were waiting to meet her. She glanced around as they walked, looking for Camille, but she must have been tucked away out of sight because Avery couldn't spot her blonde head anywhere.

'Avery, I'm very pleased to introduce you to this raucous bunch,' Tom said. 'Although I caution you to forget them all after tonight and never see them again without a chaperone.'

That made all the men around the table erupt into laughter, and Avery politely shook each of their hands and sat where they made space for her, trying her absolute hardest not to look back to the bar to see if James was still sitting there staring into his drink.

'I'm more than happy to walk the lady home,' James said, proffering his arm a few hours later when it was almost time for the hotel bar to close.

Tom was a little unsteady on his feet, but seemed determined to make the most of his last night in Portugal, and despite not knowing James, Avery felt walking with him was preferable to making her way alone. She also had no interest in joining her group to gamble – they had supposedly arranged a car to take them to the Hotel Palácio Estoril and then the nearby casino. Portugal was proving to be an entirely different world to anything she'd ever imagined, so she was thankful James had noticed her predicament.

'You're certain it's not an imposition?' she asked.

'I'd be grateful for the company, truly.'

Avery gave Tom a quick kiss goodnight on the cheek and took the arm James offered, and after pausing briefly to make small talk with the doorman, they were walking the cobbled streets towards her apartment, the night air so fresh it made Avery want to gulp down mouthfuls of it after the thick, pungent smoke in the bar.

'There's something magical about Lisbon at night, don't you think?' James said. 'I've still never quite got used to it, and I've been here for months.'

'I can't believe the twinkle of lights,' she said. 'It's as if the rest of the world is sleeping, and yet Lisbon is alive.' Avery laughed. 'Sorry, I sound like a young girl transfixed with the magic of it all, don't I?'

'I'll never forget how enchanted you looked when I first saw you,' he said. 'There's something innocent about seeing a person enjoy something as simple as lights, and in a world as dark as the one we're currently living in? There's something rather refreshing about it. Reminds me what we're fighting for I suppose.'

James stopped walking then and took off his jacket, placing it around her shoulders before she could protest.

'I don't expect you to be cold so that I can be warm,' she said.

'Well, that's where we differ in opinion,' he said with a chuckle. 'Besides, I have four sisters.'

'You're telling me you'd give up your jacket for them?'

He snorted. 'Not a chance! I'd let them freeze. But I'd expect their young men to give up theirs if they were walking with them at night.'

Avery wasn't sure if it was the alcohol or the night air, or a combination of both, but she had the most overwhelming urge to drop her head to James's shoulder as they walked.

'How long are you in Portugal?' she asked, instead.

'As long as I need to be,' he said. 'And I'm not trying to be cryptic. I honestly don't know. You?'

'At least a year, I think,' she said. 'But I suppose none of us really knows what will happen with the war or how things will change. My father thought our boys would be home by Christmas, and now he thinks it'll be before next Thanksgiving, but I tend to think he's being overly optimistic.'

They walked in silence for a long time, their steps quiet. She realised that this was the very first time she'd been alone with a man at night, especially one she barely knew, but she felt oddly comfortable. Even with Michael, they'd never really been together alone. They were always on a double date or at home with her parents or his.

Being alone with James felt different, more grown-up somehow. She suddenly felt a long way from the naive girl who'd left New York.

'Thank you for walking me home tonight,' Avery said, as they neared her apartment. 'I certainly didn't expect it.'

'I think your friend was rather too inebriated to be trusted with your safety,' he said. 'He's certainly going to have a sore head come morning, but his loss was my gain.'

'Well, I guess this is goodnight,' Avery said, reluctantly letting go of James's arm as they reached her door. 'This is me.'

He took the jacket from her shoulders, which immediately made her shiver, and then he reached for her, his hand gently closing over her bare shoulder as he leaned in to kiss her cheek, his skin soft as it brushed hers.

'Second rule of being a spy, Avery,' James whispered, his cheek hovering next to hers.

She went still, feeling the warmth of his breath on her skin.

'Don't let another spy find out so easily where you live.'

Avery shook her head as he took a step back, watching a smile play across his lips as he held up his hand in a wave.

'I told you, I'm just a librarian,' she said, but this time when she said it she started to laugh, which made him shake his head as if she'd given herself away.

'Avery, can I be frank with you?' he asked.

She nodded.

'For all my teasing, this can be a dangerous city. Don't let the parties and twinkling lights fool you into a sense of safety. You must keep your wits about you at all times.'

Avery swallowed as his eyes met hers, not liking the seriousness of his tone. If he'd wanted to scare her, he'd succeeded.

'I wouldn't want anything untoward to happen to you, that's all.'

They stared at each other for a moment longer, before he shook his head and took a few more steps backwards.

'Goodnight, Avery the librarian,' he said, standing beneath a street light as he put his jacket on, his eyes still never leaving hers.

'Goodnight, James the journalist,' she replied, unlocking her door and going through it before she did or said anything she might regret.

But when she was on the other side of it, she pressed her back to the timber and closed her eyes, her heart beating fast as she thought about the man who'd brought her home. He was obviously a rogue, a man who talked to single women at hotels, probably on his way now to warm his lover's bed after bidding her farewell, so she knew nothing could come of it, but she certainly wasn't minding the flutter in her stomach when she thought about the way he'd so boldly kissed her cheek, or the touch of his fingers against her shoulder.

But what he'd said to her about staying safe had rattled her, despite her excitement, especially when she'd received no such warnings during her training. And she couldn't help but wonder whether he was actually a spy or not. Were they all spies? Had the hotel truly been full of them? Was she really in jeopardy if she was walking the streets alone?

Upstairs, as she slipped out of her dress and put on her nightgown, she also thought about the woman from the bookstore, and wondered just how she fitted in with the mysterious crowd at the Hotel Avenida. She'd been drawn to Camille in her bookshop, despite how blunt the French woman had been, but Avery was starting to understand that she needed to be less trusting and more suspicious in Lisbon. After all, what had James said? Something about enemies all smiling politely under the same roof? That meant she shouldn't trust him, either, no matter how much she was drawn to the handsome Brit who'd so chivalrously walked her home with his jacket draped around her shoulders.

Chapter Eight

CAMILLE

Camille was at the front of the bookstore rearranging a table when she saw a familiar face outside. The American woman raised her hand in a wave before entering, making the little bell above the door tinkle. There was no one else in the store – it had been a quiet morning so far except for a few newspaper sales – and Camille stopped what she was doing to greet her, grateful for the distraction.

'You decided to come back,' Camille said.

'I did.'

'The newspapers were suitable for your work?' she asked, starting to return to the counter.

'They were. I'm interested in all publications from anywhere in the world, so if you come by anything else . . .'

'Predominantly *enemy* publications, by chance?'

She saw the flush of colour in Avery's face, but quickly glanced away so it wasn't obvious she'd noticed. It hadn't been Camille's intention to catch her out so easily, but quick words had shown Avery's lie. So it was enemy newspapers Avery really wanted, not all newspapers and books as she'd first claimed.

'Unfortunately I don't have anything, but perhaps I could put some aside if they do come in.' Camille still couldn't decide how she felt about the American. They were both Allies, so in theory she wasn't opposed to helping her, but before she did that, she'd need to trust her.

'That's fine,' Avery said. 'I'll call in another day. Thursday perhaps?'

Camille went to nod, but she froze when she saw who was poised to come through her door. She immediately went through an inventory in her mind of what she had out in her office, of what could be found in the shop. Camille was always careful, but she didn't doubt how thorough they could be if they suspected her of conducting illegal activity.

'Avery, the PVDE are—' Her whisper was cut short when two men marched more quickly than expected through her store towards them.

'Can I help either of you with a book?' Camille asked, refusing to let them see how rattled she was.

'A book?' One of them laughed and nudged the other man with his elbow. 'She thinks we're here looking for something to read.'

'I didn't realise it was so funny. This is a bookstore after all,' she said. 'Most people who walk through my door are looking for a book to purchase, or a newspaper. I can't interest you in either?'

The man who hadn't spoken yet took a piece of paper from his pocket and held it out, slamming it on to the counter with a bang that made her jump. 'Suppose if we took a look around,' he said. 'Would we find any documents that looked like this one?'

Camille swallowed, seeing from the corner of her eye that Avery had quietly moved to the back of the shop. They were holding papers, but she knew immediately that they weren't papers forged by her hand. She breathed a sigh of relief.

'I have my own identification papers that look very similar to that, if that's what you're asking?'

'So you wouldn't mind if we took a look around then? Just in case you have papers that don't belong to you?' he asked. 'And while you're at it, how about you show us those papers that you're so confident about.'

Her heart was pounding. She'd hidden the visas in her apartment, and one she was still working on was tucked away under the floorboards, but her pot of ink and pen were still on display. There could be many reasons for her to have ink, but she was worried it might add to their suspicions about her, and she couldn't recall what else she might have left out.

'My purse is in my office in the back room. Please give me a moment to retrieve it.'

It was then that Camille realised she didn't know where Avery was, until she walked straight out of the office that Camille was striding towards.

'Stop!' the PVDE man shouted. 'Who are you?'

Avery stopped, and her cheeks turned a deep shade of pink. 'I'm sorry, I—'

'This woman is a customer. I sold her a book just this week.'

His gaze narrowed. 'What were you doing back there?'

'Looking for a restroom to powder my nose,' Avery said, before laughing and giving a little shrug. 'Sorry, I don't actually think you call it a restroom here, do you? What would I—'

'Leave,' he ordered, immediately ignoring Avery. Camille glanced after her, wondering what game she was playing, before going into her office and taking out her purse. She found her papers and handed them over, barely breathing as she watched the two men give a cursory glance around her office.

Camille noticed that some items were missing – a pair of tweezers that she used to place photos on doctored identification papers, and the ink pen that had taken her some time to procure, as well as her ink pot, but she kept her chin high, not letting on that anything was amiss. She must have put them away earlier and forgotten. She stood still as the men checked her papers and walked around the small space, opening drawers, and finally turning around to look at her.

'Next time we come here, we won't be so polite.'

She watched them go, refusing to acknowledge the wobble in her knees until the front door had opened and closed. Camille slumped against the wall then, eyes shut, realising how easily everything could collapse around her, how much her being caught would affect the families who were counting on her. And all she could see in her mind was the old man, the pain in his eyes; the faith he had showed in her to create the documents he needed for his daughter and grandchildren when he'd stood before her earlier in the week. Or the mother from the camp the other night, who'd been so desperate for her help.

The tinkle of the bookshop's bell made her jump, her eyes flying open as she pushed off from the wall. But it wasn't just any customer, it was the American again.

'Avery, what are you doing back here?' Camille asked, irritated at having to talk to her when all she wanted was a moment alone.

'I thought you might want these back,' Avery said, her voice soft as she reached into her pocket and took out Camille's tweezers, pen and small pot. 'I heard what they said to you and I thought these might—'

'You took these from my office?'

Avery nodded.

'Thank you,' Camille said, her voice catching in her throat. 'You saved me there, you did, but if you'd been caught . . .' *I don't need anything else to keep me awake at night, I have enough memories haunting me as it is.* 'Just, thank you.'

'I was worried these things might implicate you, and I didn't think they'd even look twice at me.'

Camille sighed, placing the items on the counter and reaching out to her. 'What you did was very brave, and I'm so grateful. But I don't want anyone else to be punished instead of me. If you'd been caught, I'd never have forgiven myself, and being an American doesn't mean they won't question you. It's as dangerous for you as it is for anyone else.'

Avery nodded. 'I understand.'

Camille wasn't so sure she did, but she didn't press the subject any more. 'Come with me. I might just have one of those newspapers you were asking about earlier.'

A smile brightened Avery's face. 'You do? I thought—'

'Don't ask questions,' Camille said, as she walked across the store to the counter and reached beneath it, passing Avery a Portuguese newspaper, as well as recent copies of both *Das Reich* and *Der Stürmer*. She watched Avery's eyes widen at the sight of the German newspapers.

'Thank you, this is excellent.' Avery laughed. 'I had no idea it would be so easy to obtain these German newspapers. I expected it would take a great deal of searching.'

Camille gave her a little shrug. 'You'd be surprised what comes into Portugal each week. I take copies of everything, and there's a newspaper vendor a few streets over that usually has whatever I don't.'

'Well, this is very much appreciated. I honestly can't believe it.'

'I do need something from you though,' Camille said. 'I have other customers looking for your American *Time* magazines. Is there any way you could have some sent to you, if someone from home were to send you a parcel?'

Avery was quick to smile. 'I'll try my best. Leave it with me.'

Camille rang up the sale and Avery paid, before tucking the papers beneath her arm. 'I'm sorry, about what happened before.'

'So am I.'

'Camille, if you were caught with the forged papers they were asking about, what would happen?'

'The PVDE are ruthless,' Camille said, hearing the catch in her own voice. 'I'd be sent to jail.'

Avery visibly swallowed. 'Has your shop been subject to a raid before, or was this the first time?'

Camille nodded. 'It has. I don't think there's a bookshop in Portugal that's been exempt, although they've come looking in mine perhaps more than others.' She didn't tell her why: that the PVDE likely had suspicions about her that were unrelated to the books she stocked.

'Camille, please feel that you can say no, but would you like to have lunch together?' Avery asked, managing to take Camille completely by surprise. 'I don't know anyone here, and I'd love the company.'

Camille hesitated. Earlier, when Avery had walked into the shop, she would never have said yes, but this American woman had taken a risk for her, and she'd also heard the PVDE were poking around. She quickly realised that it would be better to have her as a friend than foe.

'I could close for an hour at one p.m. if you'd like to meet at Pastelaria Suíça?'

Avery's eyes lit up. 'Fantastic. That gives me time to work before we meet. I might need directions to the café though. Is it far?'

'Oh, *mon Dieu*,' Camille said with a laugh, taking herself by surprise.

'You're surprised?'

Camille smiled. 'I forgot you spoke French! It's only you're the first person I've met here who doesn't know the Pastelaria Suíça.'

'It's famous?' Avery asked, looking confused.

'Famous in Lisbon, yes,' Camille said, returning to the counter to write down directions.

The bell tinkled to announce the arrival of more customers, and Avery took the note and slipped it into her pocket. 'I'll see you there,' Camille said, shaking her head at the American's enthusiasm and wondering if she might regret her decision to meet for lunch. It had been quite some time since Camille had seen someone socially, without it being part of her work, and as she watched Avery dash from the store she couldn't deny that it would be nice to have lunch with another woman. It also hadn't been the worst feeling in the world to smile, so perhaps an hour away from the shop with the person who'd induced it wasn't such a bad idea. It wasn't as if she'd made any friends in Lisbon, other than the lovely old man who'd once owned the bookstore.

Once there were no more customers in the shop, Camille took the opportunity to go to her office in the backroom. She'd put up the bell on the door to her shop once she'd purchased the store, to alert her to any customers coming or going, which was especially helpful when she was in her office. No one could sneak up on her and see what she was doing, and as she reached for the bulky item wrapped in a man's shirt, she'd never been more grateful for that little bell.

She opened up the shirt, careful not to drop the precious wireless radio as she did so. It was beautiful, and it was going to be her way of listening and finding out what was truly happening in other parts of Europe. The foreign newspapers that she received were either out of date by the time they came in, or full of so much propaganda that she never knew what to believe. But the radio? The radio felt like her gateway to the rest of the world. It also made what she'd done with Kiefer in exchange for it almost bearable. *Almost.* She was going to be one of the lucky few who could listen to what was actually happening in the world.

She was careful to fold it back up in the shirt again, placing it beneath the floorboards with some other precious things that she didn't want anyone to find. But as she did so, bending down and looking at the few possessions she still had from her old life, the memories hit her like a wave, reminding her of what she'd lost. Of what she'd left behind. Of the life she'd once had that had meant more to her than anything else in the world. The life that she'd do *anything* to go back to.

Camille reached for the desk beside her, placing her palms flat against it as she pushed herself up, but she couldn't straighten; as Hugo came back to her, as the memories of him clawed at her, she was pulled back into the past. Usually it was at night that she twisted and turned, plagued by what had happened, but sometimes, like today, the memories came rushing into her mind as if it were only yesterday. Unable to push them away, they turned into a nightmare that replayed itself over and over no matter how hard she fought against it.

And just like that she was back in the forest, looking over her shoulder at Hugo, screaming his name, watching him crumple to the ground. She'd fought so hard to hide her identity, to leave behind the woman she once was for the woman she'd had to become in order to survive, but the pain of losing Hugo, of the betrayal they'd faced, was impossible to forget. No amount of pretending would ever stop her from thinking about that night. But it was what had happened next that kept coming back to her as she searched her memory for clues, for what she might have missed, replaying what she remembered of the family who'd stood before her and Hugo earlier that day, who they were supposed to save that fateful night – the family who had trusted her and Hugo to take them to safety.

'Please, take it,' the man said, reaching into his jacket and taking out the most beautiful pocket watch that she had ever seen.

He held it in the palm of his hand, and his eyes searched hers until she looked down again, admiring the diamonds that marked the face of the platinum watch. Just by glancing at it, she could tell how expensive it must be.

'Please, for your troubles,' he said, pleading with her as he waved his wife closer. 'My wife's rings, any of our jewellery, please, anything to keep us safe. We'll give you anything if you just help us get to Portugal.'

She reached out and closed his fingers over his watch as Hugo spoke for them.

'Keep your valuables,' he said. 'The only thing we want from you is your promise that you will listen to us at all times, and follow our lead. It's a dangerous journey, but one we've made many times now, and when you arrive in Portugal you'll need everything you have to secure passage to America.'

Tears formed in the man's eyes as their two children crowded around the couple's legs, his wife's hands falling to their small shoulders as they looked up at her with the most hopeful expressions on their faces. Camille couldn't imagine what they must be thinking as they tried to understand why they were having to leave, why they were so hated for just being them, why their parents had made them flee their home.

'But we must pay you something, for your—'

'Our reward for doing this is knowing that you're safe,' she said. 'Our network is helping Jews from all over France as best we can. Please, we don't want your valuables.'

'Why?' the woman asked, her eyes wide as she looked back at her. 'Why would you risk everything for strangers?'

Camille smiled, glancing down at the children and then reaching for the woman's arm. 'Because we know what it's like to lose those we love. Because if we don't fight against this regime, who will?'

'You know where to meet us?' Hugo asked.

The man nodded.

'Don't tell anyone where you're going. We'll meet after dark and begin our journey immediately.' Hugo's smile was kind, but she could see the worry etched on his face. 'I suggest you rest until then, because once we start, we won't stop walking until daybreak.'

They said their goodbyes and she slipped her hand into Hugo's as they made their way back to their apartment, both lost in their thoughts and neither saying a thing.

She wiped at her eyes as she remembered the steady way Hugo had held her hand, the kindness of his gaze and the warmth of his smile. But she kept thinking about the Jewish man, too, prepared to give up anything and everything just to keep his family safe; the way they'd been betrayed by someone who'd known their precise movements, by someone they should have been able to trust.

There was still a glimmer of hope that someone from that beautiful little family had survived, but so far no one had been able to tell her what had happened, and she feared that with fewer and fewer families escaping France now, she might never find out.

Camille forced herself to stand, opening her eyes, pulling herself away from the past as best she could, trying to stop the memories from haunting her. It was as if she could feel Hugo standing behind her, his steady hand on her shoulder as he coaxed her back to him, telling her everything was going to be alright, promising her that life was somehow worth living without him. Only it wasn't going to be alright, because he wasn't here. Camille's life was empty without him; every single day a painful reminder of what she'd lost.

She took a few deep breaths and bent back down to collect the notebook she kept beneath the floorboards, before carefully replacing the boards. Camille sat down and opened it, reading through her notes, trying to see if there was anything she'd missed. She did this every week, hoping that something would stand out to her or that something new would come into her mind while she read back through the words she'd penned.

British intelligence. Could be a double agent or someone who's gone rogue.

Special Operations Executive operative, which means he is most likely a spy sent for the Allies but bribed for some reason to work for Nazis. But why? What would make a man turn his back on his country. Money? Revenge? Retribution?

Resistance cell. Did someone on the inside betray us?

Did someone follow us? Did we get lazy with keeping watch?

The Jewish family. The last one. Was there something different about them? Were they of special interest to the Nazis for some reason? Was there a reason they/we were targeted?

Are there more new arrivals to question?

Camille had gone over their last days and weeks together with a fine-tooth comb, writing a diary of everything they'd done, the people they'd seen, the families they'd helped. She'd created a cross-stitched memory of their movements, but still nothing had stood out to her as being unusual – no clues as to how or why they'd been betrayed. Over the past year, she'd begun to include every tiny thing that she could recall; nothing was too insignificant – where they'd had lunch, who'd been with them, who they'd spoken to, what they'd been wearing. But nothing had helped. The only thing it had done was keep her up late at night, her mind whirring as she punished herself for her inability to figure it all out, forcing herself to recall the same few days over and over again.

There must have been something. There must be some clue, some hint, some thing *that I'm missing.* But the only thing she was certain of was that if it had been a double agent, then sooner or later he was going to show up in Lisbon – it was the only place spies from opposing sides could meet without drawing attention. *If I'm right in my suspicions, Kiefer will know him and be liaising with him. If this SOE agent worked with the Nazis in France, then if he's still alive, he'll be working with them now, even if he's still pretending to be loyal to Britain.* And if that was the case, then she intended on using Kiefer to find out everything she could.

But none of it was going to bring her Hugo back. Even if the war ended, she had no life to return to, no family or loved ones waiting for her. They were all gone. This war had taken everyone from her, and no matter what happened, she was still going to be alone. Which meant that all she could do was save as many lives as she could, while she could, before exacting her revenge.

She closed the notebook and put it back, making sure no one could tell that the floorboards had been moved, placing a chair half over them and trying her hardest not to cry. Some days were more challenging than others, and for some reason, meeting someone like Avery, making plans with Avery as if her life were normal, had only made the memories hit harder.

Camille brushed the tears from her eyes and took out her compact mirror, dusting her face with powder and applying a sweep of her favourite red lipstick in an attempt to right herself. She put everything back in her bag and stopped by the counter, making a little 'Back in an Hour' sign and taping it to the glass. Lunch sitting in the sunshine was exactly what she needed, and it wasn't as if she ever usually did anything for herself. Besides, she was still curious about the woman she was meeting. Avery had seemed so innocent and naive when they'd first met, but she'd helped Camille without hesitation earlier, and regardless of how reckless that might have been, Camille felt that she at least owed her lunch.

Not to mention Camille kept wondering whether Avery might just be the perfect recruit for her little forgery business. She'd been searching for someone she could trust for months, someone who could produce the photos she needed for brand-new identification papers, and perhaps a pretty American wouldn't be suspected of helping Jews by the PVDE. As much as she didn't want to put anyone else in danger, there could be a way to keep Avery safe *and* help others in the process, if she was careful.

Or I could be entirely wrong and she could be the reason everything comes falling down around me.

Chapter Nine

AVERY

Avery couldn't believe how busy the Pastelaria Suíça café was, but she realised the moment she found it, head down following Camille's directions before looking up and seeing it before her, why Camille had been amused at her not knowing where it was.

The café was in the middle of D. Pedro IV Square, with huge glass doors that opened wide to a large terrace that was densely filled with tables and chairs. Sunshine bathed all of the patrons, most of whom were drinking coffee, and when Avery saw a couple vacating one of the tables, she was quick to pounce, hoping there wasn't a line. But no one reprimanded her, and so she sat down, aware that she was early but not having wanted to keep Camille waiting in case she hadn't been able to find the place. Given that Camille had to close her shop to meet for lunch, Avery was pleased they weren't going to have to waste time waiting for a seat.

Many of the people around her spoke the type of rapid Portuguese that she heard every time she walked the streets, and when she'd visited the market earlier, but there were also many speaking in other languages. She heard more than a few people speaking French, and when she looked around she noticed there were a handful of women quietly sitting alone who didn't appear to be local. She immediately wondered what their stories were, imagining that maybe they felt safer in a crowded café.

Avery had observed it was easy to spot a foreign woman, more by the length of her skirt or the absence of a hat or lipstick. She tried to listen to some of the conversations as she waited.

'Well, if it isn't my favourite librarian.'

Avery knew exactly who it was before she turned, and this time she was determined not to blush.

'I'm starting to think you're following me,' she said, folding her arms across her chest. 'The first time was a coincidence, the second time was surprising, and the third time, well, I'd say you were looking for me.'

He laughed, and she found it impossible not to grin back at him, enjoying the game they played.

'May I join you?'

She didn't point out that he'd already sat down. 'You can keep that seat warm until the person I'm meeting arrives.'

'Not your wayward friend from the other night?'

'Ahh, no. Tom has left Lisbon, I'm afraid.'

James raised his brows, clearly waiting for her to tell him who she was waiting for.

'I'm meeting a female acquaintance, if you must know,' Avery said. 'For lunch.'

'Well, this is an excellent place for ladies to meet. It's not called "the nice legs café" for nothing.'

This time she did blush, and she crossed her legs and shook her head. He was charming, she'd give him that.

'I'm sorry, you're just so fun to tease,' James said. 'Can I make it up to you and buy you coffee? I'm in desperate need of something to wake me up.'

She nodded and forced herself not to watch him as he walked away, just in case he happened to turn and catch her. But he was back within minutes and she was grateful for him ordering, so she didn't have to give up her table to find their waiter, who still hadn't stopped by.

'So, Avery, are you meeting another librarian for lunch? Are there more of your kind descending upon Lisbon?'

'I'm meeting a local, actually,' she said, lifting her hand to shield her eyes from the bright midday sun. 'Well, actually she's French, but she's lived here for some time.'

James suddenly stilled, his smile disappearing. 'The woman from the bookstore?'

'Camille, yes,' she said. 'Do you know her?'

His face creased into a grimace, but it just as quickly disappeared. 'There aren't many other French women living here whose path yours might have crossed with, so it was a lucky guess.' He hesitated. 'How well do you know her?'

'I've known her about as long as I've known you, actually,' she said. 'So a few days at best.'

'Just . . . well, I'd caution you to be careful,' James said, lowering his voice as their coffees were placed on the little round table in front of them. 'It's hard to know who to trust here, and you never know who might be feeding information to the authorities – or, to be frank, to the other side.'

Avery was temporarily lost for words. She looked from her coffee up to James. 'The other side? You mean like a double agent?' she whispered. 'Surely not.'

But if James had wanted to plant a seed of doubt in her mind, he'd certainly succeeded.

'Perhaps the talk of being a double agent is a little far-fetched, but in a place like Lisbon?' He shrugged and took a sip of his coffee. 'Who knows? All I know for certain is that she goes to bed with a Nazi, which is likely where the rumours began. It's hard to decide who to trust, is all I'm trying to say, although others claim she's a Jewish sympathiser, so perhaps you have nothing to worry about at all.'

'She . . .' Avery cleared her throat and drank her coffee. What he was saying was similar to Tom's warning, although at least Tom had prefaced it by saying that it likely didn't mean anything during a time when women had to do certain things just to survive. 'I have seen her with a man. At the hotel the other night, they arrived while we were standing at the bar. And there was also a tall German man who came into the bookshop while I was there, and she seemed a little unsettled when he first walked in.'

'She was with that same man at the hotel,' James said. 'I wasn't aware you had noticed them, but clearly you received excellent training before arriving here after all.'

Avery shook her head, but before she could say it, he did.

'Then again, she chose this place to meet?'

She slowly nodded. 'It seems like a popular place to meet by the looks of it?'

Avery had the distinct feeling that James was trying to influence her thoughts, but then again, maybe he was just being friendly.

'This is the most public meeting place in all of Lisbon,' he said. 'Look around you, we can be seen from everywhere, at all angles. Everyone sitting here can be seen from the Rossio Railway Station, and they're not just looking for the great legs. There's always someone keeping an eye on the comings and goings here.'

Avery swallowed, reaching for her coffee again. It was much stronger than what she was used to at home. 'So you're saying . . .' She let her voice drift off, hoping that he'd fill in the blanks.

'I'm saying that there are spies everywhere, and this is one of the places they keep a close eye on, to see who is with who, to figure out the lay of the land so to speak.'

'You're exaggerating,' she said, looking at him over the rim of her coffee cup before lowering her voice, conscious of how close the other tables were to them. 'I don't know if you're trying to scare me or throw me off the scent or what, but I don't believe you for a second. You're making out like this entire city is teeming with spies!'

'I'm trying to give you the lay of the land, that's all,' he said, but with a smile that still made her wonder whether he was teasing or not. 'But regardless, this is an excellent place to drink coffee and people-watch. It's almost like seeing the entire world go by.'

Avery studied him, finding it amusing how easily they managed to fall into conversation with each other, even if it was usually him doing all the talking. 'Well I, for one, am definitely just here for the coffee and something to eat,' she said. 'But you're right, it does seem like an excellent place to people-watch.'

'You're just a librarian, I know, so I'm sure this is rather exciting compared to your usually dull days of filling bookshelves,' he said, draining his coffee and rising. 'I'm off to write a story about a war, but I hope to see you again soon, Avery. And I very much hope you enjoy watching people.'

'Well, thank you for keeping me company while I waited.' She realised just how naive she'd been all over again with James, and it was obvious that she was going to have to keep her wits about her.

Avery understood why he'd jumped to his feet when she saw Camille crossing the terrace, and she stood, kissing Camille on each cheek before they both sat down.

'I can see why you were surprised that I didn't know of this place,' Avery said, gesturing around them. 'It seems as if it's the very centre of Lisbon.'

Camille's smile was warmer than it had been when she'd first met her, but Avery had the distinct feeling that she was very guarded. But no matter how much James's words lingered as she stared at the beautiful woman before her, blonde hair swept elegantly off her face, she also wanted to take Camille at face value. It was nice to have another woman to talk to, especially one who knew the city so intimately. Why should she trust James over Camille, anyway?

'How do you know the man who just left?' Camille asked. 'Have you met him before?'

Avery smiled and waved the waiter over when she saw him, so Camille could order a coffee. 'It's the strangest thing, but I've run into him a few times since I arrived. Enough times that I'm almost convinced it's not accidental, but he's always been very friendly. And he's British, so I suppose there's nothing to worry about, given we're on the same side of the war.'

'Lisbon is a city full of spies,' Camille said with a shrug. 'But if he's been that obvious, I'd say it's probably coincidental. Or that he's taken a liking to you. If he was a spy and he didn't want you to know he was following you, he'd have been more discreet.'

Avery blushed. 'He said the same thing, about the spies. I was starting to think he was exaggerating if I'm honest.'

'It's true, there are many Allied and Axis spies here – it's one of the only places they can move freely, after all – but this city is much more complex. I mean, look at the women around us, those seated alone. Have you asked yourself why?'

'They could be spies?' Avery said, keeping her voice deliberately low.

'The women sitting alone? No, they're refugees. They sit here to listen for news, and because they feel safe being somewhere busy.'

'How long will they be in Lisbon for?' Avery asked. 'Are they just passing through?'

'Some will have been waiting days, others weeks, some months,' Camille said, and Avery heard her voice change, a huskiness audible as she looked away from the women, as if it caused her pain to see them. 'Some may wait forever for a boat that never arrives.'

'These women, they're mostly Jewish?' Avery was almost whispering now, not wanting their conversation to be overhead.

'Mostly. They've found their way here, to safety, but the passage they've been promised to America is constantly delayed, if it ever comes at all. So they're alive, but it's as if their lives are on hold, and they're just hoping and waiting for a chance at a new life somewhere else. They thought getting here was the hard part, but it turns out that leaving here is just as difficult as escaping wherever they came from in the first place.'

Avery found herself dabbing at her eyes, and Camille's expression softened.

'They are alive though, Avery, and that's what matters,' Camille said. 'Someone has risked their lives to help them escape the horrors of wherever they came from, and they've made it. However bad it is here waiting, it's nothing like what they left behind.'

'It's just, well, people like me read about what's happening in the newspapers from the comfort of home, and I've seen the photos of books being burned in Germany and' – Avery lowered her voice – 'of Jewish people being forced to wear the yellow star, but being here makes it feel real. I suppose I wondered if it was truly all that bad.'

'It *is* that bad, I promise you it is. I saw it with my own eyes in France,' Camille said. 'The things I've seen, the truth I know, would break your heart.'

Avery waited for Camille to continue, but she was quick to change the subject, fixing her smile and thanking the waiter when her coffee arrived.

'But Lisbon is far from all that, and here you can at least pretend that things aren't so bad. Despite its downfalls, the locals make it a haven here, for many of us.'

Avery smiled also, sensing that Camille no longer wanted to talk about the sadness of it all. 'This place, it's more alive than

112

anywhere I've ever been in my life before. New York is nothing like this.' Avery knew there was something almost ironic about her being there when all these refugees were desperate to get to New York, but it only made her more determined to ensure her work meant something – that she was doing something useful for the war effort.

'So, tell me about yourself,' Camille said, glancing down at Avery's hand. 'No husband? No fiancé waiting at home for you to return?'

Avery felt a sense of calm as she replied. 'No, I'm not ready for marriage. I just have this sense that I want to see the world, as silly as that might sound.'

'Not silly at all. When you meet someone who makes you feel as if your heart is going to burst from your chest if you can't be with him, that's when you'll know you're ready to get married.'

'You speak from experience?' Avery asked, hoping she wasn't overstepping.

'I do,' Camille said, before reaching for the menu and artfully changing the subject again. 'Shall we order something to eat?'

'Thank you for lunch, Avery, and for your assistance earlier, but I'd best get back to the shop. My regulars often call by in the afternoon,' Camille said, slowly rising and reaching for her purse an hour or so later.

Avery stood, too, kissing Camille on each cheek. 'Shall we do it again sometime? It's nice having another woman to spend time with.'

Camille nodded, her smile polite, but Avery found her hard to read. She hoped that Camille had enjoyed their time together as much as she had.

'I'll come by on Thursday and see if you have any more newspapers for me,' Avery said.

Camille nodded and said goodbye, and Avery watched her go before heading off in the other direction, towards her apartment. She wanted to see for herself the families displaced and waiting that Camille had spoken of.

Early that evening, Avery set off to look for the square. It was very central, and it didn't take her long to find where they all were – a city of families living in makeshift shelters covering the entire area. Avery walked slowly to take it all in, noticing the differences between the locals and the refugees, the women with baskets held high on their heads carrying produce and the mothers with children clinging to their skirts.

Lisbon was sad in one way and vibrant in another, and it made Avery realise that no one back home in America could possibly imagine what it was like here. Without the refugees, Lisbon was a city of music, smiles and happiness, a place that was somehow completely untouched by war, an oasis for the people who lived there and were able to continue their day-to-day lives. But on the other hand, it was also a place that vividly showed the truth of war and the people displaced by it, which made something inside of her burn: a desire to do something, *anything*, to help them. Only, she had no idea what or how to go about it.

Avery stood for a long time just watching, until the heat from the sun began to fade and a coolness brushed her shoulders, as if to tell her she'd been there long enough.

She sighed, and decided to make her way back to her apartment. She had hours of microfilming ahead of her, and she wanted to write home while the day was still vivid in her mind, to tell her sister about Camille, and also write to Jack to remind him that she was thinking of him. It had been ages since she'd received a letter in return, but then she imagined it would take some time for him to receive news of her change of address, or for her family to forward anything to her, so she was trying her best to be patient.

As she walked, she couldn't help but notice a tall, handsome man with light-brown hair coming towards her. She was so distracted by him that she didn't feel the tug on her handbag until it was too late.

'No!' she shouted, as fingers clenched tight around her wrist, so tightly that she felt as if they were going to pierce her skin.

She spun around and came face to face with a haggard-looking woman, the desperation in her eyes terrifying Avery more than the hold she had on her.

'Please!' she cried, fighting with the woman as her fingers moved up Avery's arm, digging in.

'Let go of her!' came a deep voice, followed by large hands forcing the woman away.

Avery's body trembled as she clutched her bag tightly to her chest, the woman backing away but not leaving as she gasped to catch her breath.

'Please, just have this,' Avery said, reaching into her bag and taking out some gum and a square of wrapped chocolate and throwing it towards the woman. It was only then that she realised her rescuer had his hand on her shoulder.

'Are you alright?' he asked, studying her with the warmest brown eyes she'd ever seen, as the woman scurried away.

'I, ah, I'll be fine,' she stammered. 'Thank you. I think she would have had my purse if you hadn't intervened.'

His hand fell away and he stepped back. 'Desperation brings out the worst in people,' he said. 'But I'm pleased you're alright. You were coming from the square?'

'Yes. I was just wanting to see the, ah, the situation there with my own eyes.'

The man nodded. 'I understand. I've just returned from delivering some supplies there myself.'

Avery watched him as he held up his hand in a wave and then turned to walk away, looking over his shoulder to give her a quick smile that she couldn't help but return.

What is it about this city and handsome men? First James and now this fine-looking stranger, and both British, too.

Avery rubbed at her wrist, glancing down and seeing that an ugly blue mark was appearing and her hands were still shaking. She turned on her heel and hurried home, lest she be the target of another hungry person desperate enough to rob her.

But as scared as she was, her curiosity had been piqued, and she knew that she would be back at the square before long to observe the comings and goings again. *Only I won't be stupid enough to bring a purse next time.*

Chapter Ten

CAMILLE

Camille glanced over her shoulder, always careful about approaching Rossio Square. Tonight she was dressed in a woollen coat and had a scarf tied over her head, trying as hard as possible not to draw attention to herself, and so far it seemed to have worked. She leaned against a tree and watched the people ahead of her, tears pricking her eyes. They were all so *grateful*, and that always managed to break something inside of her. They were just people, and yet somehow they'd ended up being so hated that they'd been driven from their homes and persecuted – despised, even. But to her, they were no different to any other human being.

I wish you were here, Hugo. I wish you could see what I see.

Camille looked behind her again, before starting to move. She was a familiar face to many, so when she lowered her scarf and showed her face, no one was alarmed to see her coming towards them. The street lights meant that the refugees were never in the dark, which she imagined added to their feeling of safety, but it made her feel as if she could be seen by anyone, and after the recent visit from the PVDE, she was more on edge than usual. But it wasn't her that she was worried about; it was the families she'd helped.

The old man she was looking for saw her first, catching her eye when he stood and gave her a nod. Behind him was a woman, perhaps a little older than Camille herself, and Camille watched as she bent to speak to her children before joining the man.

She knew immediately that the woman was his daughter.

'I have your papers,' she said in French, once the man was within earshot. 'Please embrace me, as if we are friends, and I will slide them into your jacket.'

He nodded, and once she was close enough to him, the transfer was made.

'Thank you for helping us,' said the woman, and Camille saw the glint of tears in her eyes, recognising the desperation there that was evident in the expressions of so many women just like her. 'I actually have something for you, something from France.'

The very fact they were speaking in her maiden tongue was emotional for Camille, but hearing that this woman had something for her from home was enough to make her gasp. It had been a long time since she'd had any direct communication from anyone in Paris, which meant that anything at all would be cherished.

'I've carried it in my coat since we left,' the woman said.

'You shouldn't have risked anything for me,' Camille said. 'It's not that I'm not grateful, but if you'd been caught with it . . .'

The woman stepped forward, kissing first Camille's right cheek and then her left, before putting her arms around her and giving her a warm hug. As she pulled away, she pressed something into Camille's coat, and Camille was quick to secure it in her pocket.

'You have risked so much to help us, so this was something I could do, as my way of saying thank you. Without you and your friends in France?' The woman shook her head, tears slipping rapidly down her cheeks now. 'I don't even want to think what would have happened to us.'

'Thank you,' Camille said, through her own tears. 'It might take you a long time to leave here, but those documents will keep you from being deported or arrested. Without the correct visa paperwork, the PVDE can be ruthless.'

They parted then, the old man giving her a long look that told her just how much she'd done for them, before Camille turned away. She glanced at families as she walked, wishing she could sit with them, that she could hear their stories and find a way to do more for them, but she knew that her presence would only put both herself and them in more danger. She didn't want to raise the suspicions of the PVDE any more than she already had.

But as she glanced around again, Camille realised that she'd already been seen. She lifted her scarf and wrapped her jacket tightly around herself, keeping her gaze lowered and pretending that she hadn't seen the woman standing beneath the street light.

Avery had been watching her, of that she had little doubt, and Camille could only hope that the American was who she claimed to be. Because if she wasn't, she could put everything Camille had worked so hard to keep secret in jeopardy.

The note felt as if it were burning a hole in her coat pocket as she hurried for home, and she slipped her hand inside so she could clasp it. But it wasn't until she was safe inside her apartment, the door locked behind her, that she dared open her hand and take out the little parcel of papers. There was a small note tucked inside what she recognised as the type of clandestine paper used by the Resistance.

Betrayal ran deeper than expected. Hard to know who to trust. Definitely Allied deception, confirmed British double agent. You need to be careful not to draw attention to yourself, otherwise you risk being deported alongside everyone you've helped. They know you're there and I've heard rumours of the work you're doing. You'll be treated

*the same as the Jews if you're caught. Situation in camps
even worse than we suspected, thousands dead, not just
Jews but political prisoners too. B.*

Camille read the words in Benoit's familiar scrawl three times
over before closing her eyes and sliding all the way to the floor. She
didn't even have the energy to read the other sheet of paper, not yet.

Everything came back to her then – the terror, the pain, the
sacrifice of the night when everything had changed irrevocably for
her – and she was suddenly alone again, her memories playing in
her mind, torturing her.

*She tucked into a thick area of foliage, wrapping her wool coat
tightly around her body as she tried to stay warm. She'd walked for
hours, more hesitant than usual as she followed the path she and Hugo
had taken so many times before, usually always in silence as a family
brought up the rear on their way to freedom, trudging step after step.
They'd learnt how to move soundlessly across the grass, through dense
treed areas, often guided only by the moonlight as they each focused on
putting one foot in front of the other. But it was different being alone.
This time, the silence felt deafening.*

*She began to shiver, squeezing her eyes shut as she imagined Hugo's
body pressed against hers to keep her warm, his hand covering her waist
as he pulled her against him. Every movement, every step, every decision
made her think of him, and she knew that as soon as she drifted off to
sleep, she'd be straight back to that moment in time, seeing him lying
there, choosing to leave him all over again. Wishing she could have
made any other decision but the one she'd made.*

*She sat up, tucking her legs close to her body as she reached into her
bag. She'd been too scared to go to her apartment in case someone was
waiting for her, and so she'd gone to a friend's house and let herself in
through the back door. No one had been home, and it was there she'd
hurriedly dyed her hair and packed a small bag of things, taking only*

what she absolutely needed to survive the first few days, and leaving a note of apology. One day she'd apologise in person, but right now she needed to do whatever she had to, to survive.

She took out a small piece of bread and an even smaller piece of cheese, nibbling on them slowly in an attempt to make her stomach feel more full. She was numb, but she forced herself to chew, somehow swallowing the bread even though it felt almost impossible to move around her mouth. Eventually she gave up on the rest, placing it back in her bag as birds began to chirp around her and the trees slowly came to life. The cover of darkness was her friend, which meant sleeping and hiding when everyone else was awake.

As she pulled the zipper on her bag, the edge of her wedding ring caught, and she stared down at the gold band that had been there for almost three years now. The thought of her simple wedding, with her brother and father flanking her as Hugo walked to the front of the little church, made her smile, but her happiness was short-lived when she remembered that of the four of them, she was the only one left. The war had taken everything from her.

How had this happened? It was never supposed to be like this. They were all supposed to be together. They'd had a whole life planned, a future that they were all looking forward to. Together.

She reluctantly slid the ring off her finger, knowing that she would have more luck sweet-talking Nazis or local officials as a single woman, and she fiddled with her necklace, intending on putting the band there. If anyone asked, she could say it had belonged to her mother, and no one would be any the wiser. But at least it would keep Hugo close.

Camille opened her eyes and stared down at her bare ring finger, wishing she'd never taken it off in the first place.

She also had the distinct feeling that her days were numbered.

I wish you were here, Hugo. I miss you so much.

Chapter Eleven

CAMILLE

Camille had her head bent close to the wireless as she listened, keeping the volume as low as she could. She'd closed the store temporarily, putting a 'Back in 15 Minutes' sign on the door and locking it, and she was going through all her notes, determined to try once again to piece everything together. She couldn't stop thinking about the note from Benoit, and she had it beside her, heavily crumpled, the words taunting her. She hadn't been able to sleep, tossing and turning all night, more determined than ever for Hugo's death not to have been for nothing.

She had placed the end of the pen against her lips as she closed her eyes, lost in thought, when there was a sudden banging so loud that she feared the glass door to her shop might shatter.

Camille leapt up, turning off the wireless and hurriedly placing it beneath the floorboards along with her notebook. The banging came again, along with the loud shouts of men, and she shuddered as that night came back to her – the shouts through the forest, running for her life.

She reached for Benoit's note, pushing it into her pocket before hurrying out into the store, hand shaking as she unlocked the door and stood back.

'What is the meaning of this?' she asked, as three men roughly pushed their way past her.

Camille knew exactly who they were, of course, but she stood with her hands on her hips, more to stop the shaking than anything. She'd become aware of Lourenço Santos the first time he'd marched into the shop, soon after she'd started working there. It had been no secret that the old man she'd bought the shop from had helped Jews, which was the reason she'd confessed a little about her past to him, knowing it would sway him into selling it to her. But it had also meant she faced the continued interest of PVDE men like Lourenço Santos, who seemed more intent than ever on making their position in Lisbon clear.

'We have reason to suspect that you're in possession of books that breach censorship regulations,' Santos said, sneering at her as he looked her slowly up and down, as if his police uniform gave him the right to do whatever he pleased.

Camille refused to squirm under his gaze, wishing she could slap the expression straight off his face. But men like Lourenço didn't scare her. Once upon a time they would have, but not today, not after everything she'd survived. The only part of him raiding her shop that scared her was the timing – she would never forgive herself if he knew about the family she'd met up with last night at the square, or that she'd supplied anyone with papers. It would be a death sentence for those she'd helped.

'I can assure you that I'm very much aware of what is and is not appropriate to stock in my shop.' She turned in time to see his men throw an entire row of books to the floor. 'Please tell your men to be careful. These books are very precious to me, not to mention worth a lot of money, so I'd appreciate it if they could be more careful.'

He shrugged, as if her words meant nothing, and took out a silver case from his pocket, producing a cigarette and proceeding to light it in front of her and blow the smoke in her face. She held her cough in her throat, not wanting to give him the satisfaction of knowing it had affected her – so much so that her eyes began to water.

'They were only here a few days ago and they couldn't find anything, which makes me think you're targeting me on purpose.'

His eyes were piercing when he stared back at her. 'Tell me again, Mrs—' He laughed.

'Silva,' she said, giving the false name on her papers and folding her arms, resisting the urge to cringe as more books were swept to the floor. They weren't even looking at them, just doing their best to mess up her shop.

'*Mrs Silva*, tell me again how you came to be the owner of this bookshop,' he said. 'It was owned by the same family for generations, and then suddenly, here you are, making everyone feel sorry for the widow who miraculously had enough money on her own to buy the place. Makes me wonder if you're not one of the Jews the old man was so interested in helping.'

She refused to react, keeping her mouth in the same straight line. 'If you thought I was a Jew, you'd have shut my store down by now,' Camille said. 'Let us not play silly games.'

'Maybe not a Jew, but one who sympathises with them, no?' He grunted, as if he were particularly pleased with himself. 'Now answer my question. How did you become the owner of this bookstore?'

Camille fought the tremble inside at his words. So long as he only thought she sympathised with them, she would be fine. *They* would be fine. 'As I told you last time you came to visit, I was a widow looking for a job when I first came here. I'm sure you can understand how hard it is for a woman to earn enough money to survive on her own?' she said. 'I was very fortunate to have a little money left to me by my husband, which allowed me to purchase the shop. But then I'm sure you know all of this already, don't you?'

He stroked his moustache as she spoke, the faint curve of a smile on his lips as if he were enjoying every moment. Her little diatribe certainly hadn't made him feel small, as she'd hoped it might.

'Go on,' he said. 'You look like you have more to say.'

'You make it sound as if I convinced the previous owner of Oliveira's Books to sell to me, which is not at all what happened. I worked here for months before old Mr Oliveira told me of his failing health, and he was only too happy to sell to me so that he didn't have to keep working. No one else was interested in purchasing a shop in wartime, not with such irregular shipments of books.' They didn't need to know that darling old Mr Oliveira had given her everything he owned before he died, and that he'd carefully had his bookshop and the lease on his apartment transferred into her name because he'd become so fond of her and had no family left to leave it to.

Santos's eyes narrowed. 'Why was your door locked when we arrived today? What were you doing back there in secret?'

She smiled. 'I have a very bad headache and was taking a moment to myself, which has only been made worse by your storming into my store unannounced. Is it suddenly illegal for a shop owner to take a break? I have no employees, so I can't exactly disappear and leave the door open.'

He started walking towards the back of the shop. 'You won't mind if I take a look in there then?'

Camille glared at his men when she passed, their carelessness making her want to scream, but she didn't want Santos going into her office without her. She didn't trust him not to plant something and then triumphantly march out with whatever he'd allegedly found.

'You're welcome to look, but you'll find nothing more than coffee cups and some women's magazines, which I dare say is all your men found the last time they were here,' she said, edging into the room behind him as he looked around slowly, as if he didn't want to miss anything.

But then Camille spotted the letter from Benoit on the floor. She'd been in such a hurry to hide everything that she must have dropped it.

She slowly moved closer, placing her foot over it just as Santos turned around.

'Excuse me,' he said, but Camille didn't move and he came so close to her that she could smell the onion he'd eaten for lunch on his breath.

She shook her head as he shoved past her, his shoulder colliding with hers, and while his back was still turned she dropped down low and retrieved the paper, quickly sliding it into the waistline of her skirt. She smiled sweetly when he glanced back at her and moved to the other side of the room, heart pounding.

'Did you find any books to confiscate?' Santos called out to his men, too loudly for the small room, the sound of his voice reverberating.

'Three books that need further investigating,' one of the men called back, and Camille followed him back out into the store, eyes wide at the mess that greeted her. And then she saw a movement outside the glass windows at the front. When she saw it was Avery peering in, she shook her head slowly from side to side. The sign on the door still said 'Back in 15 Minutes', and she breathed a sigh of relief when Avery stepped away and disappeared. The last thing she wanted was the American to be drawn into whatever vendetta the secret police had against her, especially when she'd been here the last time they came.

'Keep looking,' Santos ordered. 'I don't want to leave here without what we came for.'

Camille stayed still, her expression fixed. But inside, she was scared and wondering precisely what it was he'd come for. The sooner she got him out of her shop, the better.

'Camille?'

She was collapsed in a puddle on the floor, books all around her, when she heard her name being called. Camille looked up, surprised that anyone had come into the shop when the sign on the door remained. She didn't even know what time it was, but she imagined late afternoon.

'You shouldn't be here.'

Avery began picking up books and setting them up on shelves, and Camille rose to do the same. She'd been cleaning up for the past hour, determined to get her shop back in order, and she was very grateful for the help.

'I want to be here.'

Camille sighed. 'It's as if you're looking for trouble. Please, just leave me be.'

'Are they targeting you? I know you said this kind of raid is commonplace, but to be here again the same week . . .'

Camille was silent as she tried to find the right words, but Avery spoke again before she had the chance to reply.

'I went to see the Jewish people in the square – twice in fact. I went back last night because I couldn't stop thinking about them, even though I knew it wasn't my business and that my superiors would be furious at me for not keeping to myself, and . . .' Avery hesitated.

Camille stiffened. She knew what Avery was about to say. All this time she'd thought the PVDE would be her eventual downfall, yet suddenly a nosey American might be her biggest threat. The PVDE didn't have any evidence of what she was doing – not yet – but Avery did.

'I saw you there,' Avery said, softly. 'I know you're helping them. Is that why you're being investigated?'

Camille turned slightly so that Avery couldn't see how much her hand was trembling, placing the book on the shelf and reaching for another. She was still shaken up about the raid, but knowing that the American had only been at the square last night because she cared gave her the most overwhelming urge to talk to someone – to tell someone the truth so she wasn't alone in her memories. She'd spent so long alone, determined to complete what she'd set out to achieve, but knowing how easily it could all be taken away had rattled her more than she had realised.

'There are things about me, Avery, things from my past . . .'

Avery kept picking up books from the floor and shelving them, glancing up at Camille every so often, and Camille was struck by just how much empathy this woman had. She couldn't imagine anyone else she knew in Lisbon stopping to help put her bookshop back in order. But it was then she noticed a dark bruise on Avery's wrist.

'How did you get that?' Camille asked, moving closer to her.

Avery quickly pulled her arm away, her blouse covering the bruise. 'It's nothing.'

Camille reached out and nudged her sleeve back up, exposing the ugly purple welt.

'Someone did this to you? Who?'

Avery sighed. 'It seems you were right about needing to be careful, only it was another woman who grabbed me. She was looking for money or food I suppose.'

'You were attacked?' Camille blew out a breath. 'After you went to the square?'

'Yes, the first time I visited, that day we had lunch, but I'm fine now. It rattled me at the time, but I learnt my lesson and I'll be more careful next time.' Avery sighed. 'There was also a man, although I didn't catch his name, and he was passing by and intervened. I'm eternally grateful to him.'

Camille had always been a very good judge of character. And her instincts right now were to trust in Avery and her good nature.

'Well, thank goodness for your mystery man. What do you think he was doing there?'

'That's the thing, he said he'd been taking some supplies to the square. I was rather touched by his kindness.'

Avery looked rattled still and Camille watched her for a moment, before saying something she had never intended on disclosing. 'Avery, I haven't been entirely honest with you.' Avery stopped shelving, her hand hovering over a book as if she couldn't move it and listen at the same time.

'The PVDE have their suspicions about me, but nothing they can prove – yet,' Camille said, shaking her head. 'I have done things here they could arrest me for if they knew, things I don't want to implicate you in, but I had another life before this. In France. A life I'm certain that no one here knows about, and I intend on keeping it that way, no matter how badly they treat me.'

Camille was torn between telling her everything and wishing she'd never started talking in the first place. There was something about Avery that reminded her what it had been like to have friends, to have a life, to not have to hide in plain sight all on her own. But there was another part that resented Avery for the life she led, for how little risk she was taking when there was so much more she could do. 'I'm sorry, you don't want to hear all this. I'm fine, honestly. Thank you for helping, you certainly didn't need to. You don't have to stay and help.'

'I do have to stay, I *want* to stay, but I have to ask,' Avery said, 'exactly what you're doing for those people . . .'

Avery was staring at her, waiting for a response, and Camille was lost for words. She was torn between telling her the truth, and lying to put an end to her questions, but in the end, she decided to question Avery instead. She needed to know whether she was just a woman feeling a moment of empathy, or someone who would do more if she could. *Once upon a time, I was this girl. Until Hugo told me what he was doing, until he let me see the world he was part of and gave me the chance to do more. She could help me in ways that could change lives.*

'Avery, the work you're doing here in Lisbon. How much do you actually think it helps your country?'

Avery looked puzzled. 'Well, if I didn't think it was worthwhile, if my country didn't think it was worthwhile, I wouldn't be here.'

'But how much help can newspapers be? What information is actually being gleaned from those publications you're sourcing?'

Camille could see that Avery was flustered, if not downright upset, but she needed to know. She needed to know just how far Avery was willing to go, and if she pushed her away entirely, then so be it.

'All I know is that more people like me are being trained and deployed, to send back enemy publications. If our intelligence service didn't think it was useful, I doubt they would be continuing the programme, and I have to believe that they're uncovering information that's worth my time in sending it back to Washington.'

Camille nodded. 'What if I told you that someone with an eye for detail like you could be directly helping the Jews arriving in Lisbon? That you could be doing so much more to help the war effort, in a different way?' She took a breath. 'Am I correct in believing that you're highly proficient with a camera? You mentioned you had been microfilming in America.'

Avery's eyes widened. 'The allegations against you were true? You've been . . .' Avery lowered her voice. '*Forging identifications?*'

Camille nodded. There was no point in hiding any part of the truth now. 'You didn't answer my question.'

'Yes, I'm proficient with a camera. My work involves photographing documents on to microfilm.' Avery stared at her, as if she'd only just understood why Camille had asked her the question. 'You're asking if *I* would help you?' she asked. 'You want me to create false documentation with you?'

'I'm asking how far you're willing to go to help those in need,' Camille said. 'And yes, whether you'd use your camera to help others who desperately need you.'

Avery was silent for a moment, and Camille watched as she bent to pick up a missed fallen book from the floor, before finally turning back to her.

'I, well, I'd need to think about it.'

Camille could sense that Avery was interested in what she'd proposed, but she could also tell that if she wanted Avery's help, she was going to have to open up to her.

'Have you eaten today?'

Avery shook her head.

'How about we go back to my apartment as soon as it's time to close up, and I'll tell you everything you want to know.'

Less than an hour later, they walked in silence down the cobbled street to Camille's apartment, but it was a comfortable silence and

Camille found she was happy to be with Avery. She'd spent her life surrounded by men after her mother had passed – her father, her brother and his friends, and then Hugo – and she hadn't realised how much she'd been craving female companionship. But she knew that she had to tread carefully – she hadn't known Avery for long, and Camille wasn't usually so quick to trust.

When they reached her apartment she showed Avery in, careful to lock the door behind her before turning on the light. She only wished she had a gramophone to play some music on, which she'd always done when entertaining friends in Paris before the war. You never could be too careful about blocking out conversation.

'I hope you like a Merlot,' she said, taking a bottle of red wine from the little kitchen sideboard. 'One of my French customers traded it for books last week.'

'I'm going to sound incredibly unsophisticated,' Avery said as she took off her jacket and laid it on the arm of a chair, 'but I've never actually tried red wine.'

Camille thought back to when Hugo had first come to her family's home for dinner, recalling the look on his face when her father had questioned Hugo about his taste in wine, and how her father had watched Hugo trying his best Cabernet Sauvignon. She took out two glasses and pulled the cork from the bottle, pushing the thoughts away.

'You'll come to like it, I promise,' she said, before filling both glasses and turning to pass one to Avery. 'But it might take some getting used to.'

Camille laughed at Avery's expression when she took a hesitant sip, taking one herself and enjoying the familiar sensation of the wine calming her nerves. She'd missed it – opening a bottle to share, relaxing at home, preparing food for someone other than herself. It was as if opening up to Avery had broken down a barrier that had been in place ever since she'd left France, and rather than feeling uncertain about it, Camille felt a sense of relief.

'I'll put something together for us to eat. It won't take long.'

'Can I help?'

'No, you enjoy the wine and I'll prepare the food. I like having something to do.' Camille took out a knife and chopping board, deciding to slice cheese and some cold meats, along with bread and some vegetables that she had. *Like I used to do, when Papa and the boys would come home complaining of being so hungry that they couldn't wait another moment to eat. They loved cheese and cold meat, pickles and lightly toasted bread.*

She glanced behind her and saw that Avery was tucked up in an armchair, glass of wine still in hand but her shoes kicked off. Camille certainly hadn't scared her off by telling her she had secrets, which indicated that the American had more nerve than she might have previously given her credit for.

'In France, my husband and I . . .' Camille paused, her tongue stalling on his name, finding it almost impossible to say. '*Hugo* and I, we worked to transport Jews across the border to safety. He died in 1941. It was the reason I left my country and came to Portugal.'

Camille kept chopping, needing to keep doing something as she spoke. Thankfully Kiefer had never been to her apartment, because if he had, she'd be worried he might have hidden recording devices. But if he was suspicious of her at all, he'd never let on.

'When I came here, I didn't know how I'd be able to continue my work, but I soon realised that the French Jewish refugees who arrived without the correct visa paperwork or identification papers would be deported, and I couldn't stand to have that on my conscience.' Camille's fingers tightly gripped the handle of the knife. 'In France, it was my work with the Resistance that left me a widow, and I suppose that I felt as if I had nothing to lose by helping where I could here.'

'You were a member of the Resistance? The *French* Resistance?' Avery asked, her voice barely a whisper, as if she couldn't quite believe what she was hearing. 'You were never married to a Portuguese man?'

Camille grimaced. 'Today was terrifying for me not because of what they did to my shop, but because I thought someone had figured out who I really was. I thought my past had been uncovered somehow, that my work had been exposed, because everything you say is true.' She didn't go so far as to tell her about the note she'd received from Benoit – there were some things that she would keep a secret.

Silence filled the apartment, and Camille kept her back turned, half expecting to hear the door shut behind Avery. But instead of leaving, Avery had stood up and was behind her, her hand closing over Camille's shoulder. Her palm was strong, comforting.

'You were scared because you thought they might kill you, too?'

A tear slid down Camille's cheek and landed on the chopping board, narrowly missing the cheese. She quickly blinked to stop more from falling, not used to letting her emotions get the better of her.

'I was angry because I thought they'd found me before I'd found out who was responsible for betraying us in France, and before I could help more people who need me and the services I provide,' she whispered. 'I made a promise the day they killed my Hugo that I wouldn't stop until I knew, and that I would keep doing the work that was so important to both of us. But I'm no closer now to finding out who he is than I was then.' She exhaled. 'I was never scared of the work we did in France, not until the very last day, but now I'm so afraid of what might happen.'

'You're telling me that you're in Lisbon searching for the person who—'

'Killed my husband,' Camille finished for her.

Avery removed her hand from Camille's shoulder and took the plate of food, carrying it over to the small table. She went back for her glass of wine, which she'd left beside the armchair.

'I'm trusting you tonight, in telling you all this,' Camille said. 'You're the only person in Lisbon who knows the truth.'

Avery bit down on her bottom lip for a moment, before taking another sip of her drink. Camille felt as if she were holding her breath, because she certainly didn't have a plan for what to do if Avery didn't want to be confided in.

'You can trust me, Camille. You're the only friend I have here, and just hearing what happened to you, what happened to your husband, as well as seeing the refugees here, it makes me realise how little I truly understood about the war.'

Camille slipped her feet out of her shoes and tucked her legs up beneath her on the chair opposite Avery, nursing her own glass of wine.

'I suppose I'm no different than all those young men who are so desperate to go off to war and fight for their country, not really knowing what they're about to face, what it'll be like there. I was so desperate to do something, *anything*, to help, fantasising about being sent overseas, but it wasn't until I saw all those refugees in the square waiting with their families that I truly *saw* the war for what it was.' Avery exhaled. 'When I saw you, I knew you were doing something to help, that there was a reason you were there, but I never could have guessed how involved you were.'

'What did you see when you visited the square, Avery?' Camille asked.

Avery's eyes met hers, and Camille saw a change in them, an understanding in her gaze. 'I saw what the war was doing to people, even on this small scale, and it made it real to me. It made me want to do more.'

'You know,' Camille said, reaching for a piece of cheese and a small slice of bread, 'we had a saying in France, that it doesn't matter how small the role, everyone counts. Because without every part filled, without someone for every job, we will fail. The Resistance movement was testament to that saying.'

'You're trying to tell me that acquiring newspapers and books should be enough for me?' Avery laughed. 'Is that your version of an apology for asking if my work was worthwhile?'

Camille laughed back. 'I'm telling you that the fact you're doing *something* is still important, no matter how insignificant it might feel sometimes. It takes many to achieve great things, and yes, I shouldn't have been so hard on you. It's just that I've seen so much, and sometimes I can't help but want everyone to do more than they're already doing.'

They both sipped their wine and nibbled cheese, and Camille realised just how much she'd missed the simple pleasure of sharing a meal with someone whose company she enjoyed.

'Can I ask why you think the person responsible for killing your husband is here, in Lisbon?'

'Because there are very few other places where enemies can meet in person to trade secrets and double-cross one another,' Camille told her. 'All of the best spies and double agents in the world are right here in Lisbon. If I'm ever going to find the information I need, it will be here.'

They sat in silence for a moment, until Camille spoke again.

'Have you seen your British friend again?'

'James?' Avery asked, looking surprised by the question. 'Not since the day we had lunch. Why?'

'It's nothing. I'm suspicious of everyone and I just . . .' Camille rose and reached for the bottle of wine she'd left open in the kitchen. 'I think I've said quite enough for today. Let's just drink, enjoy each other's company, and hope the PVDE don't come and knock the door down.'

Poor Avery gulped down her wine so fast that Camille started to laugh, almost losing her own mouthful. She hadn't laughed or felt happy in such a long time, and she realised just how much she'd missed the feeling.

'Would it make you feel better if we barricaded the door with furniture?' Camille asked.

'Yes,' Avery said, wide-eyed. 'What shall we use?'

And within minutes they were grunting and giggling, trying their hardest to push a wooden cabinet in front of the door, and recognising that there was no way they were going to get it across the room. Which left them sitting in a heap on the floor, wiggling their toes in their stockings as they sat side by side.

'I think I'm already drunk,' Avery said. 'I feel all light-headed.'

'Shall I pour you another glass then?'

Camille stood and pulled Avery to her feet, trying not to laugh as Avery stumbled into her.

'Camille, I need to ask you something, and I need you to answer me honestly.'

She waited, keeping hold of the American.

Avery leaned into her. 'Your German boyfriend, the man I've seen you with . . .'

'He's a means to an end and nothing more,' Camille told her.

'To find out who killed your husband?'

Camille let go of the breath she was holding and it shuddered from her lungs. 'Exactly.'

Chapter Twelve

AVERY

Avery had thought she was busy when she'd been working at the library, but nothing could have possibly prepared her for the hours she was spending with her eye pressed to the viewfinder of her camera in Lisbon, documenting all of the publications she'd managed to source. She now had books and newspapers piled up around the living room and the spare bedroom – which no one had ever arrived to fill – and she was starting to see why Tom had kept the apartment in such a mess. It was impossible to keep order when she barely had time to do anything other than work, and she kept bringing bag after bag of material home with her almost every day from not just Camille's bookshop, but other vendors dotted around the city. Even those books that Avery didn't feel were important enough to microfilm were still boxed up and sent to Washington just in case, albeit without any urgency. They might not be shipped for months, until there was space on a returning aircraft.

Avery squinted, her eyes becoming tired after so many hours hunched over, but she wanted to finish photographing the current book to add to the worn, brown leather diplomatic pouch she'd prepared to send the following day. It still seemed almost unbelievable to her that the pouch would make its way by air back to the United States within days of her safely handing it over to her contact from the American Legation in Lisbon. She'd had no feedback at all on her work, receiving only her weekly stipend and a note in the post instructing her to intensify the search for books on German military strategy, but she could only imagine that no news was good news. She had sourced all sorts of books, newspapers and even maps so far, and her only worry was that she might run out of film. And she couldn't help but think about what Camille had seen, wondering if her own work *was* actually as useful to the cause as she'd thought it to be. Or whether there was indeed more that Avery could be doing, like helping to create documents that would change the lives of those Camille tried to help.

Avery glanced at her wristwatch then and realised how late it was, and she quickly checked her reflection in her bedroom mirror before grabbing her keys and rushing down the stairs. The news stand a few blocks away usually stocked German weekly papers on a Wednesday, and she didn't want to miss out on the copies for the week. But as she flung her door open, she noticed a cream envelope and quickly bent to collect it before it blew away.

She slid her nail beneath the seal, pulling out a small card in matching thick cream stock, and read the beautiful handwriting, not having any idea who it was from until her eyes flicked ahead to the last line.

Dear Avery,

I didn't want to disturb you by knocking, so thought best to deliver a note instead. Are you free for dinner tomorrow night? I'm staying at the Tivoli Avenida Liberdade, just up the street from the Hotel Avenida where we were both having drinks the other night, and I thought we could

have dinner there. I'll be at your doorstep at seven if you're
kind enough to accompany me. James.

PS I just made my first mistake, telling you where I live.

Avery put the card back in the envelope, holding it against her chest for a moment as she laughed at their little joke, before slipping it into her pocket and dashing down the street in the direction of the news stand.

'Hello,' she said when she got there, breathless from walking so fast, before switching to Portuguese. 'I'm sorry, I forget myself sometimes,' Avery apologised. 'Newspapers today?'

The man pointed towards the Portuguese paper, which was all part of the game now. He knew what she came for, and he often insisted that she buy the local newspaper before finally showing her what she really wanted.

'I have family in Germany, so I like to keep up with the news,' she said, giving him her sweetest smile. 'Do you have any newspapers that might help me find out what's happening there?'

He shrugged and she took out some money, spotting his son playing in the street as she did so. Avery had sat one day to watch the comings and goings, to observe the owner and the many customers he had throughout the day, because it helped her to understand what might work if she ever needed to bribe him.

'Your son likes American bubblegum?' she asked, taking a stick from her pocket.

The man smiled then and immediately reached for the newspaper she wanted, which he kept away until she had handed over the gum.

'I have more if you have anything else for me?' she asked. 'Chocolate?'

He bent down, and when he stood he passed her another paper. *Italian.* Avery tried not to smile too hard as she handed over the bar in her bag. *If only I'd offered chocolate before.* She often found the weekly German newspapers she was searching for, but the Italian papers were much harder to get her hands on, so this was extra special.

'Thank you!' she said, walking back the other way so she could wave to the small boy she'd just parted with the treats for. 'Make sure your papa shares the bubblegum I just gave him!'

The boy stared at her, blinking, before running over to his father, and Avery found herself grinning the whole way home, newspapers tucked beneath her arm, the sun on her face, and a cool breeze against her neck that made the temperature bearable. In her apartment it was sometimes stiflingly hot, but out here, today, the air felt magical.

She touched her pocket to feel the card there, thinking about what she possibly had in her wardrobe that was suitable to wear, and wondering what her mother would think of James. She would likely think him very dashing, although Avery couldn't imagine James being quite so eager to impress her mother as Michael had been. It was almost as if Michael were a boy, whereas James was most definitely a man.

Avery forgot all about her date though when she saw the mailman at her door, and she ran all the way to see if he had anything for her.

'Miss Avery Johnson?'

'Yes!' she gasped. 'That's me. Do you have something for me?'

He passed her three letters, and she quickly turned them over for the return address. One from Washington, one from home and . . . She let out a big breath. One from Jack. She'd been starting to panic when she hadn't heard from him in so long, always worried that something terrible might have happened to him, but a letter meant he was alive. Or at least that he had been whenever he'd sent it, which she knew could have been some time ago.

She let herself in and ran up the stairs, temporarily forgetting all about the book she had been in the middle of photographing, and tore open the envelope as quickly as she could.

Avery was on cloud nine. She'd reread the letter from Jack as she got ready, before placing it on her bedside table, alongside a letter from home, and now she was doing one final check in the mirror before going downstairs to meet James. She glanced at the clock again, seeing she had five more minutes before he was due to arrive and dabbing a little perfume on the spot just behind her ear, as well as on her wrist. Satisfied that she now smelt and looked good, she did a little turn to check her dress, before collecting her coat and purse and slipping her heels into her shoes. James was much taller than her, and she loved that no matter what shoes she'd chosen, he'd still be tall enough for her to drop her head to his shoulder if she was so inclined.

She ran down the stairs and opened her door just in time to see James walking towards her, still a few lamp posts away. Avery locked the door and waited, watching the way his rather pensive expression turned to a smile when he saw her standing there.

'On my walk here, I was convinced you wouldn't be waiting,' he said.

'Well, a girl can't say no to dinner at a swanky hotel, can she?' Avery replied. 'Not to mention your letter was very sweet.'

'You look beautiful, as always,' he said, proffering his arm.

Avery happily slipped her hand through the crook he made, feeling altogether breathless and exhilarated.

The walk to the hotel was pleasant, the temperature outside still warm as they wandered slowly enough for her to be comfortable in her heels. She'd expected to be nervous, but instead she was just happy to be in James's company, laughing at his jokes and listening to him talk about home and the things he missed about Britain.

'How about you, Avery? What are you missing?' he asked.

'Honestly? I haven't been away from home long enough to miss anyone, not really. I just . . .' She stopped.

'You just what? You can't leave me hanging wondering what it is.'

'I know this sounds silly, but I've always wanted to travel. It's not exactly a popular dream for a young unmarried woman, but I feel like I'm right where I'm supposed to be.'

'It doesn't sound silly at all, and in my opinion there's nothing wrong with wanting to see the world. How do we know what we want if we haven't seen anywhere but home?'

She was relieved from having to say any more when James slowed and gestured to the building they were approaching. 'We're here,' he said.

The Tivoli Avenida Liberdade was similar from the outside to the only other hotel she'd visited in Lisbon, only this one was across the square and with steps leading up to the entrance. She walked slightly ahead of James as he guided her past the doorman, who quickly swept the glass door back for her to walk through, into the lobby and through to the dining room. Stiff-looking white tablecloths adorned each table, and she was surprised at how many people were already there for dinner.

'Come this way, Mr Anderson,' said a well-dressed man, presumably the restaurant manager, and they were whisked away to a corner table. 'Your champagne will be with you shortly.'

'Champagne?' she asked, raising a brow. 'Are you trying to impress me?'

'It's been a successful day, that's all,' he said, sitting back in his chair and flashing her a contented smile. 'It's also been a very long time since I had dinner with a beautiful woman.'

Avery knew she was blushing but she no longer cared. She imagined that someone as elegant as Camille heard such words all the time, and Avery very much doubted she'd twist herself in knots about her face flushing. She vowed to be more like her new friend and sat confidently, her shoulders squared as she smiled at her date.

'So, tell me what you're enjoying most about Lisbon,' James asked as their waiter brought a bottle to their table and poured champagne.

'The weather, the intrigue, the work, the people . . .' Avery grinned at the surprised look on James's face.

'Perhaps I should have asked what you're *not* enjoying,' he said, before raising his glass and touching it gently to hers when she did the same. 'The list might have been shorter.'

'Considerably shorter,' she said with a laugh.

They both took a sip, and Avery couldn't help but wiggle her nose when the bubbles tickled, which only made James smile all the more.

'Tell me one thing you don't like,' he said, once they'd set their glasses down again.

'I don't like the letter I received from my boss turning down a request I made, when I know perfectly well how to do business here,' she said. 'But then that's not really something not to like about Lisbon, per se.'

'It's very easy for someone in Washington or London to tell us how to do our jobs, but we're feet on the ground here. Without being rude, I simply don't think they understand the currency in a place like Lisbon.'

Avery took another little sip of champagne and found it slightly less bubbly the second time.

'You requested items to trade, I suspect?'

She laughed. 'I did.' She wasn't even going to ask him how she knew.

James leaned forward, his hand on the tablecloth only inches from hers. If she stretched her little finger ever so slightly, she would be able to touch his. It seemed he had the same thought, because he did exactly that, brushing the edge of her finger with his.

'So what was your solution?' he asked. 'If that's not classified information, of course.'

'I wrote immediately to my sister and asked her to send a care package containing only *Time* magazines, chocolate bars and bubblegum,' Avery said. 'I was clearly told that such items weren't an approved currency and wouldn't be sent from Washington, but they never said I couldn't give personal gifts to my favourite booksellers or newspaper vendors, did they?'

James's easy laughter sent a warmth through her, and she found herself bravely moving her little finger even closer to his so that they were looped together. But then he went still.

'You have a bruise,' he said.

She glanced down at her wrist, moving it slightly so the silk of her sleeve covered it. It was barely visible now, so she was surprised he even noticed it. 'Oh, that's nothing. A story for another day.'

He gave her a long, steady look, but he must have noticed it had made her uncomfortable because he smiled and leaned closer, deftly changing the subject.

'We really should look at the menu,' he said. 'They sell out of all the best dishes most nights, and I'd hate you to go home hungry.'

Avery was happy to sit back and let James order for them, noticing that he held the menu in one hand, never moving his finger from hers even when their waiter returned to take the order.

It was then Avery understood that this feeling – the nerves in her stomach and the excitement at having her skin skim against a man's – was what had been missing when she'd been engaged. She could sit with James all night, their conversation easy and their laughter even easier. She was halfway around the world, but somehow she'd never felt more alive, or more at home.

Or more attracted to a man.

'I hope you like fish,' he said, when they were finally alone again. 'Because according to the waiter, it's divine.'

Avery giggled.

'What's so funny?'

'James, do you actually speak Portuguese?'

He cleared his throat and made a noise that she couldn't decipher, which only made her laugh more. 'I was certain it would be easier to pick up once I was living here, but in all honesty, I can only get by with the basics.' He groaned. 'He didn't actually say that, did he?'

Avery shook her head. 'He said he would have recommended the chicken, but I'm certain the fish will be excellent.'

This time when they both laughed, James placed his hand over hers, and his palm was still covering her fingers when their first course was served.

'Avery, have you had lunch with your bookshop friend again?'

'Camille? Not lunch, no, but I've seen her a few times.'

Avery glanced up at James as they walked. She liked James, a lot, but she also loved the friendship that was growing between her and Camille, and she wouldn't say anything to him that might jeopardise that.

'Do you believe she's as she seems?' he asked.

'Is anyone as they seem in Lisbon?' Avery teased. 'It certainly seems there is a lot of espionage at play.'

'*I'm* as I seem,' James said, leaning in and placing his hand over hers as they walked. She had her fingers looped through his arm, and now with him holding her hand she realised just how close their bodies were. 'You can trust me, Avery, I promise. We're both on the same side.'

She stopped resisting the urge to drop her head to his shoulder then and just did it, liking the feel of him, the warmth of him against her. Everything about being with James was new to her, and she found herself wishing the night could keep going, that it wasn't almost drawing to a close.

'You know, I think I can trust Camille, too,' she said. 'She's a good person, James, and she's doing good things that I can't talk about. I promise you, she is.'

'If you believe you can trust her, then so can I. You don't have to try to convince me.'

She sighed and listened to his breathing as she leaned even more deeply into him, pleased that he hadn't asked her questions about Camille that she wouldn't be able, or willing, to answer.

'Tonight has been quite something, Avery the librarian,' James said, slowly stopping and turning to face her. 'I would say a pleasant surprise, but then I had an inkling that it would be an evening to remember.'

He looked at her for a long moment before slowly lifting a hand and placing his palm gently against her cheek, cupping her face as he leaned down. She tilted her chin, waiting for the moment that his lips met hers. And when they did, it was so different to when she'd kissed Michael, the feeling going all the way to her toes as she slowly moved her mouth against James's and he brushed his lips back and forth against hers.

'Was that alright?' he asked.

Avery laughed, and soon they both were, foreheads touching as they stood beneath a street light and caught their breaths.

'It was definitely alright,' she eventually whispered back. It had been much better than alright, it had been the best kiss of her life, although she wasn't about to tell him that.

'I feel like I've been waiting a long time for this war to be over, Avery, so that I can get back home, but now, I'm not sure I want it to be over so soon,' he said, placing his hands on her shoulders as he stared into her eyes. 'Because that would mean you'd be back on a plane to New York and I'd be headed back to London, and that would be a great shame indeed.'

Avery bit down on her lower lip, catching it between her teeth. She knew it was a terrible thing to think, but she didn't want the war to be over so soon, either. Not now that she was finally here, although she knew how selfish it was to even have such a thought when so many were suffering.

'Well, we'd better make the most of our time here then,' she said, wishing he'd kiss her again and then feeling sorely disappointed when he put his arm around her instead.

They began to walk again, her tucked beneath his arm, heads bent close, as if they were the only two people in the world walking the streets of Lisbon after dark. Until they neared the door to her apartment and she heard a man clear his throat and saw someone step out of the shadows.

'Avery?'

She started, holding tight to James as she squinted, not seeing who it was until he moved into the light.

'Tom!' she cried, letting go of James and rushing forward to greet him. 'What are you doing here? How did you end up in Lisbon?'

'Long story, but the short of it is that I need my old room back. I've been waiting out here a while.'

'You've been sitting out here all night?'

He grimaced. 'I have. I was actually starting to consider booking a hotel room when you showed up.'

Avery looked back at James, waving him forward. 'I forgot my manners with all this excitement. James, you remember Tom? You met when—'

'Of course I recall.' She watched as James shook his hand. 'Good to see you again, Tom, and let me guess, you're a librarian too?'

Tom's laugh was easy. 'Close. How did you guess.'

Then it was James who was laughing, and Avery planted her hands on her hips and glared at him. 'All this time, you still haven't believed I'm a librarian? Why is it so hard to believe!'

'I promise, I believe you now,' James said, holding out his hand to her. 'But I fear this is goodnight for me. Thank you for a wonderful evening.'

Tom made a show of turning around and busying himself with his belongings, and Avery smiled up at James, having to tilt her head ever so slightly. 'Thank you,' she whispered. 'It was my favourite night in Lisbon so far.'

James reached out and stroked a strand of hair from her face, tucking it gently behind her ear, pausing before pressing a warm, sweet kiss to her lips.

'Goodnight, Avery,' he murmured, before taking one step backwards and then turning and disappearing into the night.

'I see you've settled in then,' Tom said with a grin when she spun around to face him. 'You seem to have made friends.'

'Not another word, or you'll be sitting on the doorstep until morning.'

He clamped his lips together and made a little motion like he was zipping his mouth closed, and Avery just groaned and picked up one of his bags for him, happy for the company but also understanding how Tom must have felt when she'd showed up earlier than expected and he'd had to make space for her.

Because finding space for Tom to move back in again was going to be no easy task.

'Oh, and Avery, before I forget,' Tom said, puffing as he hauled his luggage up the stairs behind her. 'Kilgour confirmed there's to be no trades for acquiring publications.'

'He said that to you too?' she muttered, turning around to face him when they stepped into the living room. 'He has no idea what we're up against trying to get the material Washington needs. Trades would make acquisitions so much easier.'

She realised then that Tom hadn't said another word, and she glanced back at him. Tom was surveying the room, taking in the stacks of books and small piles of Portuguese newspapers. Suddenly she could see the room through his eyes.

'Funnily enough, I don't think acquisitions has been so difficult for you, because I know for a fact that these weren't left behind by the last guy.'

Avery ignored him. It had been the most magical evening and she wanted to keep hold of it for a little bit longer before addressing her slight issue of hoarding.

'Come on, let me clear out some of my mess from your bedroom. You must be beat.'

Chapter Thirteen

Avery

Avery wandered into the bookshop as she did almost every other morning. Even if Camille didn't have anything for her, calling in and saying hello had become a favourite part of her daily routine. And she'd also been thinking a lot about what Camille had proposed – and whether she would be capable of helping her or not.

'Good morning!' she called out.

Only her voice died in her throat when she realised Camille wasn't alone. Usually there would be maybe one customer late morning – it was often busier in the afternoons – but today Camille's German friend was in the shop. When he turned, a shiver ran the length of Avery's spine, and she immediately wished she could retrace her steps and come back later. But she knew that such a move would make her look more than a little suspicious, and so instead she fixed her smile and nodded to him. She was relieved when he turned his attention back to Camille.

'Oh, good morning, Avery!' Camille said, a little too brightly. 'I have your book waiting for you out the back.'

'My b—' she began. 'Oh, thank you, I didn't expect it to be in so soon.'

Avery smiled again at the man, who was looking at her. It was most unsettling.

'Avery, I'd like you to officially meet Kiefer. Kiefer, this is one of my very good customers, Avery.'

Kiefer's smile was cool but polite, and he folded his hands behind his back as he greeted her. She was surprised he didn't offer to shake her hand.

'Pleased to meet you, Avery,' he said.

'It's a pleasure to meet you, too,' she replied. 'Are you here for business or pleasure?'

Avery cringed and immediately wished she'd kept her mouth shut when he didn't answer. She hadn't meant it to sound like that, and she quickly tried to correct herself.

'I often call in to say hello, but then I always end up buying something. It's impossible not to with such a wonderful selection of books to choose from.' Avery knew she was prattling, as she often did when she was nervous, but she couldn't seem to help it.

'Avery, would you like to browse the store while I dash out the back to get your book?' Camille suggested, saving her from having to talk to Kiefer, who was proving to be most unsettling.

She nodded and moved away, feeling as if her every move was being scrutinised. Without a doubt, this was the closest she'd ever knowingly been to a Nazi. She had no idea how Camille could be around him so easily.

'Here we go,' Camille said within a few minutes, passing Avery a book that she'd never heard of before and pressing it into her hands, giving her a strange look that she had no hope of deciphering.

Nevertheless, Avery followed her to the counter and paid, her hands trembling ever so slightly as she continued to feel Kiefer's gaze on her.

'I'll see you again soon, Avery,' Camille said brightly, and Avery found herself saying goodbye and walking straight back out the door.

When she looked down at the book, she had the strangest notion that Camille had been trying to tell her something. Was she scared? Did she need help? Was there a message in the title? But it was *Gone with the Wind*; what message could there possibly be? Unless Camille was indicating that she should be gone with the wind and flee, which she certainly hoped wasn't the case.

It wasn't until she opened the book and flicked through a few pages that a note fell out, hastily written and on paper torn from a large notepad. Avery bent to collect it from where it had fluttered to the ground.

Come back when he's long gone. Need to see you. Make sure no one's following you.

If Avery had been nervous before, now she was downright scared. Follow her? Why would anyone be following her, unless Kiefer was suspicious about their friendship for some reason? And why would Camille need to see her so urgently that she'd gone to the effort of writing a note and hiding it in a book?

Avery started to walk away, the book tucked under her arm, and glanced over her shoulder every few steps, more nervous than she'd ever been. In fact, she was so nervous that her feet walked her all the way to the square by James's hotel, but she didn't let herself go in.

You came here because you wanted to be taken seriously. If you run to him at the first roadblock, you may as well give up and go home.

So she started to walk again, counting down the minutes until she felt it was safe to go back to the shop without Kiefer knowing she'd returned. And knowing that when she did, she was going to tell Camille that she would do whatever she needed her to do. It might be dangerous, but the sight of all those families huddled together in the square when she'd last been there was imprinted in her mind now, and she knew she wouldn't be able to live with herself if she didn't do something to help them.

'You came back.'

'Of course I came back! After that cryptic message you gave me, I've been pacing the streets waiting until I could come back! Why the ruse?'

'Look, I know we don't talk about the work you do, Avery, but I have something that might be of interest to you.'

Avery leaned forward to see what Camille had under the counter, surprised to see three maps.

'What are they?'

'Maps that I've been asked to copy and bind into a book,' she said. 'It has to be ready tomorrow, so I don't have much time.'

Avery wasn't certain she understood what Camille was trying to tell her. 'So it's not for sale? You didn't ask me back because you knew I'd buy it?' She swallowed and lowered her voice. 'Your German friend left this here?'

Camille moved a little closer to her. There was one other person in the store, near the front, and she spoke in a low whisper.

'He did. And you can photograph it here, in my office, before I bind it.'

Avery hesitated, relieved when the customer had left the store and they were alone. 'You want me to bring my camera here? I can't do it at my apartment?'

'Yes. You would need to set up here, in my office in the backroom. You can't take them off-site, because if he came back

154

looking for them . . .' Camille shivered, and Avery realised it was the first time she'd seen her look truly rattled. 'I'm certain you can understand what would happen if he knew I'd broken his trust.'

Avery glanced down at the maps again, wondering what they were or whether they were worth risking so much for.

'The man I met before?' Avery asked. 'Is he your . . .' *Lover.* That's what she wanted to say, but the word simply didn't come out.

'Yes,' Camille said, holding Avery's gaze as if to challenge her to ask more.

'He was terrifying,' Avery said. 'I don't know how you can stand to be romantically linked with him.'

'I told you, it's a means to an end and nothing more,' Camille said, looking cross. 'I don't want to have to pretend with you, Avery. I have my reasons for seeing him, information I seek that only someone like him can give me, but what I do with him—'

'I'm sorry, you don't have to explain yourself to me,' Avery said, gently, seeing how upset Camille was. 'And I would love to see the map and photograph it, but it has to be our secret. No one can know that I'm working here, because if my roommate found out, I'd be on the next plane back to America. It could compromise everything I've worked so hard for.'

'I have as much to lose as you do, Avery. I won't be breathing a word, especially not to Kiefer. He'd have my head and I'm not exaggerating.'

'What are these?' Avery asked, picking up one of two newspapers that had been placed beside the maps.

'They're German papers, two copies of *Der Stürmer*, in fact.' Camille came around to stand beside her. 'They're Kiefer's as well. He has a subscription, so they arrive every week like clockwork and I keep them here for him. And he's just ordered a subscription to the daily Nazi Party paper, *Völkischer Beobachter*, too, so there's a couple of them waiting as well.'

'He doesn't come straight around to get them? That wasn't why he was here earlier?'

Camille's smile was coy. 'He comes to get them when I say they're here, but sometimes he's away. If you want to photograph them, you can do it tonight, and you can keep doing it here, too. I'll tell him they arrived first thing in the morning tomorrow to give you the time you need.'

'Why?' Avery suddenly asked. 'Why are you doing this for me?'

'Because we both want the Allies to win the war, Avery, and if sharing information helps us to do that, then I'll do anything I can to help you. Besides, you know my secrets now, so I have nothing left to hide.'

'I'd be breaking protocol if I did this,' Avery said. 'I'd lose my job if anyone found out that I wasn't completing the photography at the apartment.'

'Who's going to find out?' Camille asked.

'I live with another IDC agent!' Avery said, before clamping her hand over her mouth. She'd never told Camille who she specifically worked for before, and now she'd done more than break protocol. 'Erase that from your mind, pretend I didn't say it. But you must know that I can't fool him, he's going to realise if I'm not microfilming in my room, in our apartment.'

Camille gave her a curious look, and Avery found herself breathing hard, as if she'd just run to the bookshop.

'Photograph it or don't, it's your choice, but I'm giving you an opportunity to send back something to your people that might actually help them. These are maps that Kiefer, a German spy, wants bound for some reason, and that tells me they might be a lot more important than some old book written years ago, and *Der Stürmer* he has on subscription? Don't you want to be the only one sending back such valuable material?'

Avery didn't know whether to be grateful to Camille or annoyed by her. Or perhaps she just wasn't used to another woman having such a direct manner.

The bell to the shop jingled then, and Avery knew she didn't have long to make a decision or ask Camille any questions. Avery stood for a moment and watched as Camille greeted her new customers, and she realised then that she had no choice. She'd go home, and so long as Tom wasn't there to snoop on her, she'd be back with her camera and film within the hour. This was too good an opportunity to pass up, no matter how dangerous it might be.

When the other customers had left, she spoke to Camille again. 'The other thing you asked me to do? I need to know more about it, about what my role would be. About how it would work.' She'd thought she was all in, but standing in front of Camille, imagining that she could be involved in something that meant risking her own life, it suddenly felt overwhelming.

Camille nodded.

Avery sighed. 'I want to help, but—'

'After you've photographed the maps, wait for me until closing,' Camille said. 'I have some people I'd like you to meet, and I think they'll help you to make your decision.'

Avery nodded. It wasn't that she didn't want to help, she just couldn't stop thinking about what might happen if she were caught.

'If there are clothes I can help find for them, or even food, I know that I could—'

'Avery, once you see what I'm going to show you? Helping with food and clothes won't feel like enough. Trust me.'

Avery swallowed. That was what she was scared of.

'We're going to the square?' Avery asked, as she walked quickly alongside Camille.

They were both carrying bags of food they'd purchased from the market – the leftover produce that hadn't sold that was going for a much cheaper price than it would have done first thing in the morning. Avery moved the bag she was carrying to her other hand, struggling to keep up with Camille.

'We can't stay long once we get there,' Camille said. 'I want you to meet someone, and we'll distribute the food as quickly as possible, then leave.'

Avery was silent for the rest of the walk, her heart racing as she tried not to think about being caught or something terrible happening to her because she'd decided to throw caution to the wind. But she couldn't exactly change her mind now, not when Camille seemed so fearless.

She looked around, wide-eyed. They were across the street from the square now.

'If we are questioned, you're to say that you felt sorry for the refugees and wanted to give them food,' Camille said. 'That's all you have to say, and there is nothing illegal about giving another person a gift.'

Avery nodded, but she imagined that she looked like a deer caught in a light.

'Let's go.'

They bustled across the road and Avery watched as conversations stopped when they passed, noticing smiles and kind expressions from the people staring at Camille. It was obvious to Avery that they all knew who this woman was, and she would go so far as to guess Camille was revered for her work with them.

'They're all looking at you,' Avery whispered, bumping shoulders with Camille as she caught up with her fast pace. 'Why do you not acknowledge them?'

'The best thing I can do for them, and for me, is to pretend as if we are strangers,' Camille murmured back. 'It's not safe here, you never know who's watching.'

Avery glanced around, terrified all over again, but she didn't have time to overthink things, because soon they were at a tent and Camille was gesturing to an old man. He walked as quickly as he could over to them, taking the bags of food and calling out to a woman who hurried to join them.

'Please give this out to those who need it the most,' Camille said. 'It's not a lot, but it's something.'

Avery watched the man, the way his eyes seemed to communicate a silent thank you to Camille; the touch of another woman's hand to Camille's, a movement so fleeting that Avery could have missed it if she'd blinked.

'You've helped all these people,' Avery said, whispering. 'They are here because of you?'

Camille nodded, her chin held high. 'Without visas, they would have always been one raid away from deportation, so I've done what I can.'

Avery looked around them, at the children who flocked around their parents, edging closer to see what was happening; at the mothers staring at Camille. But it was the old man who spoke to her.

'I think I have a camera to use,' Avery heard Camille say, her voice barely audible, it was so low. 'I'll be better equipped to help those who need completely new identification papers now.'

Avery's face burned as she realised what Camille was saying. Camille would be able to help them only if *Avery* chose to use her camera alongside her.

'How have you made do without a camera up until now?' Avery asked, forcing the words out.

'I've only been able to make new identification for those who already have a photo. Usually I have to cut it from their old identification document to use on the new one.'

'But a camera would mean—'

'That I could help young children or those who've lost their paperwork on their journeys and don't have an old photo,' Camille said. 'It would mean that there would be no one I couldn't help, if you could take their photos and develop them for me.'

Avery turned on the spot and looked around at all the faces, at all the bodies, at the sheer number of displaced people in the square. When she looked back, Camille was staring at her, as if she were waiting for an answer, right then and there.

'I would take the photos at your bookshop, presumably after-hours, and then create a dark space to develop them?' she asked. 'That's what you're asking of me?'

Camille nodded. 'Yes. That way I can take the blame if we're caught.'

Avery was silent, and as she looked at Camille, her eyes glinted in the street lights.

'What do you say, Avery?' Camille asked.

Avery took a deep, shaky breath. 'Yes,' she whispered. 'I'm in.'

In that moment, Avery knew there was no other answer she could have given, not if she wanted to live with the consequences of her decision.

'Avery,' Camille suddenly said, gesturing to a man approaching. 'Is that the man who came to your aid when you were hurt?'

Avery peered into the shadowy light. 'Yes, that's him. He must be bringing more supplies.' If she'd been braver, she might have gone up to say hello to him.

Camille took hold of her hand. 'Come on, it's time for us to go,' she said.

'Do you know who he is?' Avery asked, glancing back over her shoulder at him.

'He's been in my shop before. Well-spoken British man, and clearly one with a heart.'

Avery craned her neck one last time before hurrying after Camille, and it wasn't until they had disappeared down the next street towards her apartment that the weight of what she'd agreed to really sunk in.

It was one thing to take the refugees food, but what she was going to do was illegal, and for a girl who'd never so much as returned a library book late, the thought of being caught was so overwhelming it made her stomach lurch violently.

'Are you alright?' Camille asked, slowing her pace.

Avery clutched her hand tightly, forcing a smile. 'No, but I will be.'

She only hoped she sounded more convincing than she felt.

Chapter Fourteen

CAMILLE

Camille had had some close calls in the past, but none had felt quite like this one. She swallowed, staring at the man standing before her and refusing to let him see how much he could rattle her. Now that she'd brought Avery in to help, she was responsible for yet another human life, and the pressure to keep her safe was suddenly enormous in the face of another raid.

'Avery, could you please come out here?' she called, turning her head slightly. 'We have company and I'll be closing the shop early.'

She heard a noise in the backroom, and hoped Avery could hear the urgency in her voice. When she appeared, she was carrying a bag which Camille very much hoped contained her camera, and to her credit, she didn't falter when she saw the man in uniform standing in the store.

'An American?'

Camille nodded to Avery, who stepped forward and nodded politely. 'I am. And you must be a police officer?'

'Lourenço Santos,' he said. 'Head of the PVDE.'

'It's a pleasure to meet you,' she said. 'I was feeling very light-headed earlier, and Camille here was kind enough to let me rest with a book in her office. I'm not used to such warm weather.'

He frowned and stroked his moustache. 'My men reported there being an American in here recently when they paid you a visit. I'm going to guess that was you?'

Avery nodded. 'It was. I've become a frequent customer here, like many foreigners I dare say. Browsing books is a lovely way to spend an afternoon.'

Santos turned his attention back to Camille. 'You won't mind if I take another look back there?'

Camille waved her hand for him to go, at the same time as giving Avery a pleading glance, but Avery just smiled, reassuring her that there was nothing to be seen.

'Your American friend is aware of what happens to those who don't follow our laws?' Santos asked, as if Avery wasn't standing right there.

'I most certainly do, and I hold Camille in the highest regard,' Avery said. 'She runs an excellent bookshop, don't you think?'

'I think it is time for the American to go,' he said, looking past Avery and speaking directly to Camille again.

Avery's eyes met hers, and Camille gave her a tight smile, praying that she would leave without making a fuss. It seemed that Avery understood the urgency, no matter how reluctant she might appear, because after a moment of looking between the two of them, she tucked her bag close to her body and left.

'This can be very easy, Camille,' Santos said, as she followed him into her office and stood as he walked slowly around, before going back out into her bookshop. He swept one hand violently down a bookshelf, sweeping a dozen books or so to the floor. 'You can answer my questions and I can leave, or I can come back with more men and we can turn your entire shop upside down.'

She swallowed. 'I'll answer your questions. I have nothing to hide.'

His smile pulled his lips into a thin line. 'You've been seen in the square, with the Jews.'

Camille shrugged. 'Is it now an offence to have a heart?'

'Why do they come into your shop?' he asked. 'Why are you visiting them?'

Her breath was shallow and she fought against the panic in her chest that made her want to gasp. 'They want to read like anyone else. I don't know what you want me to tell you, and if I must, I will stop selling them books. But like many of the locals, my heart breaks for the homeless women and children. It's not a crime to give them my leftovers of food, is it?'

He looked down his nose at her. 'Camille, are you familiar with the name Sousa Mendes?'

Camille maintained her expression, blinking as she slowly shook her head. *Of course I know him, you fool! He was the Portuguese diplomat who saved thousands from the Nazis by giving them visas to enter Portugal from France.*

'Since he was forcibly retired, we expected no Jews from France to arrive in Lisbon, so you can imagine my surprise at knowing there are French Jews here with visas,' he said. 'I would like to know how they came to be in possession of such paperwork, because if someone was forging documents? Then they would find themselves thrown in jail and left to rot.'

Camille leaned on the counter and reached for her silver case of cigarettes and her lighter. She lit one for herself, before offering them to Santos. To her surprise, he took one. 'I am as surprised as you are,' she said, blowing smoke into the air. 'But Lourenço – may I call you Lourenço?'

He gave her a curt nod.

'Lourenço, you must know who my boyfriend is,' she said, hating the word as she said it. 'Would I have a Nazi boyfriend if I was this sympathiser you thought I was? I am simply a woman who likes to help children sometimes, in the same way I'd throw food to an abandoned puppy on the streets. I know nothing of what you speak of.'

'If you're not the person I'm looking for, then who are you?' he asked.

'I'm a woman who will sell a book to anyone with money,' she said, nonchalantly and with an unimpressed shrug. 'I am in the business of selling books and making money, that is all.'

'And your American friend? Should I be questioning her?'

Not Avery. You can't go after Avery. Camille would take the fall before ever letting Avery get into trouble.

Camille laughed, perhaps a little too loudly. 'The American is an innocent little librarian. I can assure you that she's not who you're looking for, but if you want to question her, I'm certain she would be easy for you to find.'

He gave her a long look, taking a final draw of his cigarette before stubbing it out on her counter and striding from her store without so much as a goodbye. Camille only hoped that his presence hadn't spooked Avery.

But within minutes of his leaving, Avery marched straight back into her bookshop with angry red cheeks and two paper bags full of Portuguese pastries.

'Avery, I—'

'Whatever you need me to do, whatever help I can give, set me to work,' she said, thrusting one of the small bags towards her.

Camille gratefully took it, her eyes meeting Avery's.

'He didn't scare you away?'

'He made me more determined than ever to do more to help. I hate bullies, and that man is one of the worst.'

Camille took a bite of pastry, licking the sugar from her fingers and watching as Avery did the same.

'We're going to have to be careful. He knows who you are now, and his suspicions have been raised.' She stared into Avery's eyes. 'You need to understand the risk you're taking. If he finds out the truth, if they catch us . . .' She exhaled. 'I'll tell them it was all me, that you had nothing to do with it, but there is still a chance—'

'Stop. I told you I would do it, and I haven't changed my mind. I understand the risks.'

Avery's eyes were wide; Camille could tell she was trying very hard to be brave.

'We have the chance to do something that matters, you've shown me that now,' said Avery. 'I'm not saying I'm not scared, because I'm terrified, but this war needs to end, and if I can play a small part in doing something about it . . .'

Camille reached for her hand. 'I'm so pleased I met you, Avery. You're nothing at all like I expected.'

Avery squeezed her hand back. 'What do we do next?'

'You keep doing what you're doing, and when there's another Jewish family needing my help, we work quickly to forge the visas,' Camille said. 'Between the two of us, we'll be able to do a few documents within an evening if we work all night.'

'Then that's what we'll do. The PVDE be damned,' Avery said. 'And I'm not just taking photographs and developing them for you, I'll do anything. My penmanship is excellent, I just need you to show me what to do.'

Camille only hoped that Avery knew exactly what she was getting herself into.

'Camille, should I be scared of your Kiefer?' Avery asked.

'No, I don't think so,' she replied. 'You let me worry about Kiefer.'

'You believe that he'll help you to find out who killed your husband?'

Camille closed her eyes, her skin crawling at the thought of what she'd done, of what she'd endured, in her efforts to uncover more about the double agent she was searching for. 'I do. I would never have done what I have if I didn't believe with all my heart that he could lead me closer to what I'm searching for. We just have to be careful. Promise me you'll be careful.'

'I promise you, Camille. There's too much at stake to get caught.'

Chapter Fifteen

CAMILLE

Camille kept her eyes shut and her breathing even as Kiefer got out of bed, wanting him to believe she was still asleep. She listened as he stretched and padded across the room into the adjoining bathroom, knowing that she was going to have to time it perfectly to look through his things before he came back.

She had the distinct feeling that she was running out of time. That if she didn't find something soon, she'd lose her chance, especially with Lourenço Santos breathing down her neck at every turn. It also felt like something bigger now; that it was about more than just Hugo. She didn't want anyone else to be betrayed like she and Hugo had been, and the only thing she despised more than the enemy was a traitor.

When she heard the door click shut, she pushed the covers back and rose, tiptoeing across the room and hovering beside his things. He always took his clothes off and placed them in a specific order, and she looked carefully over everything to make sure she could put it all back in its place once she'd finished.

First she checked his jacket, keeping one ear on the bathroom to make certain she could hear him. The water was running, but she knew how easily he could deceive her if he suspected what she was doing. She pushed her hand into each pocket, but all she found was an engraved metal case, and a quick glance inside showed a few cigarettes and nothing more. She closed the case and slipped it back inside his jacket, pausing to listen and glance up again before reaching for his trousers.

Bingo.

She pulled out a photograph, and a piece of paper that was folded down into quarters. The room was dark, and she took a risk in dashing to the window and pulling back the heavy velvet drape to see what she was in possession of. If he came out of the bathroom now, she'd have to hide what she had until she could get them back in his trousers, and she knew that would prove almost impossible.

The photograph was of a woman and a very young girl, both blonde with bright smiles, staring straight into the camera. She cringed, knowing that it was probably his wife, despite the fact he'd insisted when they met that he wasn't married. She moved on to the note.

It was a letter, and as she slowly read the words in German, she realised that this too was a personal item, not the incriminating evidence she'd hoped for.

'Did you find what you were looking for?'

Camille froze. Her pulse ignited as she looked up to find Kiefer standing in the doorway to the bathroom; like a wolf that had found an intruder in its lair.

'Kiefer, I can explain . . .' she began, quickly glancing around the room and trying to find something, anything, that she could use as a weapon.

Kiefer was dressed only in a towel, which was wrapped around his waist, and he came towards her, slowly, one hand raised.

She stayed silent and took a few steps backwards, but he simply sat down on the bed and gestured for her to pass him what was in her hand. Camille hesitantly shuffled forward, dropping the photograph and letter to the bed between them, without getting close enough for him to grab hold of her. His expression was impossible to decipher.

'Is this what you expected to find when you rifled through my pockets?' he asked.

Camille blinked. He'd caught her red-handed, but she wasn't going down that easily.

'I heard a rumour you were married,' she said. 'So yes, I suppose I did find what I expected.'

'Ahh, I see. And here I was thinking you were looking for something more sinister,' he said, as if he didn't believe her for an instant.

'More sinister?' she repeated, with a laugh that she hoped was convincing. 'You thought perhaps I was working for the Allies to uncover your secrets?'

Camille pursed her lips when he shrugged, trying to read him.

'I'm just a woman who wants her man to herself.'

His gaze narrowed and it was clear that, in that moment, he trusted her as much as she trusted him.

'That is my wife, Mathilde, and my daughter, Elke, in the photograph. I know you're thinking the worst of me, but I love them both very much. I would never have been with another woman if I was still in Berlin, if that means anything.'

Camille carefully edged her way across the room and sat in the chair opposite Kiefer. She was nervous about how calm he was; he was either more relaxed than she could have imagined, or it was the calm before the storm. She kept her eyes fixed on him, almost too scared to blink, waiting for him to lash out at her for going through his personal effects. But he didn't.

'You don't have to be scared of me, Camille, I'm not going to hurt you. My secret is that I'm a married man, it's not as if I'm the first man to pretend he didn't have a wife to lure a beautiful woman to his bed.'

She wanted to tell him that he was also a Nazi, which was something she feared very much in itself, but she kept her mouth shut. She had no interest in antagonising him, given her precarious situation.

'I feared you wouldn't be interested in me if you knew about them, and I've been away for so long that . . .' His voice trailed off.

'You wanted someone to warm your bed at night,' she finished for him. 'Is that it?'

'More than that, I needed the company. It's been a long time alone for someone who's used to the warmth of a woman.'

Camille softened, but only a little. Just because she hadn't found anything sinister in his pockets didn't mean he wasn't who she thought he might be. There was every chance that Kiefer knew precisely what and who she was looking for and was playing a very clever game.

'But I'm not the only one keeping a secret, Camille, am I?'

She swallowed, considering her words. Her heart began to race again. 'I don't know what you're talking about.'

'Camille, I'm leaving at the end of next week. I'm being sent back to Berlin, so there's no need for us to keep playing this game. You answer my question and I'll let you ask me one. Fair?'

'Alright then,' Camille said, steadying herself in an effort to appear calm, her palms clasped. 'What is it you think you know about me?'

'Well, I know that you're helping French Jewish refugees and that you're under suspicion of producing false documentation for them.' His smile was hard to read. 'Perhaps you're here on false documentation too, but I'm prepared to turn a blind eye to that, given our relationship. It seems only fair.'

She tried not to react outwardly, but inside her heart was pounding. Kiefer had the power to send her to jail, to invalidate the visas of handfuls of families waiting in Rossio Square, and she would never forgive herself if he did that.

'You've followed me?'

'It's what I do,' he said with a shrug. 'I knew who you were before I invited you to my bed. I'm embarrassed that you thought anything less of me.'

'Well,' she said, trying to appear confident rather than the scared little rabbit she was inside. 'It seems that we've both been rather busy investigating each other.' She sighed. 'So, what are you going to do?'

'With you?' He laughed. 'Camille, I only have a week left here, I'm not going to *do* anything. If anything, I admire you.'

'*You* admire *me*?' She almost choked on the words.

'Standing up for what you believe in isn't easy. I'm not going to pretend I didn't grow up knowing Jewish families who look like the people out there in the streets.'

'That's why you never turned me in?' she asked. 'You'll have me believe that you're *sympathetic* to those you're accusing me of helping?'

'Those Jews are already here.' He shrugged. 'Perhaps it eased my conscience knowing that you were helping a handful of them, or perhaps I just liked you and didn't want to give you up. But what you're doing has to end.'

She let what he was saying settle, surprised at how calm he was. She also didn't correct his statement that she was only helping a handful. She'd doctored more papers than she could count since she'd arrived in Lisbon.

'Why then does what you're accusing me of have to end, if you care so little?'

He leaned forward. 'Because I've been given a promotion, and it's now my job to make sure no one uses false visas as a way of fleeing their fate. There will be no more Jews allowed entry to Lisbon, and if anyone is caught creating false documents, they will be shot.'

Camille held her composure, but only just. She didn't doubt the severity of Kiefer's words. 'You're working with the PVDE?'

'There's a reason they haven't arrested you yet, Camille. But there are no more favours, not when it comes to the documentation. It's my neck on the line now, and I need to ensure a positive reception when I arrive back in Berlin next week. I'll be telling them I found the rat I was searching for.'

She fought to breathe, her chest feeling constricted. 'Someone else will take the fall for this? If you protect me, you'll blame another?'

He stroked his chin. 'I haven't decided yet. Perhaps your little American friend could be the one?'

'No,' she said, too quickly, showing him how much Avery meant to her. 'No, not her. If someone needs to go down for this, it will be me.'

'Perhaps I can find another way. If you promise me that your little game is over, of course.'

Camille thought of the words she'd whispered the night she'd taken Avery to the square with her, the families that still needed her help. She'd only helped French families until now, but the two of them had vowed to help as many refugees as they could, wherever they came from in Europe.

'I give you my word,' she said, clearing her throat to disguise the catch in her voice. 'I won't do anything other than sell books. I promise.' Camille knew how careful she had to be now, especially when Kiefer could turn her over to the PVDE whenever he wanted if he changed his mind about her. She needed to stay on the right side of him.

'Good. I'm pleased we came to an understanding so quickly.'

'Does this mean you forgive me for going through your things?'

'It's not quite so easy for me to forgive, Camille, but I do have a proposition for you,' he said. 'A way you can make it up to me.'

She lifted her chin and looked him directly in the eye.

'My friends here have been impressed by my beautiful French girlfriend, so I would very much like you to join us for drinks and continue to see me until I go. I want to keep up pretences.'

'You want me to remain your faithful lover?' Her brows lifted. 'In exchange for . . .'

'Not turning you in to the PVDE,' he said, with a wolfish smile that told her exactly what he was capable of if she didn't agree. 'You keep me satisfied until I go, and you keep yourself safe. It is a very simple agreement, no?'

'Yes,' she replied, as if it didn't mean anything to her, that it wouldn't be hard for her to remain intimate with him when in truth it made her want to retch. 'But I still have one question to ask you.'

His smile was off-putting, but she didn't let it stop her.

'How much do you know about me, Kiefer?'

He raised an eyebrow. 'I know that you weren't married to a Portuguese man, and that your husband was killed in France.'

She baulked, taken by surprise, but she didn't bother denying it.

'Do you also know of the British double agent who was responsible for my husband's death?' Her breath was ragged, her heart pounding in her chest, hoping she wouldn't regret asking her question so boldly. But she knew this might be her only chance to ask him outright.

'I don't,' he replied, and before she could protest at his lack of answer, Kiefer leaned forward and spoke again. 'But I could find out.'

'Kiefer, if you've ever cared for me, if any part of what we've had here meant something to you—'

'We're clear about our arrangement?' he asked, interrupting her.

Camille didn't let him hear her hesitation. She knew what was expected of her. 'We are.'

'Then I will find out what I can for you.'

She hesitantly stood and then stepped forward when Kiefer held out his hand. She placed her palm against his, hoping that she could, indeed, trust his word, and that he wouldn't have her arrested the moment he was gone.

'Camille,' he said, keeping hold of her hand and staring into her eyes. 'Once I'm gone, the PVDE would only need a little provocation to arrest you or put a bullet in your head. Do you understand?'

She slowly took her hand from his. 'I know how to deal with men like Santos. He doesn't scare me.' *But you do.* Camille swallowed, watching the way Kiefer's eyes drifted to her throat before meeting hers again, unsettling her.

'Well, he should scare you,' he said. 'But from now on, no giving the Jews food, no helping them, nothing. As far as you're concerned, those refugees no longer exist.'

Camille nodded. 'I understand.'

She turned her back on him as she took her things and went into the bathroom to get changed, her mind racing. But when she came out, she crossed the room and went to Kiefer, placing her hands on his shoulders and leaning in to press a kiss to his lips, knowing how easily he could have turned her in rather than help her. And she was still playing a role, now more than ever.

'Thank you,' she murmured. 'You've turned out to be nothing like who I thought you were, even if we are on opposite sides of this war.'

He kissed her back, his hands grazing her hips, and she knew that, whatever had grown between them, it would be over in a second if he found out that she was taking copies of his maps.

'Camille, I'm going to be at the Hotel Avenida tonight. Will I see you there?'

She nodded, understanding what he was asking of her, that he wanted to know that she would be keeping up her end of the bargain. 'You will.'

Now that he knew her secrets, she would do anything she had to, to keep him on her side.

Hours later, Camille stretched her legs out, wiggling her toes in the sand as she stared out at the water. There was something about the beach that made the weight lift off her shoulders; it almost made her forget everything that had come before. *Almost.* She doubted anything would ever take away all her pain or memories, but at least being near the water stilled her mind, and for that she was grateful. Kiefer was dominating her thoughts, no matter how much she tried not to think about him, finding it hard to believe that he might willingly end up being the one to give her the information she needed. He'd been on her mind ever since she'd left his hotel room that morning.

'Do you have beaches in New York?' she asked Avery, suddenly realising how little she knew about America and wanting to talk about anything that took her mind off Kiefer and the promises she'd made.

'We do actually. They're different from this, but they're lovely. My mother would often take us there in summers for the day. They're some of my favourite memories because it was the only time we were ever allowed ice cream,' Avery said. 'Did you have any beaches near where you grew up?'

'In Paris? No. It's why I find the beach so special here, because it's like nothing I could have ever imagined when I was a child.' Camille smiled. 'But it's nice to hear about New York. I keep wondering what awaits all those families, in limbo and dreaming of a place that will be safe for them. I needed to hear that today.'

They sat, sunning themselves on the golden sand, watching two people swimming in the ocean. The beach was remarkably quiet, aside from a few couples sunbathing further down to the right, and she had a feeling that Avery sensed she needed time to just sit and think.

'You know, when I came here, I never could have imagined a place so different and beautiful,' Avery said. 'A place where a Nazi like your Kiefer could be standing on a street corner across from a Jewish mother and her children, or even browsing in a bookshop side by side. I don't suppose I understood the nuances of being in a neutral country. I simply imagined a place not at war.'

'Anywhere else in Europe . . .' Camille said, not wanting to even finish her sentence. She tried to push the thought away, something she'd never had much success at doing. 'Portugal isn't perfect, but being here gives a person hope. Or at least that's how I like to see it.'

They sat in silence for a while, before Avery spoke again.

'I have to ask you, Camille, how can you stand to be with Kiefer? Doesn't it make your stomach turn to think about what he stands for? Isn't it impossible to pretend sometimes?'

Camille nodded, staring back out at the ocean again. 'Being with him the first time almost broke me, but everything I do, everything I've done, is because it feels like my only choice at the time. It's because it helps me to get one step closer to finding out the information I need, and I think it's given me a degree of protection that I hadn't realised until now.'

'I understand. I admire you, Camille. You're the strongest person I've ever met.'

Camille closed her eyes. If Avery knew the deal she'd just made, she might not think so highly of her.

'Do you find it hard not to think of your husband when you're with him?' Avery asked, softly, as if she wasn't certain she should be asking at all.

'Hugo is never far from my thoughts. He was the only man I've ever loved, and the only man I can ever imagine loving.'

'Did you know Hugo was the one?' Avery asked, hesitantly. 'Right from the start?'

'Oh, I knew,' Camille said, closing her eyes and seeing him in her mind, smiling at her from across the table, his eyes so warm, his fingers stretching out to touch hers. 'He meant everything to me from the moment we met. Nothing could have kept us apart.'

'This world has lost so many young men,' Avery said. 'Sometimes I wonder, once it's all over, how it will ever go back to the way it was. How we'll ever rebuild what has been lost.'

Camille didn't disagree with her. 'My brother was determined to fight for France. So many young men were so excited, as if they were off to have the time of their lives without even thinking about what it was truly going to be like,' she said. 'His letters went from cheerful to sad very quickly, and when the telegram came to say he'd died, I honestly think it was too much for my father to stand.'

'They were close?' Avery asked.

'As close as could be. My mother died when we were young, and it had been the three of us for so long. Us against the world we used to say, and then when Hugo and I ended up together, he was as much part of the family as the rest of us.'

'Your father passed soon after your brother?'

Camille looked out at the water, kneading sand between her fingers as she thought back to the day he'd died. The memory was as vivid as ever.

'Hugo was home on leave when France was occupied, it's how we both ended up in the Resistance,' she told Avery. 'We visited my father as much as we could, me more than Hugo because he stayed with the other men who'd joined our cell in the countryside, but one day when I arrived home, I found my father in his favourite armchair by the window. I still hope to this day that he just passed away in his sleep and didn't feel any pain, because he looked so peaceful when I found him. As if he'd finally found his way back to my brother.'

Avery was silent, and when Camille glanced at her she saw that she was moving sand through her fingers too. It was incredibly therapeutic, and something Camille often did if she had a day off, when she'd come to the beach alone and stare out at the ocean, imagining what it would be like if she'd stayed in France.

'You've suffered so much loss,' Avery finally said. 'It doesn't seem fair.'

'Nothing about this war seems fair, and I've lost no more than so many others,' Camille said. 'But sometimes I feel as if the only thing propelling me forward is wanting to hold someone accountable.' She closed her eyes again. 'Hugo was all I had left, and I just . . . it's not just about his death, it's about everything that happened the night he died. I feel like I can't stop until I find out who took him from me, and I also have this burning desire to keep doing the work he was so passionate about. It was because of him that I became involved in Resistance work in the first place, so in a way it's like keeping his memory alive.'

Avery moved closer to her, their shoulders touching, and Camille felt the closest to breaking down as she'd ever felt. She'd never told anyone else in Lisbon the truth about what had happened to her family, and it was almost harder now that she had.

'I'm sorry, I shouldn't have burdened you with all that.'

'You're wrong,' Avery said, bumping her shoulder this time with Camille's. 'My mother has this little saying that a problem shared is a problem halved. My sister and I used to always whisper to each other at night, following that advice, knowing how much better we'd feel if we told the other our worries.'

'You miss her?'

'I miss what we had as children,' Avery said. 'We're so different now, but there was a time we were so similar, we were like twins.'

They were silent for a while, the only sound the water lapping softly nearby.

'Avery, have you seen James?' Camille asked. 'I know you have feelings for him, but I don't trust him. I'd prefer you not to see him alone, just in case.' She paused. '*Have* you seen him again?'

Avery was silent, and Camille hoped she hadn't upset her. But when their eyes met, Avery held her gaze.

'I haven't, not since we had dinner. I fear that he's left and I won't ever see him again, but if James was playing a duplicitous game, then he's very good at it,' Avery said. 'But I promise, I'll be careful. And if it was him who was involved in what happened to you . . .'

The words didn't need to be said. Camille reached for her hand and gave it a quick squeeze.

'On a lighter note, don't look now, but it appears we have company,' Camille murmured, recognising the tall, broad-shouldered man coming towards them.

'Hello ladies,' he said, his shoes in one hand as he walked barefoot across the sand.

Avery sat up, shielding her eyes from the sun, and Camille realised just how inexperienced her American friend was. They

180

may only be a few years apart in age, but sometimes Avery seemed much younger.

'Ahh, hello,' Avery said, as Camille smiled and said 'hello' back to him.

'I thought I recognised you from the square,' he said, his gaze trained on Avery. 'How's the wrist?'

'Fine, thank you.'

Camille tried not to laugh at how obviously flustered Avery was over her handsome friend. There went her naive little librarian all over again.

'I'm Camille,' she said, watching as Avery quickly pushed her skirt down so she wasn't showing so much leg. 'And this is my friend Avery, although I believe you've met before.'

'William,' he said, although he never took his eyes off Avery. 'Pleased to meet you, and under nicer circumstances this time.'

Camille exchanged a look with Avery, who looked like she wanted the ground to open up and swallow her.

'You ladies are enjoying the sun?' William asked, rolling up his trousers. 'Do you mind if I sit for a moment?'

Avery made a noise that was impossible to decipher, but Camille covered for her. 'Of course. It's not every day we have a handsome man wanting to keep us company.'

He made a face as if he was trying to remember something, before clicking his fingers. 'You're the French bookshop lady, am I right?'

She smiled. 'I am French, although I've been in Portugal long enough to think I'm one of the locals, and yes, I'm from the bookshop a few blocks from Rossio Square.'

'I thought you looked familiar.' He nodded and turned to Avery. 'And what brings you to Portugal, Avery? I'm guessing you're not abroad on holiday in the middle of a war.'

'Ah no, I'm here on behalf of the Library of Congress, actually,' she said. 'I specialise in cataloguing books and other publications, so I'm making sure we have a record of the war, for historical purposes of course.'

'Ahh, well, that's very interesting work, I'm sure.' He glanced at his watch. 'It's later than I thought, ladies, so I'm going to have to leave you. But are you going out tonight? It is Friday, after all.'

'We are,' Camille said, before Avery could interject. 'The bar at Hotel Avenida, actually. You?'

'It seems that I might see you there.'

Camille watched as his eyes flickered over to Avery again, and she waved goodbye to him while trying not to laugh. After everything that had ensued with Kiefer this morning, it was nice to have something to be amused about.

'That man was very interested in you,' she whispered as soon as he was out of earshot. 'But you need to relax, he's just a man.'

'Oh stop it, he was *not* interested,' Avery said, still flustered and rolling her eyes at Camille.

'You never look so hot under the collar when you're talking to your other British man.'

'James is different, he's very easy to talk to, but trust me when I say that I'm *very* hot under the collar around James. I feel like my face is on fire every time we have a conversation.'

They both laughed and Camille lay back in the sand, even though the sun was starting to fade. She just wanted a moment longer to close her eyes and relax.

'Are we really going out tonight?' Avery asked. 'I thought you wouldn't trust him either, given that he's British.'

'It's because he's British that we're going to meet him,' Camille said. 'We need to extract every bit of information from all of the men we come across. Besides, how many other men have you seen helping the Jews? I don't think he's my target.'

'Including Kiefer and his friends?' Avery asked. 'Aren't you at all nervous, pretending to be interested when really you're not? I know you said it's all a means to an end, but how do you do it?'

Sometimes I can barely breathe when I'm with Kiefer and his Nazi friends. That was what she should have told Avery.

'I already know Kiefer and his countrymen are the enemy; it's the ones pretending they're not that scare me. But yes, Kiefer will be there with his friends tonight too, and I'm keen to use them to my advantage.' She paused. 'Kiefer is leaving soon actually, he told me so this morning, so this might be my last chance to extract some information from him.'

What she didn't tell Avery was that Kiefer knew more about Camille than he'd let on, and that it could put them both in danger if he didn't keep his word.

Avery stood and held out her hand to help Camille to her feet. 'Come on then.'

'So you'll come?'

'Yes, I'll come, but don't go thinking I'm going to be useful to you tonight in extracting information from anyone, because I can assure you that I won't be. It is most definitely not one of my strengths.'

Camille smiled to herself, starting to see Avery for the woman she could be. *We'll see about that.* But she knew she couldn't part ways with her friend without telling her the truth about what she'd agreed to. It should have been the first thing she'd told her when they'd met at the beach, and she didn't want to, *couldn't wait,* any longer.

'Avery, something happened today, something I wish I'd told you the moment we sat down.'

Avery's eyes met hers. 'Nothing happened to any of the families, did it? Please tell me they're—'

'Kiefer knows what I'm doing. He found out.'

Avery visibly paled. 'About the work we're doing? About the . . .' Her voice fell away.

'He doesn't know anything about your involvement, but I made a deal with him.' She hated herself for what she was about to say. 'In exchange for information, I promised to stop forging documents or going near the Jewish area.'

Avery's eyes widened. 'You're not going to help them anymore? You're just going to stop when—'

'No, Avery,' she said. 'What I agreed to and what I'm going to do are two very different things, but I might need your help more than I thought. I'm going to have to be careful. You might have to deliver any documents to them, depending on how closely I'm being watched.'

Avery was silent.

'Nothing will stop me from helping those families, but I can't be seen going near them again. I have to believe he's having me followed. I know it's a lot to ask, but—'

'I'll do it. Whatever you need from me, however I can help them, I will do it.'

Camille reached for her hand and searched her face. 'You're certain?'

'I don't see that I have any other choice.'

Chapter Sixteen

AVERY

Avery was already second-guessing why she'd agreed to meet Camille at the hotel, and she'd only just walked in the door. The Hotel Avenida was familiar to her now, and she no longer felt so out of place in Lisbon as she had done that very first night she'd come out, but she doubted that she'd ever get used to arriving at a bar alone. The fact that there were so many men there, and so few women, was off-putting to say the least.

Helping to forge documents and taking photos in the relative safety of Camille's bookshop didn't feel such a stretch for her, but pretending she was a confident woman in a bar full of men? That was something more challenging.

'Avery?'

She turned at her name, delighted to see James standing by her with a drink in hand. She'd been hoping to see him, especially after not hearing from him since their date a few weeks ago, and she'd almost given up all hope.

'James! You're a sight for sore eyes.'

He came closer and kissed her cheek, and she found herself leaning into his touch, truly pleased to just be near him again. She might not know him well, but every time she was with him she found herself thinking that there was no way this charming man could possibly be a person of suspicion.

'I had to leave Lisbon unexpectedly, in case you were wondering why I wasn't following you and appearing wherever you were.'

Avery laughed. 'And here I was thinking you were just avoiding me.'

'Avoiding you? I'd have been making sure we bumped into each other at least once a day if I'd been here.'

She'd almost forgotten how easy it was between them, James's banter somehow always putting her at ease, and she realised just how much she'd missed him. Their date had been one of the best evenings of her life, but she'd started to wonder if he'd felt differently when she hadn't heard from him again. It was reassuring to know that wasn't the case.

'Unfortunately, I'm only here for a couple of days. I'm heading off again shortly.'

'How long will you be gone for this time?' she asked, disappointed to think she wouldn't see him again. 'You will be coming back, right?'

'I promise that I'll be coming back, I'm just not entirely sure when that will be.' He smiled. 'I'd tell you more if I could.'

Avery wasn't quite sure what to do with her hands, wishing she had a drink to hold, and she went to fold them in front of her at the same time as James reached out. He caught her fingers in his, his eyes meeting hers.

'I've missed you,' he said.

She opened her mouth to reply, but didn't get the chance to say what she'd intended.

'Avery! There you are.'

William's voice was loud, and she saw the frown cross James's face for a split second before he let go of her. When James's eyes met hers, she saw something in his gaze that made her feel as if she'd let him down, and she wished they'd just had a moment longer alone, together, for her to tell him how she felt. If it had been up to her, she'd have held on to James's hand for hours without letting go.

'I'm so pleased you came,' William said when he reached her, passing her a glass of champagne. 'James, how are you?'

James looked prickly, but he held out his hand anyway. 'Ah, William, right? Good to see you.'

'You know Avery?' William asked, moving closer to her.

James just looked at her, and she felt a sense of hurt, knowing how it looked. William was making out as if they'd come together, and it wasn't a lie, she had come to see him, but if she'd known James was going to be there . . . She swallowed. Avery had very little experience with the politics of dating, but she very much wished that James hadn't seen her with William. If she could have chosen any man in the world to spend an evening with, it was James; every time, it would be James.

'James and I have known each other since my very first night in Lisbon,' Avery said, not about to let him go thinking that she'd chosen William over him. 'Without him, I fear I would have been completely lost in this town.' She stared into James's eyes for a moment. 'He made me feel at home when I was otherwise very lost.'

'Well, you two enjoy your evening,' James said, looking away from her to down the rest of the amber liquid in his glass, before placing it a little too heavily on the bar. 'I'll see you soon, Avery.'

William took her hand then to pull her away, and Avery watched as James's gaze dropped, looking at the way William touched her. It was then that she wondered if James had come to the hotel bar to search for her, to tell her that he'd been unexpectedly sent away again, but she didn't get the chance to ask before William was pulling her through the crowd of men to where Camille was waving at her, gesturing to a bottle of champagne on the table.

There was no sign of Kiefer, and for that Avery was pleased, but she found herself craning her neck for one last glimpse of James, to see if he was looking after her, to wave. She might have even braved the crowded room by herself and gone to say goodbye properly. But the spot where he'd been standing was now vacant, and she couldn't see him anywhere.

'Avery, who are you looking for?' Camille asked.

She glanced back and saw that William and Camille were both watching her, and she smiled and shrugged. 'No one. Sorry, I was just distracted.'

'Come and enjoy your champagne with us,' William said, beckoning for her to sit beside him. 'It's not often I get to enjoy drinks with *two* beautiful women.'

Avery blushed and took the spot beside him as Camille gave her a tell-tale look. And she would have enjoyed herself if she didn't have such a sinking feeling in her stomach that she'd hurt James. She had the most overwhelming sense that she was never going to see him again, that he thought she'd taken up with William when it couldn't have been further from the truth, but she also couldn't quite figure out why the two men had been so frosty towards one another. They were both British, after all, and either there was something between them already that she didn't know about, or James was simply prickly over William being with her.

'Ahh, I can see my date,' Camille suddenly said. 'Would you mind terribly if Kiefer joins us? I know you're technically enemies with him, William, but surely we can put all our differences aside for an hour?'

'So long as we keep the conversation neutral and no one tries to steal secrets, I'm certain I can make an exception,' William said. 'Avery, are you comfortable with that?'

She found herself shuffling a little closer to him as Kiefer neared. There was something about the German officer that put her on edge from just seeing him, and she was even more cautious now that she was photographing his maps. She didn't even want to think about what he might do if he found out.

'Of course,' Avery said. 'Just promise me that neither of you will leave me alone with him.'

When Avery arrived home later that night, having been out all day and in such a hurry to get ready when she'd dashed home in the late afternoon that she hadn't seen her roommate, she was surprised to see Tom waiting up for her.

'Tom! What are you doing up? Have you just got home, too?'

The expression on his face told her that he wasn't happy with her, and the pleasant tingle through her body from the champagne she'd consumed disappeared the moment she stepped into the living room.

'I stayed in, but Avery, we need to talk.'

She took off her coat and placed it over one of the dining chairs, along with her bag. She saw a letter there then, addressed to her, and reached for it. 'This came for me?'

He nodded. 'Can we talk first, before you read it?'

She was itching to open it, especially when she saw that it was her mother's handwriting, but she set it back down and took a seat opposite Tom.

'Should I make us a coffee or—'

'Avery, where's your camera?'

'My camera?' Avery clenched her fingers and dug her nails into her palms. 'You've been looking in my room?'

Tom stared straight at her. 'I haven't just looked in your room, Avery, I've searched the entire apartment and your camera isn't here.' He paused. 'I'd hoped it was with you, that you'd somehow decided it was safer to keep it on you, but I can see from the size of your purse that's not the case, so I'm going to ask you one more time. I need you to tell me where your camera is.'

'How dare you go through my room! You have no right to look through my things.'

'Even if I'm looking for government property?' he asked. 'Because I'm sure Kilgour would like to know why your camera isn't here, Avery. Are you even completing the work you were sent here to do? You haven't been working in your room all week, which is the only reason I looked in the first place.'

'Don't you dare accuse me of not taking my work seriously, Tom, and threatening me is not going to work. You wouldn't dare contact Kilgour.' But her pulse was racing just thinking about it, because she was starting to wonder if perhaps he would be so bold. It wasn't as if she knew him well enough to know that he wouldn't. 'Do you think you'll get a promotion by telling on me? Because I doubt a man as busy as Kilgour would care for gossip.'

'Tell me where it is then,' he said, not backing down. 'Where have you been using it? Why are you being so secretive?'

'I have a new source of information, if you must know,' she said, standing up to make herself a drink so she didn't have to sit in front of her colleague as if she were being interrogated. Her heart was pounding, and she hoped he didn't know about the other work she was doing with Camille. 'You know how difficult it's becoming to find material, especially with the latest directive asking us to reduce the amount of film we're using, and I was fortunate enough to find a new source of sensitive information that I very much believe is worth photographing.'

'You weren't sent here as a spy, Avery. If that's what you're playing at—'

'I'm microfilming documents and other items of great sensitivity, if you must know,' she said. 'But to do so, I have to work away from here. I have very limited time in which to complete these tasks.'

'I know you didn't spend long at training, but you do realise this is against protocol, don't you? I have an obligation to tell our superiors that you're breaching the very purpose of our—'

'You wouldn't dare.'

He narrowed his gaze, and she thought for a moment that he might apologise and acknowledge that she hadn't done anything so terrible, but instead he just stood and glared at her. Perhaps she shouldn't have called his bluff.

'Either you tell Kilgour or I do. The choice is yours, but you know that our work here is classified. What you're doing is showing our hand, that we're trying to source important Axis information to send home.'

'You're prepared to sacrifice the work I'm doing for what? A promotion? To somehow prove yourself to Kilgour and make yourself look better than me? I'm doing my job, Tom, I've just had to find a more creative way to do it well!'

'Goodnight, Avery,' he said.

She wanted to scream and throw something at him, but she forced herself to stand and stay calm, to breathe through the curses mounting up in her mind. *Screw you, Tom.* She'd thought they'd become friends in the short time they'd known each other, and she'd never have guessed that he might have the nerve to go into her room or search through her possessions.

Avery picked the letter up then, tucking it under her arm. Camille had given her a small jar of cocoa, and she made herself a hot drink and took it to her room, closing the door behind her and curling up on her bed to read the news from home. The confrontation with Tom had rattled her, but the fact her mother had chosen to write to her made her hopeful that she might finally be missing her enough to forgive her. A letter from home was just what she needed tonight.

She put her cocoa down on the small bedside table and opened the envelope, taking out two folded pieces of paper.

Dear Avery,

I'm so sorry I haven't written to you properly until now. I miss you so much, and I should have told you how proud I was of you before you left, because I am so incredibly proud of how much you've accomplished. Since you were a little girl, you worried me with your determination, but I can see that it is what has made you the confident, strong young woman you are today.

I promise to write again soon, but today I'm writing because we've had some sad news. Your cousin Jack arrived home today, and Avery, it's not so good. We're all relieved that he's alive, but he suffered terrible injuries and he's been in hospital in Europe until now. They patched him up as best they could over there, but I fear he'll have to have more surgeries now that he's home, and I only hope he can get his head in the right place. Anyway, talking about you is the only thing that's making him smile, and I promised that he could dictate a letter to send you. So the other letter is from him, even though it's in my handwriting.

I hope you're staying well and not missing home too much. I love you, darling, and I can't wait until you're home.

From Mother.

P.S. You stay safe and make sure you come home in one piece!

Avery pressed her balled fist to her mouth as she stifled a cry. Not Jack. She couldn't bear to think of something awful happening to Jack, of him not being able to travel like he wanted to after the war, or what it would be like for him if he couldn't ever fly a plane again. But if he was injured, at least it meant he was alive.

She heard Tom banging around in the living room but didn't care. He could threaten her all he wanted; nothing could shake her as much as something happening to Jack. Her fingers quivered as she opened the second letter, as she tried not to think about why her cousin couldn't write to her himself, what sort of injuries he might have.

Dear Avery,

Well, I bet you never thought I'd have your mother write a letter for me. But I knew if I didn't write to you, you'd only worry too much and probably want to come home, and I don't want you to do that. You're on your own adventure, remember? This is your chance to see the world, and I'm just grateful that you're well away from the fighting.

I was shot in my stomach and my leg, and I have my right arm in a cast still which is why I can't write you myself. It was touch and go there for a while, maybe it still is, and I lost a lot of blood and even sitting up in bed feels exhausting right now, but I refused to let them take my leg. We have adventures to go on, remember? That's what's

193

keeping me going. Because if I don't make it, who will keep your adventurous spirit alive?

Your mother is starting to cry now so I'm going to wrap this up. If she was the one writing she'd probably tell you that I look terrible and that she can't imagine how things are going to turn out for me, but I made it home, Avery, and so many of the men I fought with didn't. So I'm going to do my best to keep living, don't you worry. Nothing is going to stop me from keeping on putting one foot in front of the other, even if I need a walking stick.

Keep having fun over there and don't forget to write, because I have a whole lot of nothing to do and I need to hear from you.

Jack.

Avery wiped the tears from her eyes and read the letter a second time, before setting it down and forgetting all about her cocoa drink as she marched out of her bedroom, finding the living room empty and changing course. She stood outside Tom's room and banged on the door with her fist.

Something about reading Jack's letter had set a fire inside of her, and she wasn't going to stand by while anyone made threats.

'Open the door!' she shouted, surprised at how loud her voice was.

She thumped again until he answered it, and she imagined she looked like a wild woman standing there with tears in her eyes and her face feeling like it was on fire from being so angry. But she didn't let him get the first word in.

'You're right, Tom. I am working outside of the framework we were given in order to do my job to the absolute best of my ability, and because of that I'm sending material off that I don't think anyone else would be able to source. Information that I very much think could help the Allies win this damn war, otherwise I wouldn't be taking the risk.'

He folded his arms over his chest. 'That doesn't change the fact that you're breaching protocol and that I have a duty to report it. You don't get to make the rules, Avery. You could be putting yourself in danger and I'm only trying to protect you.'

'Oh, spare me the righteous crap, Tom! We're in the middle of a goddamn war, in case you hadn't noticed. Do you think the guys in Washington have ever been in the field? Don't you think that, after all these weeks, I know what I'm doing? I've figured out a way of sourcing exceptionally useful intelligence, and if you don't like it, then how about you just keep your mouth shut and let me do my job.'

'I think you need to take a breath.'

'Do you want to know what I think?' she asked, with an edge to her voice that she'd never heard before. 'I think it's time for you to mind your own business, and if you ever come into my room again and look through my personal things? It'll be me writing to Kilgour about *you* and your inappropriate behaviour. Are we clear?'

Tom looked at the ground, and Avery had never been so proud of herself.

'We're clear.'

She turned on her heel and stormed back to her bedroom, resisting the urge to slam her door behind her. Avery flopped down on her bed and reached for the letter, placing it over her chest, wanting Jack close to her as she shut her eyes and prayed that he would recover from his injuries. Because he was right, they had adventures to go on, and in the morning she'd write to him and tell him that she wouldn't accept anything less than a full recovery.

Chapter Seventeen

CAMILLE

Camille had never worked alongside anyone in the bookshop before. When she'd started there, she'd had a few days of being shown what to do, but the previous owner had been very elderly and unwell, and had soon left her in sole charge. She found that the shop felt different on the days that Avery was there, with just the noise of having someone else present making her feel a sense of comradeship that had been missing since she lost Hugo, and for the first time she truly realised how alone she'd been since she'd left France. She only wished that they could continue in their happy little bubble together, without her having to break Avery's heart. They'd only known each other a few months, but it already felt like they'd be friends for a lifetime.

As the last customer left, Camille wandered through the shop and locked the door, turning the sign around to 'Closed' and going back slowly so she could right any fallen books and check all her displays.

'How are you doing back there?' Camille asked, knowing there was only so long until she had to share her news with Avery. 'I feel like you've been clicking away for hours without a break.'

Avery set her camera down. 'I'm going as quickly as I can, but it's taking forever.'

'I should have asked you to come here sooner,' Camille said. 'Then you wouldn't have so much catching up to do.'

She went over to the two maps on Avery's left. 'You've photographed these already?'

She had the camera raised again. 'I have. Anything that you need to bind tonight has already been photographed, and this film will be winging its way back to Washington in the morning, all things going to plan.'

Camille glanced over the newest batch of maps that Kiefer had entrusted her with. She didn't know how helpful they'd be to Avery, but if they were important to him, then there had to be a reason. Her only worry was that he'd arrive at the shop and find Avery there, but he knew they were friends and she would find a way of explaining it. The PVDE, on the other hand . . . that would be harder to explain away. And every day that passed made her even more convinced they were going to come back and raid her store again. But next time, she doubted they were just going to turn over a few rows of books. Next time she feared they might trash everything she'd worked so hard for, turn the entire place over top to bottom, and make it impossible for her to pick up the pieces.

'Avery, I know we've gone over this before, but just in case,' Camille said, picking up the maps and taking them over to the workstation she'd set up. 'If the PVDE do another surprise raid . . .'

'I'm here as your friend visiting. I put the film in my bag beneath the books and I carry my camera and say I'm off sightseeing,' she said. 'I was fine the first time, and I'll be fine the next time, if there is a next time.'

Camille nodded. 'And most importantly, you don't say anything else. You don't ask any questions, you just quietly leave the shop,' she said. 'I don't want you tangled up in anything with them, it's just not worth it, and I don't want you coming back to help me. I knew the risks when I chose to do what I'm doing.'

'It must be awful worrying about them doing another raid, but if their sympathies are with the Nazis, surely the fact that you're doing work for Kiefer must help the situation? It must offer you a degree of protection?'

'I certainly hope so.' She sighed. 'He assured me that he put in a good word for me, but there's no guarantee they'll listen to him, and he won't be here much longer to help me anyway.'

'When does Kiefer leave?'

'In a few days. He's ended up staying on so much longer than expected,' she said. 'The funny thing is, I can't work out if I'm relieved or worried that I'll never see him again.'

'I'm going to be worried not to have his material to photograph, but if I'm honest, he's always set my nerves on edge.'

Camille grimaced. 'Mine too. Trust me, I know how you feel, and if he ever found out that I'd shown you these . . .'

They exchanged a glance – no words were needed. They knew what they were risking.

They both went back to work then, focusing quietly together for the next hour, until Camille was finished with her binding. She'd had two maps and some documents to bind for Kiefer, as well as finishing off visas for a newly arrived French couple that she and Avery had been working on, and when Camille was done she set the water to boil to make a drink and placed his things in a paper bag for him, ready to collect in the morning. The forged documents went directly into her undergarments now; she'd decided not to keep anything contraband in her office anymore, for fear of what might happen if she was caught. There were too many people relying on her for her to be arrested, especially when another raid felt imminent.

When she heard Avery stretch and yawn, Camille knew her friend was probably ready for a break.

'There's something I'd like to show you, before you go,' Camille said, indicating to Avery that she needed to take a step back. She dropped to her haunches and pulled up the two loose floorboards, wiggling them out and reaching down into the cavity. She had more than a few things down there, but nothing was more important to her than the three items she'd originally hidden when she'd first begun to work at the shop. Back then, she'd taken a huge risk in keeping anything on the premises, but something had told her that it was the safest place for the things that were most precious. Things that meant something to her, but not to anyone else. Not even the PVDE would be interested in what she was about to show her friend.

Camille felt for the items she wanted and stood, holding them out to Avery.

'I've never shown these things to anyone else, but I want you to see them,' she said. 'I thought it might help you to understand who I am, and why I'm doing what I'm doing.'

'What am I looking at?' Avery asked, as she glanced from Camille and down to what she was holding and back again.

'This is my wedding ring,' Camille told her, indicating the slender gold band tied to a piece of ribbon. 'I took it off when I fled France, and I originally had it on a necklace, but when I arrived in Lisbon I took it off completely. It just didn't feel right to be wearing it for some reason.'

It was a slight stretch of the truth. She'd actually kept it around her neck when she'd first arrived, but when she'd decided to seduce Kiefer, she'd felt sick at the thought of having something from her marriage with her. Which is how she'd ended up hiding it, in an attempt to ease her conscience.

'You have a photo as well?'

'This is the only photo I have of the four of us. My father, my brother, Hugo and me.'

'Your wedding day?' Avery asked, reaching out for it and holding it close to her face as she studied it.

'It was one of the happiest days of my life, for all of us, and I often think if I could have only frozen time that day . . .'

'Your Hugo was gorgeous,' Avery said, as Camille teared up. 'Your brother was very handsome, too. He has the same eyes as you, I think that's what it is.'

Camille stared at the photograph, unable to take her eyes from it.

'And what's that?'

Camille didn't pass this to Avery. 'It was a letter he wrote me, when we first joined the Resistance. Or should I say when he joined it,' she said. 'He joined first and it took me more than a week to decide to do the same and join him.'

'It must be so comforting having this, as a memory of him.'

'I kept it to remind me why I joined the Resistance in the first place. I always kept it in my jacket pocket in case my confidence or commitment ever wavered, but now I keep it because it's one of my only reminders of the man I loved. I suppose it's all I have left of him.'

Avery looked at the photo again before passing it back to her.

'Camille, why are you showing me all this?' Avery asked. 'Why now?'

'Because I want you to understand who I am and why I am so determined to find out who was responsible for my husband's death. And I want you to know that when I have been with Kiefer, that I mean no disrespect to my husband. I could never fall in love with a man like him, could never have true feelings for someone I've given everything to fight against.' She shook her head. 'He's a Nazi, and no matter how nice he can be at times, or whatever kindness he might have shown me, nothing will ever change what he is.'

They stood facing each other for a long moment, before Camille pressed a kiss to the photograph and placed the items back beneath the floorboards.

'Are you any closer to discovering who you're looking for?' Avery asked. 'Do you truly think you can find out who it was who betrayed you?'

It was as if Avery knew she was holding something back. Camille took a breath and slowly let it go before answering her. 'Kiefer confronted me that morning before I met you at the beach. He agreed to give me information about the double agent I'm searching for.'

Avery's eyebrows shot up. 'He did?'

'In exchange for keeping up our little romance until he left,' Camille told her. 'But this morning he came to me and told me that the spy I'm searching for left Lisbon for Portugal recently.' She paused, wishing there was another way. 'Avery, he believes that this man is on his way to France.'

She let the words hang between them, watching as Avery's face fell, and Camille hated that she was responsible for her pain. But she wouldn't be a true friend if she kept it from her.

'James?' Avery whispered, her voice coming out as a gasp.

'I'm sorry,' Camille said, tears pricking her eyes as she saw how heartbroken Avery was. 'I know how you feel about him, and I've been trying to figure out a way to tell you all day. I'm sorry.'

Avery blinked away tears, wiping at her eyes as Camille's own heart broke for her. If there was one person in the world she didn't want to hurt, it was Avery.

'I truly believed you were wrong about him,' Avery said. 'He was so charming, when I was with him, when . . .' She shook her head. 'Well, none of that matters, does it? I should have trusted your instincts from the start and listened to it.'

'If it helps,' Camille said, 'I wish I was wrong.'

Avery nodded. 'Do you think he'll come back to Lisbon? Or is he long gone?'

'I wish I knew, but trust me, if he returns, he's going to wish he hadn't.' Camille reached for Avery's hand. 'Please don't hate me for telling you.'

There was a steely determination in Avery as she looked back at her, and Camille marvelled at how much her American friend had changed since the day they'd first met. She had a resilience that Camille would never have guessed at. When Camille closed her eyes at night, the nightmares were slower to come, and she knew it was because of their friendship. Only last night, she'd lain awake seeing Avery usher the little Jewish girl and her mother into the bookshop as she kept lookout, listening to the click of her camera. She hadn't been able to stop thinking about the way Avery had kissed the child's head, her eyes shining with unshed tears as she'd said goodbye to them – the work they were doing helping people in ways that would never be forgotten.

'I'm proud of you, Avery,' Camille said. 'I know I was hard on you at first, but everything we do, all of us, is worth it. Every little thing, right? And the photographs you've taken, the documents you've helped me with . . .' She paused. 'What you've done for those people is life-changing.'

Avery smiled back at her, and the words settled between them. The thing about her and Avery was that they seemed able to let their feelings be known without even saying the words these days, and not for the first time, Camille had the notion that she finally knew what it would have been like to have a sister.

Chapter Eighteen

AVERY

'You look beautiful.'

Avery frowned at her reflection in the mirror. It wasn't that she didn't think she looked nice, because she had put a huge effort into her appearance, but she wasn't convinced about going out at all. Ever since finding out about James a few days ago, she'd found it hard to be interested in doing anything other than work, and she'd rather curl up on her bed and eat dinner with a book balanced between her knees than go out.

'Thanks. I just, I don't know, I wish I hadn't said yes. It doesn't feel right.'

'Avery, look at me,' Camille said. 'You're going to have a wonderful night out with a gorgeous man. Just enjoy it. You deserve it.'

Avery nodded.

'I know you're still feeling distraught about it all,' Camille said. 'But you need to give William a chance. He's shown himself to be kind, and he's rather gorgeous to look at. James fooled you, don't you forget that, so you shouldn't waste any time thinking about him.'

Avery knew Camille was right, but she still found it almost impossible to believe that the man who'd kissed her beneath the street light, the man who had made her laugh whenever she was with him, was capable of such duplicity. Because of that, she wasn't convinced she was the best judge of character, or that she should be going out with any man.

'You saw Kiefer this morning, before he left?'

'I did. It was strange saying goodbye to him, I had this overwhelming sense of relief when he walked away from me. Like that part of my life, pretending to be someone I wasn't, was finally over.'

'That you no longer had to keep up the charade?'

Camille nodded. 'I suppose that's what it was. But also that all of this, the search that's driven me almost crazy, is almost over. That it will soon come to an end.' Her eyes met Avery's in the mirror.

'What does that mean?' Avery asked. She hadn't actually imagined what Camille might do to James if he ever came back to Lisbon. She hated what he'd done, her stomach turned whenever she thought of how easily she'd fallen for the man, yet her heart still hurt when she thought about him. 'You've never actually talked to me about what you'll do next.'

'Nothing. Just, nothing. Please don't worry about it,' Camille said. 'Now come on, otherwise you'll be late.'

Avery hesitated, staring at Camille, wondering what she could possibly mean by that, but a quick glance at her watch told her that she would indeed be late if they didn't hurry. She'd wanted to ask her how careful they would have to be going forward, now that Kiefer wasn't there to offer at least some degree of protection, but that could be a conversation for another day.

She'd agreed to meet William outside the hotel and Avery was going to chaperone her there. What James had said in jest that first night, about not letting a spy know where she lived, had stopped her from giving William her address. Camille might believe that

William was trustworthy, but Avery had decided to be much more careful moving forward.

Tom was sitting in the living room, his feet up on the coffee table, and she gave him a cursory glance as she passed. She reluctantly stopped when he cleared his throat, clearly trying to get her attention.

'Avery, you have a letter from Washington,' he said. 'I left it on the table for you.'

She raised a brow. 'You didn't open it for me?'

He let out an audible breath. 'No, Avery, I didn't open it for you. Of *course* I didn't open it.'

She turned to Camille. 'Can I meet you downstairs?'

Camille didn't need to be asked twice, and Avery saw how Tom kept glancing at her friend.

'She's the bookshop owner?'

'She is indeed. Her name is Camille.'

'She's the one I've seen with a Nazi.'

Avery laughed and resisted the urge to roll her eyes. 'So have I, Tom. Anyone who doesn't live under a rock would have seen her with a Nazi at the hotel. We all do what we have to do, no?'

He looked uncomfortable and she almost felt sorry for him, but she still hadn't forgiven him for the threats he'd made, and she didn't want to let him off the hook too easily. She used a knife to slice the envelope open, taking out the letter, which appeared brief.

Avery, excellent work. I don't know how you're sourcing these maps and other documents, so I won't ask questions. Washington wants to commend you, so from now on please preserve your film and focus only on your most recent work. I'm certain you'll know what I'm referring to. You were certainly the right person for the job.

Stay safe. Kilgour.

She looked up, seeing that Tom was watching her intently.

'Everything alright?' he asked.

'Everything is just peachy,' she said. *With no thanks to you.*

'Avery, about what happened the other night, about what I said . . .'

She folded her arms and waited for him to finish.

'I wanted to say that I'm sorry. I was out of line, threatening you like that, but I am worried about you,' he said. 'I would hate for something to happen to you, that's all, and I felt like I owed it to you to keep you safe. To preserve the integrity of what we were sent here to do.'

'I appreciate your concern, but I know what I'm doing,' Avery said. 'All I've ever wanted was to do this job to the very best of my ability – to prove that it wasn't a mistake, my being chosen to come here.'

'That letter confirms that for you?' he asked.

She nodded, not able to resist a small smile. 'As a matter of fact, it does.'

'Well, then I'm pleased for you. Whatever you're doing, it must be worth the risk,' he said.

Avery slipped the letter back into the envelope and placed it in her purse, deciding she didn't want to leave it on the table for any prying eyes, despite the contents being so glowing.

'Avery?'

She glanced back at Tom.

'I want you to know that I'm here for you. Whatever was said between us, we're on the same side. You can always come to me if you need me, no questions asked.'

'Thanks, Tom,' she said, smiling as she walked past him and heading down the stairs and out the door to where Camille was waiting. It would certainly be nice not to have so much tension between them, and she knew it couldn't have been easy for him to back down like that.

'Nothing you couldn't handle?' Camille asked, offering her arm.

Avery slipped her arm through Camille's as they set off down the road. 'Nothing I couldn't handle,' she repeated.

And she meant it. When she'd been picked for the job and sent to Lisbon, she'd wavered between being excited and wondering how anyone could possibly think she had the right skills for the job. But she no longer felt like that. Avery knew she was the right woman for the job now, and so long as she could keep finding exclusive material to send back to Washington, she knew that she'd never doubt herself again. Or at least she hoped so.

'I have to say, I was surprised when you agreed to see me tonight.'

Avery glanced up, her hand on the stem of her wine glass. William had been nothing other than charming and sweet so far, and she was pleased she'd come, although it was abundantly obvious that he was interested in being more than just friends.

'Why were you surprised? I'm fairly certain you don't have a problem with ladies agreeing to dates.'

He grazed her hand with his knuckles, and she fought to hold his gaze. He was bold, and she wasn't used to bold. She slowly pulled her hand away to put some distance between them.

'Let's just say that I thought your interests might be elsewhere,' he said. 'Either way I'm very pleased to be spending the evening in your company.'

Avery had already had a glass of wine, and she was being careful not to take more than tiny sips of her second, but she feared that if their dinner didn't come soon, she would start to feel light-headed. Certainly she was going to wait until she'd had her first course before she attempted to stand and walk to the bathroom. William was well through his second drink and had already waved the waiter over for another.

'My sources tell me you're rather good at acquiring newspapers and the like,' William said, as their dinner finally arrived.

The plate of food in front of her smelt amazing, and Avery stalled by taking a small mouthful as she tried to figure out how to reply. He was certainly very direct, but she was used to telling her cover story and he wasn't going to rattle her so easily.

'Your source is correct,' she said. 'I'm here to acquire books of interest from all countries, as well as relevant newspapers, to ensure that our central library at home has a full record of the war.'

'Our government has a similar initiative, although I do wonder if it's slightly more clandestine than they care to admit.'

'Really?' She purposely let her eyebrows shoot up in surprise. 'That's interesting, because my instructions are very clear, and I'm to ensure zero involvement in anything covert, so to speak. It's all very much above board and transparent.'

'I take it you've heard about the Allied operative arrested in Spain?'

Avery swallowed, her food suddenly very dry in her mouth. 'When you say *operative* . . .'

'Sorry, my terminology was too loose. She may well have had a job similar to yours. I believe she did something called microphotography, although I may have the terminology wrong. Anyway, she was arrested just last month on suspicion of being a spy for some of the materials she'd managed to acquire. I thought you would have heard?'

William spoke as if he were talking about the weather or some other trivia, and she had the distinct feeling that he'd told her to see how she would react.

She immediately thought of the maps of Kiefer's that she'd copied. 'Will she be released, once they realise it was all a misunderstanding?'

William picked up his knife and fork and took a mouthful, as she sat frozen still, her fork hovering over her plate with a piece of warm ham on it.

'Of course, I'm certain she will. I just thought it was admirable, that a woman such as yourself was prepared to risk so much for her country. Although I suppose it's about setting up a network you can trust, right? Although it's hard to know who to trust in some places, and you certainly wouldn't want to do anything outside of what you've been sent to do, am I right?'

Avery felt torn inside, and she wasn't certain if it was Camille's ongoing suspicions about British men or her own concerns that made her wonder if William was purposely toying with her. It was almost as if he wanted to warn her, scare her off perhaps, and it was certainly working.

'You never did tell me what you were doing in Lisbon,' she asked, knowing it was bold but realising that he'd never actually told her.

'I'm a journalist, actually,' he said. 'I thought I'd already told you that.'

She watched as he took his napkin from his lap and dabbed carefully at the corners of his mouth. Avery had a second realisation then, that it was particularly strange for a journalist to be stationed in a country that wasn't at war. What were they possibly reporting on, or was it simply their base? She'd never given it much thought when James had told her his occupation. *Or cover story.* Now she wondered if anything James had told her was true.

'That's how you know James, presumably?' she asked. 'Although I'm guessing you're rivals, not colleagues, if you're both fighting to report on the same stories?'

'Ahh yes, my fellow countryman James,' William said, collecting his drink again and sitting back in his chair, looking as relaxed as could be.

Avery's stomach was churning. She forced herself to pick at her food, despite her distinct lack of appetite, waiting for him to continue.

'We're competitors, that's all. Sometimes he gets the best stories back to London before I do, other times it's me. The only bad blood between us is that we're always against each other when it comes to work. That's all.'

She finished her mouthful. 'That's all? You're not going to try to warn me off him or . . .' Avery didn't actually know what she expected him to say.

'You know him well?' William asked.

'We met a couple of times,' she lied. 'Nothing more.'

If he was worried about her friendship with James, he didn't show it. 'Anyway, how's that ham? I could eat a second plate it was so good.'

'It's lovely, thank you,' Avery said. 'I just don't have a very big appetite. But you help yourself to what I can't eat, if you like, while I use the restroom and powder my nose.'

She smiled as William stood for her, tucking her purse under her arm and heading for the bathroom, her legs a little wobbly. Once she was there, she went to the toilet and then stared at herself in the mirror while she washed her hands, keeping them under the water for much longer than she needed to.

Stop doubting yourself. You deserve to be here. No one is going to arrest you, you're not doing anything wrong. Just try to enjoy dinner and then find a way to end the night early before he tries anything on.

But she couldn't stop thinking about the PVDE and what might happen to Camille if they found a reason to raid her shop again, and when she finally went to turn the water off, she realised her hands were shaking.

Just go back out there and enjoy the rest of your date. You're being silly. William is handsome and charming, he's the perfect date.

And so she did. Avery walked back out to the table and found William had ordered another drink, and that their main course had arrived.

'Sorry to keep you waiting, I think I had too much to drink on a very empty stomach,' she said. 'But this food looks delicious. I've never tasted fish so nice as I have in Lisbon.'

William reached for her hand and she let him. 'How about I order you an orange juice, so you don't have to worry about drinking too much wine?'

'That's incredibly thoughtful of you. Thank you.'

He waved the waiter over and ordered, before taking a pocket watch from inside his jacket to check the time, the diamonds around the watch face glinting under the lights.

'William, do you mind if we don't talk about our work tonight?' she said. 'I find myself so consumed by what I do each day, that it'd be nice to just pretend we're not in the middle of a war.'

'A woman after my own heart if ever there was one,' he said. 'I knew there was a reason I was drawn to you.'

Avery turned her attention to her dinner, feeling slightly more at ease already. But when she looked up, she saw a familiar figure walk past the door to the restaurant. Avery quickly glanced away, not wanting William to see, but she clearly hadn't been quick enough, for he turned to look. It might have been her mind playing tricks on her, but she was certain that James had just passed by, and her stomach lurched violently.

Avery blinked away a tear, her eyes down, and hoped that William hadn't noticed.

'Did you see someone you know?' he asked.

'No, I was just . . .' She cleared her throat and leaned in, even as her mind was racing, as she tried to come up with another lie. 'I feel very unsettled knowing that we're surrounded by the enemy, and a Japanese man just walked past the door.'

211

That seemed to be enough to placate William. 'It is unsettling, I'll give you that.'

'My father would have a heart attack to know I was virtually rubbing shoulders with the enemy here. I wouldn't put it past him to demand a seat on the next plane heading to Portugal to drag me home himself.'

William laughed, and they both went back to eating their meals, although it took every inch of Avery's willpower not to keep looking out for James, her heart racing as she tried not to panic that he was back. Because it didn't matter what Camille had told her, she still found it hard to believe that he'd been a traitor to his country, and she was tempted to ask James outright to explain himself if she could find him before Camille did.

A commotion near the door caught her attention then, and William stood, dropping his napkin to the table as men in uniform approached their table. Avery's breath caught in her throat.

'What is the meaning of this interruption?' William asked, stepping slightly in front of her to obscure her view of the men. But she immediately knew who they were, recognising the shorter, overweight man who'd been in Camille's shop on the day of the raid.

They were from the PVDE.

'We would like to speak to the young woman behind you, about her association with a French woman by the name of Camille, who we believe may be illegally assisting Jewish refugees and selling contraband books from her bookshop.'

'And you have evidence of this, or are you merely on a fishing expedition?'

'The lady behind you has been seen at the square, and frequenting the bookshop, which is why we'd like to have a word.'

'It is now a crime to be charitable to the needy or indeed indulge in buying books?' William laughed. 'Because if that's the case, then you may as well arrest me while you're here.'

Avery's entire body trembled, but she refused to let anyone else see how scared she was. And if ever she'd been grateful, she felt eternally so to the man protecting her in that moment. She glanced around the room and saw that everyone else dining in the restaurant was watching them.

'No sir, neither of those things is a crime, but—'

'I'm sorry, but as you can see, we're in the middle of dinner, and unless you intend on arresting one of us, then I suggest that you calm down and leave us be until a more convenient time.'

The man leaned around William, dropping a card on to the table as his beady eyes met hers.

'I suggest you make an appointment to see me at your earliest convenience,' he said.

Avery glanced at it and saw that his name was Lourenço Santos. She reached for it, her fingers curling around the stiff card. She'd heard Camille mutter his name after the raid on her shop.

'Yes sir,' she said. 'I will.'

He gave her a long, unsettling kind of stare, before turning sharply on his heel and taking his two men with him.

'Avery?' William asked, his brows furrowed as he reached for her hand.

She couldn't stop thinking about the young child whose photograph she'd taken recently, watching the film come to life as she developed it; the maps she'd photographed; the documents she'd carefully forged as she sat shoulder to shoulder with Camille at the little desk in the backroom of the bookshop, black ink pens in their hands. Thankfully the other people dining had resumed their conversations and were no longer staring at them.

'Avery?' William repeated.

'I think I've lost my appetite,' she said. 'I'm sorry, but I need to go home.'

Chapter Nineteen

CAMILLE

Camille never felt so vulnerable as when she spent time with Lisbon's refugees. They reminded her of home, of Hugo, of what she'd lost. But they also reminded her why her work was important, and why it was worth risking so much to save them. Only now she felt more nervy than usual, knowing that someone could be watching her. Kiefer had been clear in his warnings – if she was caught here, if anyone could prove she'd been doing the work, no one would be able to save her. And now he was gone.

She sat in the square, a book in hand as she pretended to read. In actual fact, her eyes were barely dancing over the words as she waited for her contact to meet her. In helping the French arrivals, she wasn't just risking her own life, but theirs, too. Only, they didn't have much choice if they ever wanted to escape the clutches of Europe for America.

Within minutes, a woman sat down beside her. She, too, held a book, which she opened in her lap.

'The man in the uniform has been following you again,' the woman said. 'I saw him last time you tried to come.'

'I have to be more careful than ever. This has to be my last forgery for a while. And you need to spread word that it's too dangerous for anyone to come to my shop looking for me, for the time being.'

'What if someone needs you?'

Camille blinked away tears. This was what she'd feared the most. 'It's just for now. But you have to do what I ask, for their safety as much as mine. If they're caught looking for me, without a visa, they'll be deported immediately.'

They were careful not to speak too much, and Camille suddenly felt overcome with sadness. The woman's children played nearby, and they reminded her of that last family they'd tried to help in France; the fear in the mother's eyes as she'd stood before Camille and Hugo asking them to help her, putting their lives in her hands. She knew that no matter what happened in her own life, that moment would play through her mind for as long as she lived; wishing things could have been different, that they'd made another choice.

'The papers are tucked inside this book,' she told the woman. 'I'm going to put mine down for a moment, you do the same, and then we will carefully swap books.'

The woman was silent, and when Camille put her book down, the woman did the same, though she caught Camille's hand, her fingers brushing hers for the briefest second, lingering, her only way of showing Camille just how much the papers meant to her.

A tear trickled down Camille's cheek then, followed by another, and she sat silently as they began to stream down her cheeks.

'What you've done, for so many of us, it will never be forgotten,' the woman whispered. 'Even if you can't help anyone else, what you've done is a miracle for those you've helped.'

Camille quickly wiped her cheeks. 'It will never feel like enough.'

'You will remain in the hearts and prayers of families like ours forever, Camille. Don't you ever forget that.'

They sat for a while longer, side by side, in silence, until the woman finally rose to leave. Camille knew she was right, but she also knew that she would always wish she could have done more. Just as she would always wish she'd found out what had happened to the family who'd been waiting for her and her husband that night, and whether any of them had survived. Although, in her heart, she knew.

Camille's last customer for the morning left and she walked out the back into the office, perplexed at why Avery was packing up her things. They'd barely spoken since Avery had arrived, as Camille had had people in the shop all afternoon, but she went to seek her out now to see how she was.

'Avery? Is everything alright?'

Avery looked unsure of herself, which was not something Camille was used to. When they'd first met, certainly Avery had been very green, but the more time they'd spent together and the longer she'd done her job, the more confident she'd become. But today, Avery looked plain scared.

'I just need to get back to working at the apartment,' Avery said. 'Now that Kiefer is gone and we won't have anything from him to photograph, it—'

'Avery,' Camille said, frowning. 'Tell me what's wrong.'

Avery looked like she was about to cry. 'That PVDE officer came looking for me, Camille. I was having dinner with William and they came into the restaurant and . . .' Avery reached into her handbag and produced a card. 'He left me this. He wants to talk to me.'

'About?' Camille asked, taking the card and knowing without even looking who the card belonged to. *Lourenço Santos.* The one man in Lisbon who could ruin everything she'd worked so hard for. 'What would he want to talk to you about?'

'You,' Avery said, her voice a whisper. 'He wants to talk to me about *you.*'

'Did you tell him anything?' Camille asked, glancing up and out into the shop to check that no one had entered. 'Do you think he knows you've been working with me?'

'No! I barely spoke to him, William tried to make him feel rude for interrupting us, but I'm so nervous of everything. Of what could happen to me, of being arrested, of—' Avery gasped. 'I feel like I don't know what I'm doing anymore, as if I shouldn't even be here. One moment I was feeling as if I'd gained this newfound confidence, and now I'm questioning everything. And William told me about a woman just like me who'd been arrested in Spain, and I can't stop thinking that it could have been me, it could *still* be me. They could send me to jail, Camille, and throw away the key!'

Camille took Avery's camera from her and placed it on the table, wrapping her in her arms and holding her in a long hug. Camille stroked her hair, sensing that something more had happened to warrant her sudden change of heart, but not knowing what.

'What happened to my brave American girl?' Camille asked, still holding her, trying to tease. 'I will never let anything happen to you, I promise. I told you I'd take the fall for both of us if it ever came to that, and I meant it.'

Avery pulled back and Camille saw tears shining in her eyes. 'The brave American girl is scared, Camille. She's scared that she's very much out of her depth.' Avery blew out a breath. 'But I will always help you with the documents. I know it's dangerous work, but I would never forgive myself if I didn't help those poor people. I just, I don't know what to do. I'm terrible at lying, and if they question me properly, I . . .'

Avery stayed silent, and Camille let go of her, watching as Avery finished tidying up the area she'd been working in. She'd miss her not being there every day, not having someone to talk to or just have nearby to remind her that she wasn't alone.

'I don't think there will be many more refugees arriving from France, it's so difficult for anyone to get through now, but regardless, we won't be doing any more of that work for a while, not until the heat is off us.'

Avery didn't hide her surprise. 'We're stopping?'

'For now. I don't see that we have any other choice.'

'What you've done for those people, Camille, even if that work is finished for now, it's meant so much to so many people. I've seen it first-hand, the way they look at you . . .' Avery put her arms around Camille and hugged her. 'I'm so proud to have played a small part in helping you. Every little thing, right?'

'Every little thing,' Camille repeated. Her smile was small, but it was there, and Camille realised, not for the first time, just how much Avery had come to mean to her.

'I actually came looking for you last night after I left William,' Avery said. 'I went to your apartment, but you weren't there.'

'Come on, let's close the shop and get some fresh air,' Camille said. 'We can talk while we walk.'

They stepped outside into the warm sunshine together, Avery carrying the bag with her camera in it, and Camille swinging the keys to her shop from her fingers. They walked down the street and crossed over to stare out at the water, and it reminded Camille of the day they'd spent at the beach together.

'The PVDE followed me last night,' Camille said. 'I went to the square, but it didn't feel safe to hand the documents over.'

'Do you think they were following you before they came looking for me?' Avery asked.

'Perhaps,' Camille said. 'I didn't risk handing over the papers, they were sewn safely into my jacket, but when I realised how hungry so many of the families were, how desperate their children were, I went back and took them everything I had in my kitchen. It was too dangerous to hand over the papers, I had a feeling I was being watched, but I knew I couldn't be arrested for giving them food.'

Kiefer had warned Camille away from the refugee families, told her she wasn't to go back, but even with his words of warning ringing in her ears she'd still returned.

Avery reached for her, putting an arm around her. 'You have the kindest heart, Camille. Is there more we can do for them? I have a little more money stashed away that we can use to buy more supplies if that would help?'

'There's just so many of them,' Camille whispered. 'You can fill the bellies of one family, and turn around to see another watching. It's enough to break a heart.' Hers felt as if it were cracking wide open, although she didn't tell Avery that. 'I know you've seen it too, but something about last night, it just all felt so much worse. There are so many of them here waiting, and I don't believe the boats are even coming for them.'

'We can't give up hope, and I know it's not ideal but they're here. The ones with the correct paperwork are at least safe – that's what you told me when you first took me there, and it's as true today as it was then.'

Avery breathed deeply, but after a moment of just standing together, Camille turned to her. 'Why were you looking for me last night, Avery? To tell me about the PVDE?'

'That, and I was coming to tell you that . . .' Avery shook her head, as if she didn't want to tell Camille. She looked torn. 'I was coming to tell you that I thought I saw James.'

'You're certain?' Camille asked, grabbing hold of her arm. 'Where was he? Tell me where you saw him?'

'He walked past the restaurant last night. I'm guessing he'd just returned from—'

'France. He must have just returned from France.' She paced a few steps away then came straight back. 'You're certain it was him you saw? You couldn't have made a mistake?'

Avery shook her head. 'I didn't make a mistake. It was him.'

Camille took Avery's hand in hers and pressed their palms together, looking out at the water as tears burned in her eyes. She'd waited so long to hold someone accountable, and she might finally have her chance.

'Will you turn him in to the authorities? How does this even work?' Avery asked. 'You have to tell me what happens next.'

'No,' Camille replied. 'I'm going to take care of it myself.'

'Meaning?' Avery asked.

'That I'm the only person in Lisbon who cares about what he's done, and I intend on making him pay.'

Avery pulled her hand away. '*Meaning?*'

'Meaning that I've been waiting for this day since the moment my husband was murdered beside me to hold someone accountable, and no one is going to stop me.' *Not even you, Avery. Even you couldn't stop me.*

'What if I told you that I was in love with him?'

Camille's heart skipped a beat, but it didn't matter what Avery said, she already knew what she had to do. 'Are you?'

'I think I'm in love with the man I thought he was,' Avery said, and Camille saw the shine of tears in her eyes. 'I still can't bear to think of him being hurt, even though I know that's terribly naive of me.'

'I understand that, truly I do, more than you can imagine.' Camille gripped her hand again, more tightly this time. 'But you said you'd help me, and I need your help tonight.'

Avery looked more uncertain than Camille had ever seen her look, but she didn't pull away.

'What would you need me to do?'

'I'd need you to come out with me, to the hotel.'

'To draw James out?' Avery asked, her voice small. 'You want to use me as bait?'

'If I'm wrong about him, then he can prove himself to me tonight.' But Camille knew she wasn't wrong. The information Kiefer had given her was good – James was the man she was searching for.

'But if you're right?'

They were both silent. Camille chose not to fill in the blank.

'Just tell me you'll think about it. I'll be at the Hotel Avenida tonight, at one of the back tables,' Camille said. 'If you want to join me, meet me there at six.'

Avery started to walk away, but after a few steps she turned and gave Camille a look she couldn't decipher, that she very much hoped meant Avery was thinking about it.

'Avery, it's me. Whatever doubts you have, whoever you think is trying to deceive you, it's not me. You have to believe that.'

Avery slowly nodded, and Camille watched her walk off, but Avery was only a few feet away when she stopped and turned back around.

'What happens if the PVDE raid your shop again?'

'They won't find anything,' Camille said. 'They can turn the place over again and again, but there's nothing to find.'

'Promise?'

Camille placed her hand on her heart. 'I promise, Avery. I'm being more careful than I've ever been before, and there is nothing left for them to find.'

All they'll find are memories. There is nothing there they can arrest me for, unless they've discovered that I'm not the Portuguese widow I've been pretending to be.

'You came.'

Camille had never been so relieved to see someone before.

'Of course I came,' Avery said. 'Besides, I don't think even the PVDE could arrest me just for having a drink, could they?'

Camille gave her a hug and she listened to Avery's big sigh, which she hoped was one of relief that they were together.

'Has there been any sign of him?' Avery asked.

'No, but your friend William is here. He's heading our way now, and I think I'll leave you so that I can watch from a better vantage point, to see if James arrives. If he's here, you'll be the one to draw him out.'

William arrived at their table then, a bottle of champagne in one hand, and glasses in the other.

'Avery,' he said. 'What a pleasant surprise.'

'It's lovely to see you, too, William,' she said, finding that she was happy to see him. He was at least a nice distraction from everything else.

'If you'll both excuse me, I have to go and powder my nose,' Camille said. 'I'll see you soon.'

She went to pick up her handbag, but Avery's hand reached out.

'You can leave that here if you want me to look after it.'

Camille quickly grabbed hold of her bag and pulled it closer, sliding it over her shoulder and keeping it snug to her body.

'What on earth do you have in there?' Avery asked as she let it go.

'Just what I usually have,' Camille said, patting it innocently and praying that William's attention wasn't drawn to what she might be carrying. 'I'll be back soon.'

As she walked, she slipped her hand inside and let it rest on the cool metal of the pistol, and even though she'd expected to be nervous, the strangest sense of calm settled over her as she crossed the room to search for her target.

Chapter Twenty

AVERY

'Avery, I owe you an apology for last night,' William said, as he took the seat beside her.

'You have nothing to apologise for, it was a lovely dinner,' she said. 'I was the one to leave early, so it's me who should be apologising.'

'I fear I had a little too much to drink and the result was a loose tongue,' he said. 'I'd like very much if we could start over.'

'As friends?'

He nodded. 'If that's what you'd like, then certainly, as friends.'

Avery considered him, and for the first time she forced herself to push James completely from her mind, which was no easy task. But if James was who Camille said he was, if everything she'd said was true, then she needed to stop thinking about him altogether. William was handsome, charming, and most importantly interested in her, and she needed to give him a chance without constantly comparing him to James.

'I'd very much like that,' she said. 'I don't think I was entirely present when we had dinner, I had a lot on my mind, but if we can start as friends, then I'd like that very much.' She craned her neck to look for Camille, but her friend seemed to have disappeared. 'And I'm sorry you were drawn into that business with the PVDE. For some reason, they've always been suspicious of my friend, but I'm hoping she's cleared all that up now.'

'Well, let's pour a glass and relax,' William said, extending his arm and putting it around her. 'We could start by you telling me all about yourself, and I'll reluctantly tell you about me, and we can put last night behind us.'

She moved a little closer, inhaling the woodsy scent of his cologne and happily taking the half-glass of champagne offered to her. And just as she was starting to enjoy herself, laughing at William recounting tales of his childhood, Camille appeared. She still hadn't shared precisely what she was intending on doing once she found James, and Avery found herself wondering just what Camille might be capable of. The thought of violence terrified her, but what scared her even more was what might happen to Camille.

'I hope you two don't mind me re-joining you,' she said.

'Not at all,' William said, leaning forward to retrieve the empty glass on the table. 'Champagne?'

'Yes, please. I'll only have the one glass though. I fear it's been a series of late nights, and I'm almost ready to turn in.'

William took out his watch from his pocket. 'It's not even seven. Surely you'll stay and join us for dinner?'

Avery didn't even remember what she and William had been talking about, but she saw the way Camille's face changed, as if she'd seen something she didn't like. Avery followed her gaze and realised that Camille was staring at William's watch.

'That's a beautiful watch,' Camille said, studying it, her face hovering in a frown as Avery looked on. 'I've never seen anything quite like it.'

William's smile was easy, and Avery found herself looking at the watch too, until he slipped it back into his jacket, passing Camille her glass of champagne.

'It was passed down to me from my grandfather,' he said. 'I was tempted to leave it at home when I received my orders to go abroad, but I figured it was better to have it with me than leave it behind.'

Camille took the glass, and Avery didn't know why or how, but it was as if a cloud had settled over their table, stealing the laughter and most definitely stealing the light mood that had existed only moments before.

'Camille, are you alright?' Avery asked.

A look crossed Camille's face that Avery couldn't place, but William quickly filled the silence.

'Camille, Avery and I were just talking about our childhoods. It seems we both had fathers who liked to keep us out of mischief.'

Camille downed half of her champagne in a few hurried sips, and Avery wondered again why she now appeared so agitated. It was almost as if she'd seen someone or something and was in a rush to get to them, and just then she unexpectedly excused herself without an explanation.

'Is she usually in such a hurry?' William asked, looking perplexed. 'Was it something I said?'

Avery stared after her until she couldn't see her anymore, before turning back to William. Her heart was hammering in her chest, as she assumed that Camille had darted off for one reason and one reason only.

She had to have seen James.

'Not at all, but . . .' She sighed. 'I'm sure it's nothing. I can only guess that she saw someone she recognised.'

'Well, how about we forget all about your friend and see if we can get a table in the restaurant,' William suggested.

Avery must have looked as uncertain as she felt, because he suddenly covered her hand with his.

'Just so we can talk some more away from all this noise and cigarette smoke, and enjoy our champagne,' he said. 'What do you say? I promise I'll behave.'

Avery took a deep breath, torn between wanting to go with him and not being entirely certain she even wanted to have dinner with him. But the way he was looking at her, the way his eyes traced over her face . . . She needed to push James from her mind and enjoy the company of the man before her. Camille had made it clear she didn't want her help beyond drawing James out, and Avery's preference was to remain distracted so she didn't have to think about what might happen to him.

'Of course, that would be lovely.'

William held out his arm and she took it, letting him lead her through the bar and out into the lobby of the restaurant. She stood back while he spoke to someone about a table, but when he returned, he was frowning.

'They have a table for us, but not for another half hour,' he said. 'Would you mind terribly if we went upstairs to my room while we wait? I'm out of cigarettes and I thought we could have a drink and . . .'

He clearly noted her taken-aback expression, because he laughed and held up his hands.

'Or not,' he said. 'I can see that I've made you uncomfortable, but I can assure you that I didn't mean anything by it.'

She tilted her chin and looked up at him, telling herself that she wasn't the same girl who'd left New York. She was a strong, independent woman, and if she wanted to go with him, she had nothing to be fearful of.

'I'll come with you, but just for one drink. And just to make it clear, I'm not the kind of girl who goes to hotel rooms with men, so don't take this the wrong way,' she said, firmly. 'Please don't get any ideas.'

His smile was immediate.

'I'll be a perfect gentleman, I promise.'

Avery's heart started to race as he led her across the lobby, although she had to stifle a giggle as she imagined her mother's reaction if she knew what her daughter was doing. The poor woman would be making the sign of the cross on her chest and sending a prayer skywards.

Avery was nervous as they walked down the hallway to William's hotel room, but she was relieved that he'd done nothing more than offer her his arm. Part of her was worried that someone might see them and think less of her, but she had to keep reminding herself that it was an innocent drink, nothing more.

He unlocked his door and stood back for her to walk in ahead of him, and she did, surprised that his room smelt like his cologne, and that it was as neat as a pin. 'I'm impressed,' she said. 'It's so tidy I'd almost suspect it was a woman's room.'

William just laughed and took off his jacket, placing it over a chair and then loosening his tie and undoing his top button. She watched as he also unbuttoned his cuffs and rolled up his sleeves two turns, while she stood in the middle of the room, uncertain why he was taking off his tie when they were going down for dinner soon.

'That's better,' he said. 'Feel free to make yourself at home.'

Avery suddenly wished the IDC had put her up somewhere as luxurious as William's hotel room. It was making her apartment in Lisbon seem very much inferior. She crossed the room and sat down on the bed when William gestured for her to do so.

'I hope I haven't made you uncomfortable, asking you up here.'

He sat down beside her, close, but not close enough that their legs touched, and she found herself turning to face him.

'It's not that, it's just I recently found out that a friend of mine isn't who he says he is,' Avery said, studying William's face to gauge his reaction. 'I've been trying to enjoy myself tonight, but it's hard to push from my mind.'

'He lied to you for personal reasons, or are you talking something bigger?'

She felt as if her lungs were constricted, almost as if her body didn't want her to tell William, but she fought against it. 'Can I trust you?'

His smile was sweet and he gently placed his hand on hers. 'Of course you can trust me, Avery.'

She took a big breath. 'I'm told that he's a traitor, a double agent in fact, working with the Nazis.'

William appeared to stiffen. 'Can you share with me who this friend is?'

'*James*,' she whispered. 'The traitor is your fellow British countryman James, and I've found it incredibly hard to believe, but I know now that it's true. It's just taken me a long time to accept it.'

He looked surprised. 'Well, that's certainly news to me,' William said. 'I'll have to alert the authorities in the morning if your intelligence is correct. But you can leave it with me, Avery, it's not something you should have to be worrying about.'

'The person who told me is someone of the utmost character, and she has no reason not to tell the truth about it.'

He nodded. 'I understand, and I'll make sure the situation is dealt with just as soon as I can.'

'Thank you,' she whispered, feeling as if a great weight had been lifted from her shoulders. 'Would you excuse me just a moment, though?'

She rose and went to the adjoining bathroom, checking her reflection and dabbing some perfume on to her wrists and behind her ears, and putting on a little more lipstick. She was nervous, but not so nervous that she didn't want to impress him, and she'd just needed a moment to get thoughts of James out of her head.

When she walked back out into the room, William was leaning back on the bed, but he rose when he saw her and took a few steps forward.

'Has anyone ever told you how beautiful you are, Avery?'

She blushed, about to remind him that they were supposed to be friends, and that she'd only come up to pass the time and have a drink with him. But William took her hand, and his fingers were soft as they stroked her skin. When his gaze lowered to her mouth, she faltered.

'May I kiss you?' he asked.

Avery nodded, just the slightest incline of her head, and his lips crushed against hers within seconds, moving softly then more firmly, kissing her passionately until she pulled away, gasping for breath. William smiled down at her, running his fingers along her jawline and then slowly down the soft skin of her neck, sending shivers through every part of her.

'I realised while you were in the bathroom that I'm out of Scotch or anything else for us to drink,' he said, his voice low and almost raspy, as if he'd been smoking too many cigarettes. 'I'm going to go down to rustle up a bottle of champagne for us, if you don't mind being left alone for a moment?'

Avery dabbed at her mouth, hoping her lipstick wasn't all over her face. 'Of course.' She was happy to have a moment alone to right herself, and to try to make sense of what had just happened.

'I'll be back shortly, don't go anywhere,' he said, taking her hand and pressing a quick kiss there before taking a few steps backwards and then disappearing out of the door. 'And then dinner, I promise!'

Avery dashed into the bathroom and checked her appearance again, righting her smudged lip colour, before going back out into the room. She sat on the bed and then promptly stood again, not wanting to be on the bed when he came back into the room in case that gave him any ideas. So for something to do, she opened his closet, took out a spare coat-hanger, and picked up his jacket to hang it up for him. But something fluttered from the pocket and she bent to collect it, wondering what he had in there, expecting it to be a letter.

It was a map, crudely drawn and folded down to roughly the size of her palm, and when she turned it over she saw names written there. But it was when she saw the name *Camille* that a shiver ran through her. Avery had no idea what she was looking at, or why he'd have her friend's name on there, but she knew that something wasn't right, that it wasn't something he should have in his possession. And then she turned cold, as if ice was trickling its way down her spine.

It always pays to ask the doorman on the way in who's ordered champagne. You see, whoever orders a celebratory drink was the winner of today's battle.

She swallowed, still gripping the coat-hanger in one hand as she dropped the jacket to the floor, James's words echoing in her mind. He'd told her that night at the hotel, when he was teasing her about becoming a good spy, and it was something she'd never forgotten. The Germans were the ones drinking champagne downstairs in the hotel bar – she'd seen Camille walking past them and recognised them as Kiefer's Nazi friends. And when she and William had passed them to reach the hotel lobby, she'd noticed multiple empty bottles discarded on the table.

So why was William so insistent on them drinking champagne? What success could he have possibly had, if it hadn't been a good day for the Allies?

Avery bent down and picked up his jacket again, feeling all the pockets, and this time she found a receipt for a large amount of money, dated today, as well as a small handful of loose diamonds. Why would he have diamonds on him?

She set them on the table as the truth dawned on her, as everything slowly fell into place in her mind. Suddenly nothing about William added up, and she realised that the only reason a man like him would have loose diamonds in his pocket would be if he had been paid for something with them.

The double agent wasn't James. It had never been James. The double agent was the man ordering champagne when the other Allied men in the bar were drinking whisky, the man who seemed too good to be true, who'd slipped past Camille's defences and convinced both of them that he was nothing more than a charming Brit.

She knew that it was him, just as she knew her original instincts about James had been right, too. William was the traitor, and instead of trusting her gut, she'd turned her back on James and blindly followed the real double agent all the way to his room. *To his lair.*

William is the British man responsible for the death of Camille's husband. It's been William all long!

But Avery didn't have long to think about her discovery, as just then she heard footsteps and the sound of the doorknob turning. She considered leaping across the room and trying to lock it, but she didn't know where the key was and she wanted to avoid a confrontation at all costs. She could plead a sore stomach or a headache, she could dash past him as soon as it opened, anything but try to barricade the door and let him know that she knew.

But when the door opened, it was clear that William did know. His eyes scanned the room, taking in the fallen jacket, the coat-hanger dangling from her fingers, the table and, she imagined, the fear reflected in her gaze.

He was holding a champagne bottle in one hand, two glasses in the other, but the second his eyes met hers, he kicked the door shut behind him and calmly set the glasses on the table. He was still holding the neck of the champagne bottle as he began to slowly stalk towards her, and even if she'd wanted to scream, the lump in her throat stole her voice and left her powerless to make a sound.

Chapter Twenty-One

CAMILLE

Camille reached into her bag as she walked through the hotel, placing her hand on the pistol and wrapping her fingers around it. She felt calm, as if every step of the past year had been building up to this moment, and she was ready for it. She'd made peace with the fact that it might not make her feel any better, that it would do nothing to ease the pain that ached so deeply inside of her, but at least she'd know that she'd done everything she could to avenge her husband's death. And to stop anyone else being deceived – to prevent more lives being lost.

When she neared the bar, Camille slowly and steadily took the gun from her bag and pressed it into the man's back, snug against his spine.

'Hello James,' she murmured.

He stilled and she didn't move, careful to keep her body tucked close to his so that no one could see what she was holding. But the men in the hotel bar were too busy drinking and smoking to notice a woman with a gun, anyway – she may as well have been invisible. All they saw was a pretty face – beyond that, they didn't seem to register a thing. She might have been amused if the situation were different.

'Turn around. Slowly,' she said, taking the pressure off a little but still keeping the pistol closely trained on him.

'Camille, what are you doing?' he asked, staring steadily into her eyes when he turned.

She was surprised by how calm he was, but then she supposed that a man like him was used to talking his way out of tricky situations, of deceiving those around him. But she wasn't going to let him talk his way out of this one, and she most definitely wasn't going to let him do anything that took her attention off the gun in her hand.

'I know who you are, James. I know that you're a double agent, that you've been working for the Nazis,' she said, keeping her voice low as she glared at him. 'I know you've been in France.'

It seemed that he was an even better actor than she had thought. His eyes widened, and a look passed over his face that seemed like pure disbelief. Camille could see why Avery had been so easily fooled by him.

'You're the man responsible for my husband's death, for betraying us, for the deaths of countless Jewish families,' she hissed. 'Don't even try to deny it.'

James used his head to indicate the drink he was holding, a short glass still a quarter full of liquor. 'May I?'

She nodded, but she didn't look at the glass, keeping her gaze on him. It would be too easy for him to knock the gun from her hand or even turn it on her with one swift movement.

James downed the drink and gently placed it on the bar, his movements slow.

'Camille, I'm not your double agent,' he said. 'You have the wrong man.'

She just stared at him.

'You're lying. I know where you've been, I've been tracking you.'

'Camille, please,' he said, grunting when she pushed the pistol into his stomach, moving closer to him, making it look to anyone else like she was about to press a kiss to his jaw.

'I'm telling you, you have the wrong man.'

'Shut up,' she muttered. 'You're going to turn when I tell you to, and we're going to walk towards the lobby and out on to the street. You're not going to call for help or try to be your own hero. You're going to do as I say.'

'Camille,' he said. 'I can prove I'm not your double agent, but I know who is. I can explain where I've been, I—'

'You've been in France, James. I know exactly where you've been and what you've done. I have proof.'

'I had to pretend I was in France to convince the real double agent that he could trust me. I fed him false information, to plant a trap before having him arrested. I can walk you through every step of it if you want, but you have to believe me.' He paused. 'Just lower the gun and we can go somewhere quiet and talk.'

Her instincts were to soften her hold on the gun, but she ignored them, clenching her fingers even tighter. He was trying to sow doubt in her mind, and it was working.

'You're lying.'

'I'm here at this bar tonight waiting for him. My instructions are to keep a close eye, not let him know that we're on to him, and then my station head will have him arrested, but I haven't been able to find him yet,' James said. 'You have to believe me, Camille.'

'I've spent so long trying to understand what happened the night my husband died, who betrayed us, how someone could have infiltrated our network and used information against us,' she said, blinking away tears now, 'and I'm determined to understand why no one saw this coming.'

'Camille, I don't know how your husband died, but I do know that this man is responsible for selling classified information to the Nazis for personal gain. He is paid predominantly in jewellery stolen from wealthy Jewish families, which he sends home to London, and we've just intercepted one such parcel. The evidence I have is irrefutable, and if you'd give me the chance to explain myself without that gun trained on me, I will explain everything. *I promise.*'

Camille took a step back then, her hand starting to shake as James's words ran through her mind. She closed her eyes for a split second, saw the family standing before her, the family whose faces had haunted her ever since that night, coming to her in her dreams, leaving her wondering if they were already dead. Imagining their fates and making her more determined than ever to find out who was responsible. Benoit had told her to focus on staying alive, and to do everything in her power to get what he was covertly sending her from France to their Allied friends, which she'd been doing through Avery.

The pocket watch. The diamond and platinum pocket watch. She pressed the gun against James again even as her thoughts jumbled. What he'd said about being paid in jewellery had set off a light bulb in her mind.

'The watch,' she gasped. 'He had the watch.'

'Who had what watch?' James asked, looking confused.

'William was wearing the watch,' she whispered. 'On the night my husband was killed, when we were ambushed, we were meeting a Jewish family to help them escape France to safety. The man had a watch, he'd shown it to us when we'd agreed to help him. He'd tried to give it to us as payment, to ensure their safety, but we told him that he'd need all his valuables to secure safe passage to America when he reached Portugal.'

James was intently staring at her, listening.

'He was pouring champagne and he checked the time, the diamonds were glittering under the lights, and I recognised it but I couldn't put my finger on it.'

'Who, Camille? Who had this watch? When?'

'William,' she murmured. 'William had the watch.'

'*William* is the double agent, Camille, not me. He's the man I'm after. I can show you all the evidence I have. You can have whatever you need for me to prove this to you, but you have to believe me that the person you're hunting is the very same person I'm following. He's our mutual enemy here.'

William had played her like a fool! He'd even flaunted the stolen watch, not realising that she'd seen it before, not knowing what it meant to her.

But worst of all, she'd trusted him with Avery.

James reached out and placed his hand slowly on the pistol, gently pushing it away, and she let him, until it was hanging from her fingertips at her side.

'Put that back in your bag before someone sees it,' he said. 'And tell me everything you know about William and his whereabouts. If he thinks you recognised the watch, it's anyone's guess what he'll do next.'

'He couldn't know. There's no way he'd make that connection, I'm certain of it.'

James shook his head. 'He's known for some time who you are, Camille. It's one of the reasons I was so determined to catch him out, to protect you from him, so I wouldn't leave anything to chance.'

Her blood ran cold. 'You think he'd hurt me? Here, in Lisbon?'

'I don't know what a man like him is capable of, and if I'm honest, I don't want to find out. But I'd say he's the type to do anything he has to in order to hide his tracks.'

James turned to order drinks for them, calling out to the bartender and holding up two fingers, but Camille was frozen to the spot. When he passed her a glass, she just lifted her gaze to meet his.

'James,' she whispered, her heart beginning to hammer in her chest. 'Do you think he'd hurt Avery?'

She thought he was going to drop the glass he was holding. His entire face drained of colour, going white as a sheet, as he stared back at her.

'*Avery?* What does Avery have to do with this?'

'She was here with him tonight, when I saw his watch,' Camille said. 'They left together.'

'Avery is with William? She's with him now?'

Camille nodded, fear racing through her body as James put his glass back on the bar and grabbed hold of her hand.

'Which way did they go? Where were they heading?'

'I saw them walk out into the lobby, that's all I know. They might have gone elsewhere in the hotel, but equally he could have walked her home.' Camille racked her brain. 'No, she told me that he doesn't know where she lives. She has a thing about wanting to keep her address secret, something about someone giving her a tip when she first arrived.'

'Quickly, follow me.'

They ran out to the lobby and James shouted to the concierge, the panic in his voice palpable.

'Have you seen a pretty woman with dark-blonde hair and a British man? He has mid-brown hair, blue eyes, taller than me,' James asked. 'I need you to think very carefully about who came through the lobby.'

'She was wearing a calf-length navy dress, her hair was twisted up and he was in a suit,' Camille added. 'They would have passed through here perhaps half an hour ago, maybe less.'

The man frowned. 'I can't give out personal information about our guests. You must understand—'

James took a step closer, and for the first time Camille saw his temper. 'A woman's life is in danger, so spare me the privacy speech. Did you see them or not? I need to know who's come past you tonight.'

The concierge shook his head. 'No, I didn't see them come through the lobby together, but a British man fitting your description came down from his room asking for champagne not ten minutes ago. He'd left his bottle in the bar and we arranged a new one for him.'

'That's him! He had champagne, I had a glass before I left.'

'Where did he go?' James demanded, and she noticed his fists balled at his sides, his jaw clenched.

'To his room, sir. He went up in the elevator five minutes ago.'

'Which room!' James demanded. 'Tell me what floor he's on!'

The man went to hold up his hands but James reached into his pocket and pulled out a handful of cash, slamming it on to the counter. 'Tell me the room he's in, and if he hurts her before I get there, then I will hold you personally responsible.'

The man reached for his book, frantically flicking through pages, tracing his finger down a row of names. It felt like it took forever, but the more James glowered at him, the more the poor man's hands shook.

'Room 305.'

Camille turned to James, but he was already gone, running through the hotel lobby, past the door to the elevator and heading up the stairs. Any doubts she might have had about him completely disappeared, and she thanked the concierge, took off her heels, and ran after him. Her whole body was trembling, her mind racing, imagining the very worst of scenarios.

If anything happened to Avery, she'd never forgive herself.

Chapter Twenty-Two

AVERY

Avery edged backwards until her shoulders touched the wall. William had known the moment he'd walked into the room, his eyes flashing with recognition, like a wolf cornering its prey.

He reached behind him and pushed the door shut, and Avery tried to count how many steps it would be if she ran to the bathroom. But William was tall, and she imagined he was fast, and even if he didn't manage to intercept her, he'd surely grab hold of the door and stop her from slamming it shut.

Her heart was pounding, her fingers reaching behind her for something, *anything*, that she might use to protect herself, but all she had was the coat-hanger, and she doubted that was going to do her any good against a man considerably bigger than her.

'Avery, Avery,' he said, shaking his head. 'I never thought you were the kind of girl to snoop, otherwise I wouldn't have left you in here alone. But you couldn't help yourself, could you?'

'I went to hang your jacket up,' she said, hating the shake in her voice. 'That's all.'

'But you had to take a look in the pocket, is that it?'

'Why do you have Camille's name on your list?' she asked, deciding there was no point in pretending she didn't know what he was talking about.

He edged closer, moving slowly, his eyes never leaving hers, and for the first time in her life, Avery understood fear. She understood what it was to see her life flash before her eyes, to wonder if she was ever going to see her parents again; her sister, Jack. All the things she wished she could say to them echoed through her mind.

You need to talk him down. Focus on calming him. Make him think you're on his side. Don't ask him anything.

'William, you can trust me,' she said. 'The way I feel about you hasn't changed, I just want to understand what I'm getting myself into, what you're involved in. That's all.'

His smile scared her, and she knew then that he wasn't going to let her out of this room. The only way she was leaving was if she could find a way past him, to fight her way to the door, and if she'd been a betting woman, she wouldn't have liked the odds.

'William, please. Can we not sit down and talk about this like adults? Can we not just have a conversation?'

'It didn't have to be like this, Avery,' he said, taking another step forward and placing the champagne bottle on the bedside table. 'We could have been happy, you and I, but now I have to figure out what to do with the American girl who ruined everything.'

Anger flared inside of her, and she realised that if she had no chance of making it out there alive, then she wasn't going to waste her last breaths trying to placate him. 'I could never be happy with someone like you, William. The kind of weak, despicable man who would turn his back on his own country, who could have blood on his hands, and for what? Money? You make me sick.'

He laughed and started to clap, and she moved when he did, edging her way along the wall.

'What a courageous speech. Bravo, Avery. Who would have thought you had that in you?' His grin chilled her to the bone. 'A weak man wouldn't make a deal with the devil though,' he said, his voice getting louder and louder until he was almost shouting. 'A weak man wouldn't be rolling in seized jewellery or have priceless French paintings being shipped to his house in London. Do you hear me? Only a man with a backbone could do what I've done. Could *get away* with what I've done.'

Avery took her chance when he lunged forward, darting to the right, taking her further away from the bathroom but closer to the door of the room. She moved as quickly as she could, a scream lodged in her throat as William reached out to catch her.

He missed, tripping as he did so, but just when the door handle was almost within reach, he caught her around the ankle, his fingers closing tightly around the bone as she fell and hit the ground, landing hard on her hip.

William dragged her towards him as she clawed frantically at the ground, kicking as hard as she could and hearing a grunt from him that suggested at least one of her feet had connected. But he was too strong for her, and his knee was on her thigh, digging into her flesh, his hands reaching for her throat.

'No!' she screamed, finding her voice, crying for help. 'Get off me!'

But his hands found their target then as he straddled her, as she kicked and flailed and tried with everything she had to get away from him while he pressed so hard on her windpipe that she thought it would snap.

Do something! Fight harder! Make him stop!

The voice in Avery's head became louder, and as he choked her she reached up and clawed at his eyes, stretching so far and so hard that it felt like her shoulders were going to pop from their sockets. But she was not giving in this easily. He was not going to strangle

241

her on the floor of his hotel room and get away with her murder and everything else he'd done.

Her nails connected with his eyes and his howl of pain gave her the strength she needed, and as his fingers loosened she kept on clawing, a wild cat fighting for her life.

Avery scratched and kicked, sinking her teeth into his arm when it came close enough. And it was all she needed to get away, kicking hard at him when he lunged at her, scrambling on her hands and knees towards the door. He caught her but she kept on kicking with all her might, knowing that if she didn't get away this time, she might not have another chance.

She reached for the door, her fingers closing around the knob, and she turned and yanked it open, pulling herself up and falling into the hallway, landing hard and slamming her head against the opposite wall as he grabbed her. She felt her body being pulled back into the room as she frantically tried to dig her nails into the wallpaper so he couldn't get her in there again.

'Let go!' she screamed, fighting with everything she had as William hauled her into the room.

But as he pulled her, as Avery frantically looked up for help, screaming, she saw James running towards her.

'Let go of her!' James shouted.

William didn't relent, and when she glanced at him, kicking as hard as she could, she didn't see the man she'd only an hour earlier been sitting with in the hotel bar: charming, engaging and sophisticated. The man who'd so easily convinced her to come upstairs with him. Now, she saw a man with his hair sticking up and his eyes wide, his mouth pulled back into a sneer. This man was fighting for his life as much as she was fighting for hers.

'I said let go of her!' James shouted again, as he grabbed hold of her arms.

But it wasn't James who stopped William.

A gunshot echoed out, the noise so loud that Avery felt as if the bullet had whirred past her head. It was a bang that reverberated through her and left her ear ringing, her jaw aching as she tried to move it up and down to clear her ear canal; as if she'd travelled up a mountain and it was blocked.

But it was the violent hold on her ankle disappearing that surprised her the most, then the feeling of James pulling her forward, tugging her to the safety of his arms, holding her against his chest.

Avery stared over his shoulder at Camille, who was standing, her arm raised, a pistol held steady in her hand, until her shoulders slumped as if she couldn't believe what she'd done. Or perhaps she did know, and she was collapsing in relief. It was William she'd shot, and not James.

'You bitch.'

Avery had just closed her eyes when she was yanked backwards, and she turned in horror to see William, blood soaking through the shoulder of his shirt, trying to pull her away from James. She was flung to the floor when James shoved him, the two of them tumbling backwards into the hotel room, a blur of limbs as punches were thrown and they fought on the ground.

Avery scrambled back on her heels, palms to the floor, scooting close to Camille who had the pistol raised again. But Camille didn't have a clear line of sight. If she fired, it would be anyone's guess who she would shoot.

'Camille, no,' Avery cried.

But James was on the ground now. William was taller and bigger than him, and even with a gunshot wound to the shoulder, Avery knew there was a chance that he could kill James with his bare hands and then come for her again.

She wanted to run and scream for help, couldn't stop wondering how no one had come out of their rooms, but it was mostly men staying here and she could only guess that they were downstairs in the bar.

Avery closed her eyes, too scared to watch, wrapping her arms around her knees and squeezing as hard as she could, trying to ignore the searing pain from where William had grabbed her. The pain in her throat was even worse, on fire from when he'd tried to choke her, and she wondered if her voice would ever return to normal.

But then the pistol fired again. The noise was as loud as the first time, but it sounded different, as if it had been fired at close range. When Avery opened her eyes, she saw William had fallen, blood seeping through his shirt, but he wasn't the only one bleeding.

Somehow, while Avery's eyes were squeezed tightly shut, he'd turned the gun on Camille. Camille was staggering towards her, her dress pooling with blood, her hands already red from pressing against her wound. William's eyes were open but vacant, as if they were made of glass, and James was lying on the ground, breathing heavily, a knife beside him.

'Camille?' Avery cried, forcing her legs to work as she launched herself forward to catch her, guiding her body to the ground.

'Shot me,' she whispered. 'The bastard shot me.'

Avery placed Camille's hand firmly over her wound, cradling her for a moment, easing her back so she could lean against the wall. Then she got up and raced over to James, just as he was getting up, his cheek bruised and his eye already swelling over.

'James?' she whispered, hovering over him. 'Where are you hurt?'

'I'm fine. You?' He ran his eyes over her, as if to inspect every inch of her to make sure she was intact.

'Go to her,' he urged, his fingers against William's neck.

Avery had to look away. She couldn't stand to see William's body like that, his eyes open, the blood pooling on the carpet beneath him. But she knew she had to have a stronger stomach for Camille – her friend's life might depend on her being capable, and she had no intention of letting her down.

'You saved my life back there,' Avery whispered, scared to see how much blood was trickling through Camille's fingers as she held her wound.

'You would have done the same for me,' Camille whispered back.

Avery didn't know what to do. She crouched down, her hands fluttering, wanting to take care of her friend but not knowing how. She looked back to James and saw that he was now striding towards them, his face tense, set in a line that told her he was as worried as she was.

'You need to get Camille out of here,' James ordered, as he tore off his jacket and shirt, ripping it in half to tie it around her wound, stemming the blood flow. 'Take her somewhere safe and do everything you can to stop her bleeding.'

Avery could only imagine how helpless she looked as she stared up at James, but he caught her hand in his and stared deep into her eyes.

'I don't have any medical training other than basic first aid,' she said quietly, not wanting Camille to hear. 'She needs to go to a hospital, she needs a doctor or at the very least a nurse who knows what she's doing, but that person isn't me.'

'No hospital,' Camille whispered.

Avery shook her head. 'No, she *needs* a hospital. I don't see that it's a choice!'

'Hospital means questions, and I'm guessing you're here on false papers?' James asked, looking past Avery to Camille. 'She'll be arrested if we're not careful, we all could be, and you're more capable than you're giving yourself credit for.'

Camille nodded, then groaned as she writhed on the spot, her hands still pressed against her side as Avery watched, feeling more helpless than she ever had in her life.

'Your job is to stop the bleeding, make sure she's warm and keep her fluids up,' James instructed.

'I can't do this without you, James. You need to help me, to—'

'I have to clean up here, Avery. There are going to be questions, and if I don't stay here and deal with the mess, the PVDE will be searching for all three of us and charging us with murder,' James said. 'You need to get her out of here before anyone sees you, and leave the rest to me. I'll be there to help just as soon as I can, but you can do this. I believe in you.'

He went into William's hotel room then, stepping over the body and emerging with a coat.

'Put this over her so no one sees the blood, and take her to the bookshop. Do you hear me?'

Avery swallowed, tears burning her eyes as James hauled Camille to her feet, and Avery put her arm around her friend to support her weight.

'I'll help you get her into the elevator, then it's over to you.'

She nodded, keeping a hold around Camille's waist, knowing that she'd find the strength to carry her if she had to, to get her to safety. It wasn't that she didn't want to help, she just had no idea if she'd be able to save her.

Camille wobbled to the elevator, her feet dragging. James took most of her weight, pressing the button then standing back, his eyes meeting Avery's.

'You can do this, Avery. You're all she's got. Now go.'

Chapter Twenty-Three

CAMILLE

Every step hurt. Every time Camille lifted her left foot, she felt more pain than ever before as it ran up her leg and exploded in her side.

She placed her hand there again, and it came away wet. Sticky. She recoiled, lurching forward and being sick all over the pavement.

'Come on, we have to keep going. Just one step after another.'

'Can't. Keep. Going.' Each word was painful, almost impossible to push out, and Camille groaned as Avery adjusted her hold on her.

'I can't carry you. You have to keep moving.' She could hear the pain in Avery's voice, hear her start to cry. 'I can't lose you, Camille. Please, just keep going. Do it for me.'

Tears slipped down her cheeks as she held on to Avery, trying so hard to stay upright. But it was just so, so hard.

'Just a few more steps,' Avery whispered. 'Keep going. Keep walking.'

Camille stumbled, falling against a door as Avery fumbled in her pockets, cursing as more pain spiralled through her. Then she realised they were at the bookshop. But when she tried to speak, the words caught in her throat, the pain in her side so severe that it was like she'd been set on fire, the agony searing straight through her insides.

The pain only intensified when the door opened and she fell through, and suddenly she was being dragged across the floor in the dark, heard the sound of a door shutting, of someone crying, panting, breathing too heavily, and she wondered if it was her or someone else.

'Hugo?' she murmured, reaching out when she heard a voice. 'Hugo, is that you?'

'It's me. Camille, it's me, Avery?'

'Avery?' She wasn't sure if the word had even come out of her mouth. *Avery*. Of course it was Avery. But she'd been so certain she'd heard Hugo's voice, that she'd felt him beside her.

'You've lost a lot of blood and the bullet wound . . .' She could hear Avery, but her friend was starting to sound as if she were talking to Camille from far away, her voice almost like it was disappearing down a tunnel.

'So tired,' Camille whispered as her eyes fluttered shut. 'I'm just so tired.'

'Stay awake!' she heard Avery cry. 'You have to hold this here, against your side. We have to stop the bleeding so I can figure out what to do next.'

Camille tried to keep her hand where Avery had placed it, against her side, but it hurt so much, and every time she pressed it, she cried out in pain. She thought she heard someone else crying too, but everything seemed blurry, as if the room and Avery and what had happened were all mixing together while she tried to focus.

'Where's James?' she asked, suddenly confused. 'Did something happen to him? I—'

'Shhh, James is fine. Remember we left him to, well, to clean everything up,' Avery said. 'Now this might hurt, but I'm going to tie this sheet around you, tightly, to try to stop the bleeding.'

Camille wondered then if Avery had taken her starched white tablecloth from her display at the front of the store, but she didn't have long to wonder before Avery moved her, positioning the sheet beneath her and tying it so tight that Camille fell into darkness, as if she were tumbling down a hole that went on and on, each spasm of pain sending her deeper, further away from Avery.

'Hugo?'

Camille reached out a hand, smiling as he came towards her, his wide grin telling her that it had to be him, that he was really there. She tried to touch his face, to palm his cheek, but every time she reached for him, he was just a little too far away.

'Hugo?' she said again, stepping forward as she tried to get to him.

She was so certain he was there, that if she could just move a little faster, just reach a little further, she'd be able to connect with him.

'Hugo!' she cried this time, as something started shaking her, and her husband faded away as if he'd never been there in the first place.

But when she opened her eyes, it wasn't Hugo staring down at her, it was Avery; her eyes were wide and she looked like she'd been crying, they were so red.

'Hugo was here,' Camille murmured.

But as Avery stroked her forehead and whispered something she couldn't hear, she realised that Hugo had never been there. Her mind was playing cruel tricks on her as her body fought to stay alive, pain continuing to ricochet through her.

'It's just you and me, Camille,' Avery said, softly, one of her hands reaching down to clasp hers. 'You just have to hang on, you have to fight this, because I'm not losing you. Do you hear me? I'm not losing you, Camille.'

'I know,' Camille whispered. Avery bent low over her, her ear almost to Camille's lips. 'I know now, who did it. I know who betrayed us.'

'And he's gone now,' Avery said, pressing a kiss to her cheek. 'Now you get to live, Camille. You get to live for Hugo; he'd want you to live.'

Camille nodded, slowly, but it was a nod. Seeing Hugo had made her want to slide away from the world and reach out to him, but Avery was right. She needed to live now. She needed Hugo's death not to have been for nothing.

She heard a noise then, turning her head as far as she could to see what Avery was doing. Avery was on her hands and knees, and Camille watched as she lifted the loose floorboard and took something out.

It wasn't until Avery lifted Camille's hand that she knew what she was doing.

Camille stared down at her hand as Avery slipped the gold band on her finger. Her wedding ring. The ring she'd taken off the day Hugo was killed.

'You stay alive for him, Camille,' Avery cried, leaning over her. 'He would want you to live, do you hear me? He wouldn't want this to be the end.'

Camille moved her thumb enough to touch the ring, the familiar round edges, the coolness against her skin. And she couldn't help but wish she'd never taken it off in the first place.

Chapter Twenty-Four

AVERY

'I'm sorry,' Camille gasped, her fingers sliding against Avery's as she regained consciousness, her eyes fluttering open. 'I'm so sorry.'

Avery held her tightly in her arms, collapsed on the floor of the shop. There was nothing more she could do other than pray. She was no medic, and Camille's injuries were beyond her basic first-aid training, but it was heartening to see her with her eyes open and managing to talk again.

'You have nothing to apologise for,' Avery told her, trying to smile but failing. Her body kept shaking, and she was terrified, not able to stop her tears even though she was trying so, so hard to be brave.

'But he wasn't, he . . .' Camille gasped. 'Tell James I'm sorry, that I never should have doubted him.'

'Shhh,' Avery whispered. 'James is fine. All I care about is you pulling through this. You need to conserve your energy.'

Camille was gasping now, and Avery's shoulders shuddered as she tried to stop crying, the pain in Camille's every breath impossible to ignore. She couldn't help but think about Jack and how many friends he'd lost when he was overseas, about all the men serving and the horrors they were faced with.

'How did I miss him? He was right in front of me, he—'

'Shhh,' Avery tried again. 'Please, Camille, just rest. You need to rest.' *I don't give a damn about anything else now, Camille. I just want you to live. Live, goddamn it!* 'None of it matters anymore.'

'You're . . . a good friend, Avery,' Camille murmured as her eyes fluttered shut. 'You're the best friend I've ever had.'

Avery slumped low over Camille, her tears merging with the blood on Camille's skin, smeared all across her hands. *How did this happen? How was I such a fool that I didn't see who,* what *he was?*

There was a thump, thump on the door then, sending a shiver of terror through her.

'Don't let them in,' Camille whispered, lucid, her eyes wide. 'You can't trust them.'

Avery nodded and kissed her forehead. 'I won't let them in. I'll fight until my very last breath to keep you safe, Camille. I promise.'

But when she peered out from the office, creeping through the store to see out into the almost-dark, her heart leapt. It wasn't the PVDE, it was James. She dashed through the shop as quickly as she could, fumbling with the key as she hurried to open it for him.

'James!' She threw her arms around him, holding him as tightly as she could.

He kept one arm around her and manoeuvred them both inside, shutting the door and locking it behind them before engulfing her in his arms. His mouth was pressed to her neck, his embrace warm and solid as she cried.

'I don't think she's going to make it. I don't—'

'Where is she?' he asked.

Avery took his hand and led him to the backroom where she had Camille on the floor, her head propped up on a blanket she'd found folded in the office and the coat they'd taken from William over her to keep her warm.

'There was so much blood, and I've done my best but she's . . .' Avery didn't even want to say it. *She looks like she's dying. James. My friend is lying on the floor dying and there's nothing I can do about it other than watch her slip away.* 'She needs to go to a hospital,' she said, instead. Because it was true; if Camille had any chance at all of surviving, she needed proper medical treatment. 'I know you said we couldn't, but she's going to die if we don't,' she whispered.

'Can you see the bullet?' James asked. 'If we can get the bullet out, she has a chance at pulling through.'

Avery's stomach turned at the thought of looking at all that blood again, of touching her friend's flesh and trying to fish out a piece of metal from inside of her. 'I couldn't see it, I just tried to stop the blood and—'

'James,' Camille gasped, her eyes suddenly flickering open. 'I'm sorry.'

'You'll have plenty of time to apologise to me another day. Right now, I'm going to get Avery to hold you down and I'm going to try to get this bullet out of you.'

Camille groaned.

'Avery, we need boiled water, anything that resembles a clean cloth, and something sterile to dig the bullet out.'

Avery's eyes widened. 'Do you even know what you're doing? Do you—'

'I know enough, and right now I'm the best she's got,' he said with a grimace. 'Can you find those supplies? And we're going to need a needle and thread. We can sterilise the needle in a flame.'

Avery started to nod her head, unable to stop, her body in shock.

'We don't have long, Avery. Every minute counts.'

An hour later, Avery and James sat side by side, shoulder to shoulder, backs against the wall and their knees drawn up. She'd cried so many tears she was dry, her eyes raw, her skin still covered in her friend's blood. All they could do now was wait – to see if Camille would pull through, or perish right there on the floor of the bookshop she loved so much.

'Do you think she's going to make it?' Avery whispered.

James had his head tipped back against the wall, his eyes shut, arms resting on his knees. Camille's blood was dried beneath his nails and streaking the skin of his arms. He even had it on his jawline, and if she hadn't been so exhausted, so drained of every ounce of energy, Avery would have lifted her hand and turned to him to wipe it away. But instead she just sat, turning her gaze back to Camille, who was lying on the floor still, covered in two jackets in an effort to keep her warm.

'James?' Avery asked, her voice husky and sounding like it belonged to someone else.

'I don't know,' he said. 'I want to tell you that she'll be fine, but I honestly just don't know.'

Tears filled Avery's eyes again, just when she'd thought she had none left, but she appreciated him telling her the truth.

'I'm sorry about what happened, about William, about—'

'Avery, we're long past apologies,' James said, reaching for her hand without even looking at her. He linked their fingers, his hold firm. 'You're alive, we're both here now, that's all that matters. All I care about is that you're right here beside me, right now.'

Avery didn't even have the words to tell him how deeply, truly sorry she was for not believing in him. She'd owed him that, and instead she'd let herself be swayed from what she'd known in her heart. 'I can't believe I ever doubted you.'

He pulled her against him, his arm around her shoulders as she nestled closer, placing her cheek to his chest. James was steady. He made her heart flutter at the same time as making her feel as if she'd found her way home; strong enough to protect her yet soft enough to wrap his arms around her and kiss her under a street light for everyone to see. She'd fallen in love with James from the night they'd talked at the hotel, blushing under his gaze as he'd teased her for being a librarian, only she hadn't wanted to admit it.

'Camille had every reason to suspect me,' he said. 'I was feeding William information about the Allies; it's why I had to leave Lisbon for a while, it was all part of my ruse to draw William in. I needed him to believe that I was playing the same game as he was, that I was prepared to trade information for my own personal gain. So she wasn't wrong.'

'I wish you could have told me, that I'd known something about what you were doing.'

'So do I, but I couldn't tell anyone, Avery. I've been closing in on him for months, it's why I was sent to Lisbon in the first place.' He sighed. 'It's been a long time waiting him out. He was clever, I'll give him that, but we knew someone was betraying us and it only took so long for me to put two and two together.'

'How did you figure out it was him? I mean, before tonight, before he tried to . . .' Her voice trailed off. She didn't even want to talk about what had almost happened to her, what *had* happened to Camille.

'I fed him false information,' he said. 'Then, just as expected, he told his Nazi friends.'

She was silent as she considered what he'd just told her, tilting her head to look up at him. 'James, do you think we're going to win this war?'

'Yes,' he said, without hesitation. 'If you'd asked me six months ago, I might have given you a different answer. But yes, Avery, I very much think we're going to win this war.'

'And William?' she asked, trying to push the thoughts of his crumpled body on the floor outside the hotel room from her mind, hating that she'd been so close to doing something she would regret earlier that night, wishing she'd never gone to his room.

'It's been taken care of. That's all you have to know.'

Avery glanced over at Camille, who still had her eyes shut, and she was thankful she'd passed out before James had pulled the bullet from her side. But she was worried that Camille might not wake up at all, and that she might never look into her beautiful blue eyes or feel the warmth of her smile ever again. Avery couldn't imagine never walking into the bookshop again, or how she'd even stay in Lisbon if Camille didn't make it.

'How about you get some rest,' James said. 'I'll keep an eye on Camille.'

She wanted to resist, but she was so desperately tired, and as James's fingers stroked back and forth against her skin, Avery couldn't help but shut her eyes. *Please be alive when I wake up, Camille. It's not your time to go yet, you have to stay alive.*

'In the morning I'll find her the painkillers and antibiotics she needs,' James murmured, as Avery pressed herself against him and finally drifted off to sleep. 'We just have to pray that she wakes up.'

Chapter Twenty-Five

AVERY

Avery walked into the bookshop, trying not to think about it being the last time she'd ever do so. She'd been overwhelmed with emotion all morning, but with only a few hours left on Portuguese soil, she was trying to tell herself to soak up every last second. She could collapse later, when she was on the dreaded plane back to New York.

'Avery?'

Her face broke out into a smile as Camille called her name. Avery hurried towards her, not wanting Camille to have to move. She was still slower than usual after what had happened a month ago, but one thing that had never changed was her beautiful smile that still managed to light up the shop.

'I was worried you'd left without saying goodbye.'

'Never,' Avery said as she wrapped her arms around Camille. 'I could never leave without saying goodbye to you.'

They held on for longer than usual; the kind of tight, heartfelt hug that was reserved for loved ones. When they finally let go of each other, Avery found herself brushing away tears.

'I can't believe they're sending you home,' Camille said.

'It didn't matter what I said, after everything that's happened, they wanted me back. I have to go to Washington for a full debrief,' she said. 'But Tom is staying on for now, and he knows you're the best little bookshop in Lisbon.'

'It's not going to be the same without you here, Avery.'

She knew exactly how Camille felt, because it wasn't going to be the same for her either.

'I don't know when or how, but I have to believe that we'll see each other again,' Avery said. 'I can't imagine that this is the last time.'

'Who knows, I might get passage on one of those big ships heading for New York with everyone else. America doesn't sound so bad, you know?'

Avery's eyebrows shot up in surprise. 'You've considered it?'

'For one fleeting moment when I saw the refugees all lined up yesterday, and again right now when I realised my dearest friend was actually leaving.'

Avery sighed and brushed away a fresh batch of tears. 'You could, you know,' she said, softly. 'If you ever wanted to, if it was something you wanted to consider . . .'

Camille caught her hand and squeezed it. 'I know. But until all the refugees are gone, my work here isn't complete. I can't turn my back on them when someone new might still need me.'

'Well, you put that camera to good use for me, and know that if I could have stayed to help, I would have.'

'You're sure you won't be in trouble for not returning it?'

'I intend on telling them I was robbed on the streets of Lisbon. They can't blame me for that, can they?'

When she finally let go, Camille reached under the counter and took out a book.

'I actually have a parting gift for you. Something to remember me by,' Camille said, handing it to Avery. 'It's an old book, but I wanted to give you something French.'

'*Madame Bovary*, by Gustave Flaubert,' Avery said out loud, and then she felt her cheeks heat. Trust Camille. 'I know this one.'

Camille laughed. 'It's naughty but worth the read. I thought it might keep you occupied on your travels home.'

Avery glanced at her wristwatch then and knew she had to leave. She only had an hour before she had to be back at her apartment to collect her luggage.

'It's time for you to go, isn't it?' Camille asked.

'It is,' she said, tucking the book into her bag and embracing Camille one last time. 'I'm going to miss you, so much. Just promise me you'll stay out of trouble; I can't stand the thought of anything happening to you without me here.'

'I will, and I'm going to miss you, too,' Camille whispered. 'More than you'll ever know.'

When Avery began to pull away, Camille placed her hands on Avery's elbows and drew her in for a kiss on each cheek.

'Safe travels, my friend.'

Avery took a deep, shaky breath and blew a kiss to Camille as she walked away, knowing that if she dared look back, she might never leave.

The tables at the Pastelaria Suíça were as crowded as ever, and Avery sat at one in the sunshine and opened the book Camille had given her, smiling when the note fell out. It reminded her of the last time Camille had done that. Avery still had her copy of *Gone with the Wind*, packed safely in her luggage, from that day.

Dear Avery,

Words are often easier to write than say out loud, or at least that's true for me. You're the closest I'll ever have to a sister, and I want you to know how much you've come to mean to me. Lisbon will not be the same without you.

Think of me every time you walk into a bookshop in New York, and know that you will never be far from my thoughts. You are the bravest and most loyal friend I've ever had. I owe my life to you.

Camille.

'I thought we'd save the tears for *after* you left.'

Avery slipped the note back into the book and closed it, tucking it into her bag before looking up at James. It gave her a moment to stop crying.

'It was a parting gift, from Camille,' she said. 'It's made me all sorts of homesick for Lisbon, and I haven't even left yet.'

'I haven't brought a gift, but I did arrange for all your favourite cakes and sweets to be brought out,' James said, waving to the waiter.

Avery was puzzled until she saw two waiters returning with four plates of cakes and pastries. 'James! There's no possible way we can eat all that.'

He shrugged. 'I remembered all the things you loved the most, and I knew you'd never find cakes as good in America. We can just have a bite of each if you like, and give the leftovers to the children playing in the square.'

'I knew there was a reason I liked you.' She sighed and picked up one of the little forks. 'And thank you. This was incredibly thoughtful.'

'I thought it might be a nice distraction from the fact you're leaving. I've never been one for goodbyes.'

Suddenly the cake went dry in her mouth and Avery found it hard to swallow.

'I don't want to go,' she said.

'I don't want you to go, either,' he replied, quickly, as if he hadn't even had to think about it.

'Are you staying in Lisbon?' she asked.

'No. I'll be recalled back to London soon and then perhaps posted elsewhere until the end of the war.'

She pushed her fork into a slice of cake, more for something to do than because she wanted a piece. It also meant James couldn't see her tears with her head down.

'Do you think we'll ever see each other again?' she asked, when she finally looked up, and he took her hand in his.

He opened his mouth and then closed it, his fingers still linked with hers. 'I hope so, Avery. I certainly hope so.'

They changed the subject and made each other laugh, and Avery fed James mouthfuls of cake on her little fork, until finally she knew it was time to leave and she stood, her hands at her sides, not knowing what to do.

But James took the lead, opening his arms and engulfing her in the kind of bear hug that she would never forget, his mouth against her hair.

'Avery, if I were to ask you to marry me, once this war is over, would you say yes?'

She grinned up at him, thinking he was teasing to begin with, but realising from the earnest way he was looking at her that he was being serious.

'I think a girl would have to be asked first, once the war was over,' she said, standing on tiptoe and kissing his cheek.

James took her hand then and they began the short stroll back to her apartment, through Rossio Square and on to the cobbled streets with buildings on one side and water on the other. Past women balancing fish baskets on their heads, and foreign women with skirts short enough to show their knees, and food markets with locals shouting to each other and laughing, and boys on the street corner polishing shoes.

It wasn't just James she was going to miss, or Camille; it was Lisbon itself. A place so vibrant that it would be etched in her mind forever. The adventure she'd always dreamed of, and the friends who'd stay in her heart until her final breath.

Chapter Twenty-Six

CAMILLE

Camille was nervous every time the bell rang now. The truth was that she was safer than she'd ever been now that she was no longer deceiving a Nazi or trying to hunt for her husband's killer, but she still shivered whenever she thought about that night and how close she'd come to death. Ever since Hugo's passing, she'd thought she wanted to join him to stop the pain, but when she'd been faced with it, she'd realised how much she still wanted to live.

When she saw who was walking towards her, she breathed a sigh of relief.

'Hello, Camille.'

Her shoulders dropped from where she'd had them hunched up. 'Bonjour, James.' She immediately went to him, opening her arms and giving him a warm hug before kissing his cheeks.

He looked surprised, or perhaps just a little bashful at the attention, his cheeks flaring a dark pink.

'I have a feeling you're not calling in just to say hello,' she said. 'But I'm pleased you're here either way.'

Camille went to the door and turned the sign to 'Closed', locking it and beckoning for James to follow her. She took him to the room in the back.

'Coffee?'

He nodded. 'Please.'

She busied herself with making them both a drink and turned around to pass him the cup, sitting on the table so he could take the single chair. It reminded her so much of Avery every time she was in the office, of hearing the constant click of her camera as she worked.

'James, I owe you a proper apology,' she said, as he took a sip of coffee and winced at the temperature. 'I distrusted you for so long, I even tried to make Avery distrust you, and I'm embarrassed my instincts were so wrong.'

His smile was easy, and she wondered how she'd ever missed that. He certainly didn't look like a man with anything to hide.

'We have a saying in English when it's time to let something go, that it's water under the bridge,' he said. 'And it is, Camille. You have nothing left to apologise for because it's already water under the bridge. Truly it is.'

Something inside of her softened and she knew that there were tears glistening in her eyes. 'Thank you.'

'I actually came here today because I have information for you,' James said. 'I thought it might give you some closure.'

Camille watched curiously as he set down his coffee and retrieved an envelope from inside the bag he was carrying. She smiled to herself. *A true spy if ever I've seen one.*

'The reason I was posted to Lisbon in the first place was to hunt for Allied double agents,' James said, tapping the folder as he spoke. 'We knew they were working in Lisbon – it's the best place for it, after all – and so I was sent here under the guise of a journalist to try to figure out the lay of the land, so to speak. I was closing in on William that night, but it all went down rather differently than I'd planned, as you well know.'

She took the envelope when he passed it to her, but James kept hold of it when he saw how much her hands were trembling.

'You don't have to look at any of this information if you don't want to. I'm sending my report back to London today, and you can forget all about my ever coming here if you want to. It's up to you.'

Camille stared at the envelope, her heart beating loudly, but she knew she'd regret it forever if she didn't look. She'd spent every day since Hugo had died seeking revenge and wanting to find out who was responsible, and James was right – it would be closure for her.

'It's time for me to move on from what happened,' she eventually said. 'But to do that, I need to see what's in this file.'

James let go of the envelope and sat back, and she took a deep breath before opening it.

'William was trained in London, recruited into the SOE after being top of his class at Cambridge University,' James said as she slowly ran her eyes over the information in front of her. 'There were no red flags at all, nothing that would have given any of his instructors reason to doubt him, and most of them are still baffled at how he was turned so easily, or that it was him at all.'

'You think he had Nazi links?' she asked, glancing up at him. 'A connection that was missed?'

'It appears he was simply bribed by the lure of wealth,' he said. 'The Nazis were giving him jewellery and other valuables looted from the Jews they arrested, in exchange for information, such as the pocket watch you recognised. It was truly as simple as him putting himself above his country for personal gain.'

Camille sat on that information, trying to digest it and finding it impossibly hard to stomach. 'All this time, I'd thought it would be more complicated. People all over the world are fighting for their country, risking everything because of what they believe in, and he was just looking out for himself?'

'It certainly appears that way,' James said, crossing his legs at the ankles as he nursed his coffee.

'You believe he was responsible for my husband's death?'

James looked at the file then back at her, his gaze steady. 'I am certain, without a doubt, that William was responsible. He's the only double agent that we've identified who was in France at the time of your husband's death.'

'And the family in France who we were supposed to help that night, do you know anything about their fate?' Camille asked. 'Is there any way to find out what happened to them? I know they would have been discovered where they were waiting for us, they would have been like sitting ducks, but I've always hoped . . .'

James shook his head. 'They are presumed dead, although there is always a chance that they made it to a camp and survived.'

Camille closed her eyes and took a deep breath. So that was it. Maybe she would never know what had happened to them, but at least she knew who was responsible for what had happened that night. When she opened her eyes, she was rewarded by James's warm, steady gaze.

'James, have you heard from Avery?' she asked.

'I haven't. Have you?'

She sighed. 'No. I've never been so eager to check the mail in all my life, but I haven't heard anything from her yet.'

They sat in silence for a long moment, James sipping his coffee and her looking over the extensive report that detailed everything James had uncovered about William's duplicity, as well as photographs of jewellery that had been recovered, including the precious watch.

'So what happens next?' she asked, closing the folder and placing it on the table. 'Will you stay in Lisbon?'

'I'm actually taking this report back with me to hand-deliver,' he said. 'I leave for London this afternoon.'

Camille felt an overwhelming sense of being lost. She'd focused on one thing for so long, and now it was over. Avery had gone. James was going. It was all over.

'What will you do?' James asked. 'Will you stay in Lisbon?'

She shrugged and swallowed away her emotion. 'I don't have anywhere else to go. France is my home, but I can't exactly go storming back to Paris, and . . .' She blew out a long, shaky breath. 'I have a bookshop to run. That's as far into the future as I can see right now.' She also had Jewish families who still needed her help until their passage to America was secured.

'I could always talk to my superiors and see if we have a role for you, if there's something you can do for the Allied cause,' James said. 'I'd personally vouch for you, of course.'

Camille rose and went to the office door, staring out at the shop that had been her life for so long now, looking at all the books before turning back to James. 'How about we agree to stay in touch, and if you need me, if you need any information at all, you know where to find me. There's nothing I wouldn't do to help the Allies win this war.'

James rose then and picked up the file, slipping it back inside his bag.

'I guess this is goodbye then,' he said.

'I guess it is,' Camille replied. 'Goodbye, James.'

He gave her a long, steady look, and she almost wondered if he was going to embrace her, but then he nodded and walked back through her store, before unlocking the door and disappearing out on to the street.

She followed slowly behind, reaching up to turn the little red sign around to 'Open' and watching until she couldn't see him any longer. It was then that she saw a little stack of mail outside, to the side of the door. Camille bent to pick it up. The mail must have come while she had the door locked, and she rifled absently through the letters to see what was there. But it was the last one, postmarked New York, that made her gasp.

Camille ran out on to the street, calling for James, searching frantically for him, but he'd already gone. She tore the envelope open, though was careful to preserve the sender's address, and walked slowly back to her shop, reading as she went. Her heart was in her throat from the second she read Avery's words.

Dear Camille,

To say that I miss you would be an understatement. From the day I left Lisbon, I've missed everything about my time there, but mostly, and with all my heart, I've missed you. I keep wondering what you're doing and how you feel, and all I can think is that I should never have left you in Portugal. I know it's not my decision to make, but if you're feeling lost or you're missing me the same way that I'm missing you, please find a way to come here. You'd love New York!

Life here seems so quiet to the life I lived in Lisbon. I'm back working at the library, which is fine, but it's certainly not Portugal, that's for sure. I find myself stacking shelves and walking along the aisles, wishing I could have been posted overseas for longer and imagining what it would be like to travel again once the war is over. But sometimes I can't stop thinking about what happened that night, the violence of it all, about how close you were to dying. Those are the times I wish you were closer so we could talk.

I'm thankful that Michael, the man I was once engaged to, has already married, because otherwise I'm certain my parents would be trying to push us back together. But I came back to America a different woman, and I think even they can sense that. I found that I couldn't live at home with them on my return, so I've found a lovely apartment to rent, with big sash windows and light-filled rooms, but it's too big for me to rent alone and I can't imagine living with anyone other than you.

Anyway, please know that I think of you often. I wanted to write you first, but as soon as I finish this I'm going to write to James. I only hope that he's still there to receive it, because if I'm honest, I miss him almost as much as I miss you, and I have no idea how I will ever see him again.

With all my love,
Avery.

By the time she finished the letter, Camille had reached her shop, and she immediately knew what she had to do. She checked there were no customers inside, since she'd left the door unlocked when she'd rushed out, turned the sign to 'Closed', locked the door and hurried back out on to the street, starting to run. She went as fast as she could, down one street and then another, until she finally reached the square and saw the hotel ahead of her. She slowed, trying to catch her breath and pushing her damp hair from her face, dashing up the steps and past the doorman, who thankfully didn't ask any questions.

She went to the front desk. 'I'm looking for a James Anderson,' she said, trying not to pant.

'He's a guest here?' the man asked.

'Yes. I believe he's checking out today, but I need to—'

'Unfortunately, Mr Anderson has already gone.'

Her heart sunk. 'You're certain?'

The man nodded and looked as if he'd rather she left him alone.

'Would you be able to check whether any mail arrived for him just now? There was a letter he was expecting, and I believe it might have only just been delivered.'

He gave her a long, uncertain look, before turning around and speaking to someone, who indicated a small stack of mail.

'Please look,' she pleaded. 'It's of the utmost importance that I know if he received it or not.'

The man held up a letter, and she could see from the beautiful writing on the back that it was from Avery. James had left without reading it, without even knowing that she'd written to him.

'Do you have a forwarding address for him? Did he leave any information at all behind?'

Camille would have asked for the letter herself, but she knew there was no chance of private correspondence being given to her, no matter how nicely she asked.

'Unfortunately no, there is no forwarding address for Mr Anderson.'

Camille nodded and turned around, walking slowly through the lobby, knowing there was nothing more she could have done. But just as she looked up to smile to the doorman, the glass door swung open and a familiar face met hers.

'James!'

'Camille? What are you doing here?'

'She wrote to us, James. Avery didn't forget us.'

His smile was as wide as hers.

'There's a letter waiting for me?'

She grinned. 'There is.'

'Lucky I forgot my coat then. I'd hate to miss a letter from my little American librarian.'

Camille stifled a laugh and placed her hand on his arm as she passed. 'It was good to see you again, James. I have a feeling we might cross paths again one day.'

He gave her a wink. 'I'm counting on it.'

Epilogue

NEW YORK, 1947

Camille stood on the pavement and stared up at the sign. She had tears in her eyes and she didn't even try to wipe them away, content to let them fall from her lashes as the men installing the lettering climbed down their ladders.

Hugo's.

They'd gone back and forth on the name so many times, trying to come up with something that sounded right for a bookstore, but when Avery had looked at her one day and simply said: 'Why don't we just call it Hugo's?', Camille had known in her heart that it was the perfect name.

'How are you holding up?'

Avery came out of the shop wearing an apron and clapping her hands together. She stood beside Camille, her hand sliding against hers as Avery stared up at the sign too.

'Hugo would have loved this,' Camille said, swallowing the emotion in her throat as she imagined his palm pressed to hers, his shoulder skimming against her own as they stood and looked up. But when she glanced sideways and saw Avery there, her smile so kind, her gaze so thoughtful, she knew how lucky she was to have found her as a friend. That she wasn't alone anymore. 'We used to lie in bed and dream about opening a restaurant one day, about finding the perfect building and seeing his name go up outside.'

'It might not be the restaurant you dreamed of, but it is ours,' Avery said, squeezing her hand. 'I can't believe we actually did it.'

Camille couldn't believe it either – any of it. That she was in New York, that she'd survived the war, that she was standing outside her very own bookshop.

'Come on, we still have some work to do before we open,' Avery said.

They'd been at the shop for the better part of the last week, and Avery had insisted they be there at daybreak to make sure everything was perfect for their opening day. They had trays of cupcakes haphazardly stacked throughout their office, and balloons still to blow up that they were going to give away to any children who visited, and still there were books to unpack.

But Camille didn't mind. There had been a time she'd wondered what her life might look like when the war ended; or more importantly, what she'd have to live for. Hugo and her family had been her life, and when they'd been taken from her, she'd fixated on finding out who was responsible for his death. But she hadn't wanted to live past that moment, hadn't imagined what might happen if she survived the war and the Allies won. Until Avery had written to her, more than once, and insisted that she come to New York.

Camille had laughed it off in the beginning, but Avery's letters had kept coming and her bossy American friend had refused to take no for an answer. Which was how she'd ended up sailing for America once her visa had been granted and moving into the second floor of Avery's rented Manhattan duplex, looking out over a city that was so different to any she'd ever seen before. It wasn't Paris, but it was a different kind of beautiful, and she'd known from her very first morning looking out at the leafy green trees and bustle of people coming and going, that it was home.

'Come on, let's set up the table at the front and then we're almost done,' Avery said. 'Everything we've been waiting on is in one of these four boxes.'

Camille followed her friend through the store to the back. Somehow, they'd managed to clean up the shop and have it sparkling for the opening day, with only the last few boxes taking up space in the middle of their office. It had helped that Avery's cousin Jack had taken a day off during the week to help them as well – without him, Camille doubted they'd have been able to open on time.

'You know, I think some of these deliveries take longer than the ones I waited on during the war,' Camille said as she bent down to collect a handful of books. 'I received newspapers from Germany faster!'

Camille looked down at the book in her hands, the one on top of the pile, and something swept through her: an emotion she hadn't experienced before. It was relief. Relief that it was all over, and that she was able to hold a novel like *Gentleman's Agreement* and know there would be no repercussions for displaying it in her store, not to mention that more Americans were buying it right now than any other book. Only last night she'd held a copy of *The Diary of a Young Girl* by Anne Frank to her chest and sobbed, crying herself to sleep as she'd realised that people all around the world were finally going to learn what it had been like for millions of Jews; that they could finally understand, through the words of someone who'd been through it, why so many people like her and Hugo had been prepared to sacrifice their lives for the cause.

'Are you alright?' Avery asked, her hand warm on Camille's shoulder.

'I will be,' she said, smiling through her tears. 'Today just, well . . .'

'It feels like a lot, I know,' Avery said. 'But we're here together, and that's all that matters.'

Camille couldn't have said it better if she'd tried.

'Can we put the Anne Frank book on the front table?' Camille asked.

'I'm already one step ahead of you,' Avery said, smiling as she gestured for her to follow. 'I have a pile there at the front, and I thought we could put that and *Gentleman's Agreement* in the window, side by side so that anyone window-shopping can see them both.'

'Perhaps we could put *Goodnight Moon* in the window too, and *The Plague*,' Camille said. 'Balance out the titles of importance with the picture books and novels we know will draw readers in.'

Avery grinned at her just as the little bell above the door jingled – the same little bell that had once hung in Camille's bookshop in Lisbon. Avery turned when she heard it, passing the stack of books in her hands to Camille and opening her arms wide to greet their first customers. James ducked low to make sure he missed the top of the door, and Avery laughed to see her son's fingers stretched high to jingle the bell, riding high on his daddy's shoulders.

'You made it!' she said, kissing James before reaching up to take Benny down. 'It's so good to see you both. Was he good for you this morning?'

'Well, this is my second change of shirt thanks to someone's excitement about breakfast, and I had to offer a shoulder ride so that we arrived before closing, but other than that, he's been excellent.'

Avery left kisses all over Benny's little head, his hair soft and fluffy against her lips. She inhaled the smell of him, holding him tight in her arms until he wriggled to get away. But he wasn't free for long, with Camille scooping him up and leaving her red lipstick on his pudgy cheek.

'I think someone might like the balloons out the back,' Avery said. 'Although we'll need to enlist Daddy here to blow most of them up.'

James slung an arm around her shoulders as Benny toddled off through the store, and Avery tucked her head into the crook of his neck.

'You girls should be very proud of this,' he said. 'It looks stunning. People are going to flock here.'

'I hope so,' Avery said with a sigh, stifling a yawn as she closed her eyes for a moment and leaned deeper into her husband. 'I feel like this is where I'm supposed to be. That everything happened for a reason to lead me to this very moment, even though I know that sounds crazy.'

'It doesn't sound crazy, not at all.' He pressed a slow, soft kiss to the top of her head and pulled away, chasing after their son when he disappeared into the back room, leaving Avery and Camille alone together again.

'You know if you ever want me to move out of your apartment, if it becomes too much for James or—'

'Stop right now,' Avery said, taking back the books she'd offloaded earlier and going to arrange them. 'You're family, and James knew the deal when he married me. You were always going to be part of our family, and you can stay with us until you can't stand us anymore.'

Camille just smiled, and then they both stood back to admire their display table.

'Besides, we're in this for life now. We own a business together in case you hadn't noticed.'

They stood side by side, shoulder to shoulder again, and Avery couldn't help but think how much her life had changed. For so long, she'd thought it was a choice between her career and marriage, that she would have to give everything up to become a mother, but that hadn't been the case at all. She'd also realised that it wasn't that she hadn't wanted to be someone's wife, she just hadn't wanted to be Michael's. But the moment James had asked her, her heart had leapt and she hadn't been able to say *yes* fast enough.

'Do you ever miss your old life?' Camille asked.

'Sometimes I miss the excitement of being in Lisbon, but I never miss being a librarian. I mean, I loved it at the time, but this?' She shook her head. 'This is the life I want.'

Avery beamed with pride as Camille walked to the front of the store and turned the sign to 'Open', hardly able to believe what they'd achieved together in just a few short years.

'I can't even imagine where I'd be now or what my life would look like if I hadn't met you, Avery,' Camille said. 'This is the life I want, too. I would give anything to have my Hugo back, but if I have to live without him, then this is the only place I want to be.'

Avery opened her arms and held Camille in a long, heartfelt hug, which would have lasted much longer if they hadn't been interrupted by a little boy with cupcake frosting smeared over his mouth and across his cheeks running directly towards their perfectly curated front table.

'Benny, no!' came a shout, as James came running behind him, scooping him up just before he crashed into the front table of books, and Ben squealed with delight.

Avery started to laugh then, and so did Camille. They laughed so hard that Avery began to cry, her cheeks and her stomach hurting as James stood there, with frosting now all through his own hair and a very naughty little boy held high in his arms.

'Darling, I think you might need to change your shirt again,' Avery said, trying so hard to keep a straight face as Camille gasped with laughter beside her.

'I don't think anyone would believe that he was once a spy for Britain,' Camille giggled.

James glared at them and Avery reached out and swiped a little icing with her finger, tasting it and then making a face at Benny, who looked as if he wasn't sure whether to cry or laugh.

'It's okay, darling, Daddy's going to take you home and get you both all cleaned up.'

She stood on tiptoe and kissed her husband's cheek. 'I love you, James. And just in case you've forgotten, your mother said he's just like you were as a child, so this is entirely your fault.'

James sighed and held Benny in one arm so he could put the other around Avery – and, despite the mess and the chaos, Avery knew she wouldn't have wanted her life to be any other way.

ACKNOWLEDGEMENTS

To an author, there is nothing quite as terrifying as a change of editor, so when my long-time editor Victoria Oundjian told me she was leaving, I was understandably scared. We'd worked on so many books together and I honestly felt like I was losing a family member. But something wonderful came from this news, and that was the chance to work with editor Victoria Pepe! The moment I received Victoria's initial notes on this novel, I had a little spark of excitement inside of me, and after we had a video call to brainstorm the story some more, I knew without a doubt that there was nothing to be worried about. In fact, I realised that this was the start of a very special relationship, one that I hope will last for many years to come.

And so, *The Secret Librarian* was born! I loved every moment of writing this novel, and I'm so grateful to have Victoria's guidance and fresh set of eyes. Victoria, thank you so much for helping me to write a book that I'm so incredibly proud of. I must also thank the incredible Sophie Wilson, who has worked with me on almost every historical fiction novel I've written – I'm so grateful to have you on this project! Both Victoria and Sophie's guidance on this novel during structural edits was invaluable, and this wouldn't be half the book it's turned out to be without their help.

It's always tricky balancing a fictional story that is based on history, and I should note that while Avery and Camille are very much born from my imagination, there are two important people in this novel who weren't. Frederick Kilgour was a very prominent historical figure, who was instrumental in the success of the Office of Strategic Services in the United States, and Sousa Mendes was a real-life Portuguese diplomat who defied his government to save thousands of Jews from the Nazis.

I have many other people to thank at Amazon Publishing UK, including Eoin Purcell, editorial director Sammia Hamer, author relations lead Nicole Wagner, copy editor Sadie Mayne, and proofreader Gemma Wain. And a very special thank you to Victoria Oundjian, who believed in this book when I first pitched it to her and made this novel possible. Thank you also to my agent, Laura Bradford. I am so lucky to have such a wonderful publishing team.

As always, I have a very small but special group of people in my day-to-day life to thank. First, to my amazing assistant, Lisa Pendle, thank you so much for all you do for me. To authors Yvonne Lindsay and Natalie Anderson – thank you for all the encouragement, the daily text messages and support. You both mean so much to me. Thank you also to my family for listening to me talk endlessly about characters and new ideas – Hamish, Mack and Hunter, you are everything to me. And thank you also to my wonderful parents, Maureen and Craig.

But the most important thanks, as ever, goes to every single one of my readers. Without you, I wouldn't be able to write the books I love, and I am endlessly grateful for your support. I love that you're as fascinated by history as I am, and I thank you for coming on this journey with me.

If you would like to find out more about me or my books, I would love you to visit my brand-new website, of which I'm enormously proud, designed by Michelle Fowler at Half Light

Studio. You can find me at sorayalane.com, and you can sign up for my newsletter at sorayalane.com/contact.

I also have a very engaged reader group where I spend time every day, and I encourage all of my readers to join. There, we discuss books and TV shows we love, and it's the first place I post news and exciting things like cover reveals. You can find us here: facebook.com/groups/sorayalanereadergroup.

Soraya x

If you enjoyed *The Secret Librarian*, why not read another of Soraya M. Lane's books? Read on for an excerpt from *The Pianist's Wife*, an unforgettable World War Two novel about those who chose to defy the Nazis from within Germany. Available now.

Chapter One

New York, 2006

Amira lifted her gaze and caught a glimpse of herself in the mirror across the room. She barely recognised the white-haired reflection looking back at her; the lines around her eyes, the narrowness of her shoulders, they seemed to belong to another. She still expected to see the thick dark hair and plump skin of her youth, but instead there was an elderly lady blinking back at her.

She turned away when the young woman beside her spoke.

'Amira, are you ready?' Madison asked.

Amira cleared her throat, reaching for the glass of water on the nightstand and taking a small sip. 'I am.'

'Is it okay if I record our interview? So I can listen to it later?'

She looked at the little machine Madison was gesturing at, her finger hovering over the button, imagining her words being played back at a later date. She hoped her voice wouldn't sound as shaky as it felt.

'Yes, I give permission for you to record me.'

Madison nodded and pressed down. 'Well then, let's begin,' she said with a warm smile. 'Amira, tonight you've been honoured for your work raising money for underprivileged and orphaned children in New York. I know you and your husband have both been very private about your joint philanthropic endeavours until now, so I very much appreciate the opportunity to speak with you.'

Amira nodded and instinctively reached out a hand to her husband's. It was warm, his skin almost feathery it was so thin, and she kept hold as she replied to Madison. When she'd agreed to the interview, her only condition was that it had to be conducted at his bedside – she didn't want to do it alone.

'Is there a reason you decided to open up about your work now, after all this time?'

'My greatest concern,' Amira said, 'is that if we don't speak now, if *I* don't speak now, then we may miss the opportunity to encourage others to step forward and follow in our footsteps. I believe that everyone is capable of making a difference in the lives of others, be it with donations or the giving of time, and I hope that in sharing my story with you, I may be able to influence others.'

Madison nodded, her pen poised above a little leather-bound notebook, taking notes even though she was recording their interview. Amira had thought about her answer to that question all day, preparing herself for what she intended on saying, but as she spoke she realised she sounded over-rehearsed.

'From what I understand, you grew up in a village in Germany and lived in Berlin during the war,' Madison said, 'which is where your passion for helping children began.'

Amira sighed. It wasn't that she hadn't expected to be asked, but hearing someone say those words after all these years . . . it made her feel as if she were somehow back there, as if she were still the little girl holding her father's hand, believing that somehow, everything would be alright.

'Can you explain to me what it was like to live in Germany, during those tumultuous years? And how that shaped the woman you are today?'

'That time in my life, it's almost indescribable,' Amira replied. 'Berlin during the war and even before, it was a place full of hate and terror, but now I look back, I suppose it was also a place just like any other. Not everyone experienced such hardship as I did.'

She reached out and took another sip of water, reluctantly letting go of her husband's hand, and when she looked up, she saw that Madison was waiting, leaning forward in anticipation of her continuing.

'In many ways, life in Berlin went on as normal, particularly for those families with what the Nazis considered pure German bloodlines, and most especially those who exemplified what the party stood for, but for others, it was a reign of terror that felt as if it would never end. For the marginalised . . .'

'But what was it like for you personally, Amira?' Madison asked. 'Could you share your own experience with me?'

'Well,' Amira said, her voice cracking slightly as she spoke, 'if I did, it would be a very long story.'

Madison's smile was kind as she leaned back in her seat, appearing to make herself comfortable. 'It just so happens that I have all day, if you're willing to share it with me, of course. I would very much like to hear as much of your story as you're willing to tell. It's why I'm here, after all.'

Amira's gaze found its way to her husband's face, as it so often did when she sat beside him, and she wished he would simply open his eyes, that he could be part of telling their story with her. But she knew that likely wouldn't happen, not now.

I think it's time, my love. After all these years, I think it's finally time that I told our story. Because if not now, then when? I only wish you could open your eyes and tell me that you give me your blessing.

'For me,' Amira finally said, looking up as a wave of nostalgia passed through her body, 'life in Germany changed in 1935, when I realised that the country I loved had a reason not to love me anymore.'

Chapter Two

AMIRA

'I don't understand,' Amira said, her hands shaking. She made them into balls at her sides as she looked up at her teacher, her fingernails digging into her palms.

'I'm sorry, but the decision has been made.'

'But why can I stay and they can't?' Amira asked. 'What makes me any different from them? It's not fair that they had to go home!'

Her teacher looked away, as if she couldn't bear to meet Amira's gaze. Tears filled Amira's eyes and she quickly brushed at her cheeks when she felt the first of many begin to fall, not wanting to appear weak in front of anyone at school, least of all her teacher. But she'd just watched a Jewish girl from her class and a handful of others from different classes being lined up in the quad outside and sent home, no longer welcome at school.

'Amira, you're different because only your mother is Jewish. Your father is German, which means that you are allowed to stay, for now. But I don't know for how much longer. You'll just have to wait and see, like everyone else, but in the meantime be grateful that you're still here.'

Amira blinked back at her, a shiver running through her body as she began to understand what was happening. She looked over her shoulder and saw some of her classmates whispering, their hands held up to cover their mouths, heads bent together. She doubted any of them had even known her mother was Jewish until she'd been singled out with the other mixed-race children that day. She'd gone from being a student just like them, to being the object of their ridicule.

'So one day you might tell me that I can no longer attend school, too?' she asked, horrified that she was in trouble for something she couldn't help. 'Even though I have the best grades in the class? How will I be a teacher one day if I cannot come to school?'

'Please, Amira, there is nothing I can do about it. The rules are the rules,' her teacher said. 'We shall have to wait and see what orders we receive, but it seems, for now at least, that we can only have a certain number of Jewish students, and our principal has decided he would prefer those Jews to be only half-bloods.'

She was left standing there when her teacher turned and walked away, but Amira didn't move. Not immediately. She'd just witnessed some of her classmates, some of the smartest children she knew, being sent home less than an hour earlier, supposedly never to return. And now she'd been told she wasn't guaranteed an ongoing place at school anymore, either.

A hand fell over her shoulder and squeezed, and she turned to find Gisele standing there, her eyes wide.

'What did she say?' Gisele whispered, her long blonde plait falling over her shoulder.

'That there are limits on the number of Jewish children allowed at schools and universities all over Germany now,' Amira whispered back.

'But what about you?'

'It's because my father isn't Jewish. I don't think anyone knows how they are going to treat us, because we're half German. She just said I shall have to wait and see.'

Gisele nodded and tucked her arm firmly through Amira's, turning them both around and steering her back to their desks. The other pupils all went silent as she walked past, most avoiding eye contact with her as if they were embarrassed and a few giving her sympathetic smiles. But it was a small group of boys who caught her attention, with one of them whispering something that made them all erupt into laughter.

'I don't understand what's happening,' Amira said as she and Gisele sat side by side, and their teacher took her place at the front of the classroom and reprimanded the students for making too much noise. The teacher didn't go so far as to tell them off for their unkindness though.

Gisele's face was tightly drawn in a way that Amira had never seen before, but she'd never in her entire life felt so grateful for her best friend. Without her, she would have been hopelessly alone.

As their teacher turned to write on the board, Gisele slipped her a piece of paper, which Amira tucked on to her lap and read, careful to be sure that no one was watching.

It won't last for long. No one will allow this to continue. It's madness.

Amira placed the note on her textbook and scribbled back.

What if it does though? What if I can't come to school anymore? What will I do?

Gisele wrote straight away when Amira passed it to her.

Your papa wouldn't allow it. He'll be at school tomorrow morning demanding you stay here, along with all the other parents whose children were sent home. They won't stand for it.

A shuffle of fear ran the length of Amira's spine. She wasn't so certain that would be the case; that Jewish parents would even be allowed on the school grounds anymore, let alone into the principal's office. She'd heard her parents arguing late at night when they thought she was asleep; had seen the silent, almost pained way they looked at each other over the dinner table some evenings. Her mother was scared, and Amira had seen it reflected in her gaze – the way she held her a little tighter now whenever they hugged, the way she said goodbye to her each morning almost as if it could be their final parting. It was as if she'd known all this was coming, as if she'd been preparing for the worst. There weren't many Jewish families in their community and no others that she knew of with only one Jewish parent, and her mother didn't practise her faith, but until recently she'd always lit her candles on Friday evenings. She'd called it her little reminder of her childhood, a tradition her mother had held close to her heart. Now, they were packed away and never spoken of, and Amira knew how much that must hurt her mother.

Gisele passed her another note.

I don't care what anyone says. I will fight for you because you're my best friend. I will always fight for you.

Gisele had only just turned thirteen, and she was one of the smallest girls in their class, but Amira had no doubt that her friend would do as she said. It was one of the reasons they were friends; because on her first day of school, as a nervous, shy five-year-old, Amira had been left in tears when an older boy had stolen her lunch and left her starving. Gisele had thrown a punch at the boy with surprising accuracy and come straight over to sit with her, halving her lunch with Amira, their legs swinging from the bench seat as they spent the rest of the recess eating and talking. They'd been best friends ever since, and no boys had ever bothered her again. Except for today in class.

But even Amira couldn't have imagined what Gisele would do next, what would *happen* next.

Every day for as long as Amira could remember, she'd walked home with Gisele. They always took the long way intentionally, dragging their feet so they could spend longer together, never running out of things to talk about, especially on sunny days. But after today, she wondered if they would ever be allowed to walk together again. If they did, it would have to be the fastest route possible, but she doubted Gisele's parents would permit it. She'd been invited into their home many times during their friendship, but lately she'd noticed the way Gisele's mother watched her and Amira no longer felt comfortable going inside.

'There's the little Jew girl,' one of the boys from school called, the very same one who'd whispered in class about her. 'Dirty little Jew girl,' he said in a sing-song voice.

'She's only half Jew,' one of the other boys said, looking down at his shoes and kicking his toes into the dirt.

Another boy looked away, and Amira at least felt heartened that they weren't all so cruel. Before all this she'd always liked the boys in her class; only a few weeks earlier she and Gisele had giggled about which of the boys they'd like to marry one day.

'She's still a *filthy* Jew,' the first boy said, his voice as high as Amira's, but the words were said with the confidence of a man.

Amira grabbed hold of Gisele's hand to quickly pull her along, scared of what was about to happen, but Gisele didn't move. Amira saw that her face had turned a deep shade of red, her anger palpable. And just like that very first day in the playground, Amira knew something was about to happen. Only, this time, she wished it wouldn't.

'Come on,' Amira insisted, trying to tug her. 'Just keep walking, don't even look at them. It doesn't matter.'

But they didn't move away fast enough. One of the boys threw an apple at Amira, which she saw just in time to duck away from it, but she didn't move quickly enough to avoid the plum that followed and hit her square on the forehead. It didn't hurt so much as embarrass her, especially when she reached to touch the spot and found some of the fruit's flesh smeared against her skin.

What she couldn't understand was why they were being so cruel. These were children she'd known for years, boys who'd never have been brave enough to behave in such a way before. When they'd been younger she'd even gone to their birthday parties and raced with them in the playground at lunchtime. But with the hatred of the new political party seeming to surge through every German household in the city, they suddenly felt they could behave differently.

'Her mama's a dirty Jew,' called the same boy, who managed to convince the others to start chanting with him.

Amira swallowed, the words leaving her with a writhing stomach that made her want to be sick. Even if she'd wanted to, she couldn't speak.

'What did you say?' Gisele asked, letting go of Amira's hand.

'Gisele, please—' Amira pleaded, whispering to her friend, but it was too late. Gisele was marching towards them.

In that moment, as she realised what was about to happen, Amira swelled with pride at the same time as wishing she could stop it. This wasn't the same as when her friend had shared her lunch, or held her hand and sat with her when some of the other girls were being mean.

This was going to change everything.

Gisele covered the ground between them quickly and swiftly swiped an ice-cream cone from one of the boys' hands, dumping it on his head so that it dripped through his hair, before he even realised what was going on. Unfortunately, neither did the next boy, who was left reeling after Gisele pulled back her arm and threw a punch into his nose that left him bleeding all down his shirt and howling in pain.

As if satisfied with the way the remaining boys ran away, Gisele turned back to Amira and smiled triumphantly, holding out her arm for Amira to loop her hand through, as if nothing had happened in the first place.

'I wouldn't worry about them anymore,' Gisele said, as if she'd simply given them a telling-off.

'You shouldn't have done that,' Amira whispered, clinging to her friend as she looked over her shoulder to make sure the boys weren't following them. Gisele might be brave, but Amira was frightened, wondering what they'd do next time now that Gisele had aggravated them. What they'd do to *her* if they found her alone. She had to be careful, that was what her papa had said. She was supposed to keep her head down and stay out of trouble, no matter what, because he said that the Jewish people were being blamed for everything that was wrong with German society. It was different for Gisele, and as much as Amira wanted to believe her, she knew that it wasn't Gisele who'd get into trouble for what had happened.

'I just did what any decent friend would do,' Gisele said, but Amira heard the tremor in her voice, as if she was just beginning to realise the severity of what she'd done.

'What if you're not allowed to see me again?' Amira whispered. 'When your parents find out what you've done for me . . .'

'They won't find out,' Gisele said. 'Those cowards aren't going to tell them that a girl gave one of them a bloody nose. Imagine one of their fathers hearing that!'

'But what if . . .' Amira's voice trailed away. She didn't want to think about any other *what ifs*. Gisele thought things would be better now, but they wouldn't be. Nothing was ever going to be the same again. Amira was never going to be asked to dances or have the chance to dress up in pretty clothes and have fun with friends, because no one was going to want her near them. These boys had made it clear that they couldn't even stand looking at her, let alone being friends with her ever again.

They walked the rest of the way in silence, stopping only to wash Gisele's hand in a little stream near their houses so that her parents wouldn't notice. Amira carefully wiped away the smear of blood and used her uniform to dry it, and Gisele did the same to get rid of the fruit stain on Amira's forehead, their walk taking them much longer than it should have, almost as if neither of them wanted to go home. But when they rounded the corner to the street they both lived on, it seemed that Gisele had been wrong about the boys being too embarrassed to tell anyone.

Gisele's mother was standing by the mailbox with another woman, waiting for them, and the boy Gisele had punched was standing beside them, a handkerchief held up to cover the blood. If it were any other day, Amira would have rolled her eyes and they would have likely giggled about what a cry-baby he was, but not today. There was something very different about today than any other day she'd lived through before.

'Oh no,' Gisele whispered, and for the very first time, Amira felt her friend's fear.

'What are we going to do?' Amira asked, as they stopped on the other side of the road, seeing the furious expression on Gisele's mother's face when she beckoned for her daughter. Her hair was swept into a dramatic up-do, her dress as fashionable as her home, which was the largest on the block. She was certainly not a woman who was going to let her daughter play with a troublesome Jewish girl.

'Go home, Amira,' Gisele whispered, letting go of her. 'It'll be fine. I promise. I'll tell her what happened and explain everything, that it was all just a misunderstanding. That it was my fault, not yours.' She smiled, as if it were nothing. 'As soon as she hears me practise the flute, she'll calm down. She always does when she sees me doing something ladylike.' Gisele rolled her eyes, before adding, 'Or hopefully my brother did something terrible at school today which will distract her attention.'

Amira nodded and stood for a moment longer as Gisele crossed the street, watching her go. But even when she turned to walk away, she couldn't help but hear the two women talking.

'You can't let her be friends with a girl like that, not anymore. You know what her mother is, don't you?'

Amira wrapped her arms around herself, wishing she hadn't heard the next part; wishing that they'd whispered and at least tried to pretend they didn't want her to hear. But of course niceties had disappeared with the announcement of the Nuremberg Laws.

'She might only be a half Jew, but I don't think it matters. They're all the same, and we'll be going to the school and telling them that we expect her to be expelled immediately, especially after what she made your daughter do today. You just can't trust them, and violence can never be tolerated.'

'I couldn't agree more. If I have it my way, Gisele won't even be setting eyes on her again, let alone spending time with her.'

Amira ran the rest of the way home, her eyes burning with tears that only fell faster when her mother caught her in her arms as she stumbled through the front door.

'Amira! Slow down. What's wrong?'

'I'm fine,' she said, quickly wiping at her eyes. 'I just—'

She looked up at her mother and felt like the little girl who'd had her lunch stolen as a five-year-old, all over again.

'It doesn't look like everything is fine,' her mother said, drawing her in and holding her close. 'Tell me what happened.'

Amira shut her eyes and let her mother hold her.

'They hate me,' she eventually said. 'Mama, they hate everyone like us.'

Her mother was silent. She rubbed Amira's back in small, comforting circles, her lips whispering against her daughter's hair when she bent down to hold her.

'They are being influenced by a monster of a man, that's all,' her mother murmured. 'But this will pass. No one will allow this to continue, your father won't allow us to be treated like this. We just have to wait.'

'You truly believe that it won't last?'

'Yes, my love, I truly believe that this will pass, we just have to be patient.'

Amira nodded, but when her mother tucked her fingers beneath her chin and lifted her face, she knew that something else was wrong. Her mother had been crying too, her eyes red and her skin blotchy; she simply hadn't noticed when she'd come racing through the door.

'Amira, I know this is going to be hard for you to hear, but I have something to tell you.'

She let her mother take her hand and guide her to the kitchen table, sitting down beside her in the afternoon sunshine as it streamed in through the window. She wondered, while she sat with her small hand in her mother's slightly larger one, whether anything could be worse than the day she'd just had.

How wrong she was to think that.

'I went to see the doctor today,' her mother said, gently; *too gently*. 'Unfortunately I received some bad news.'

Amira gulped, and she felt as if her heart were about to hammer through her body. Part of her wished to run away right then and there, so that she didn't have to hear the bad news that she knew was coming; but instead she stayed deadly still.

'I'm sick, my love. I don't know how bad it will become, but the doctor, he—' Her mother's voice wavered, and Amira threw her arms around her mother's shoulders and hugged her tighter than she'd ever hugged anyone in her life before.

'I love you, Mama,' she said, closing her eyes and pretending that her mother wasn't sick, that she hadn't just been about to tell her something terrible.

To her great relief, her mother chose not to continue speaking.

'I love you, too, Amira. With all my heart.'

Mama is going to be fine. She has to be.

ABOUT THE AUTHOR

Photo © 2022 Jemima Helmore

Soraya M. Lane graduated with a law degree before realising that law wasn't the career for her and that her future was in writing. She is the author of historical and contemporary women's fiction, and her novel *Wives of War* was an Amazon Charts bestseller. Soraya lives on a small farm in her native New Zealand with her husband, their two young sons and a collection of four-legged friends. When she's not writing, she loves to be outside playing make-believe with her children or snuggled up inside reading. For more information about Soraya and her books, visit www.sorayalane.com or www.facebook.com/SorayaLaneAuthor, or follow her on X @Soraya_Lane.

Follow the Author on Amazon

If you enjoyed this book, follow Soraya M. Lane on Amazon to be notified when the author releases a new book!
To do this, please follow these instructions:

Desktop:

1) Search for the author's name on Amazon or in the Amazon App.
2) Click on the author's name to arrive on their Amazon page.
3) Click the 'Follow' button.

Mobile and Tablet:

1) Search for the author's name on Amazon or in the Amazon App.
2) Click on one of the author's books.
3) Click on the author's name to arrive on their Amazon page.
4) Click the 'Follow' button.

Kindle eReader and Kindle App:

If you enjoyed this book on a Kindle eReader or in the Kindle App, you will find the author 'Follow' button after the last page.

Printed in Dunstable, United Kingdom